JANE AUSTEN goes to *Hollywood*

JANE AUSTEN goes to *Hollywood*

ABBY McDONALD

CANDLEWICK PRESS

This is a work of fiction. Names, characters, places, and incidents are either products of the author's imagination or, if real, are used fictitiously.

First edition 2013

Library of Congress Catalog Card Number 2012947263
ISBN 978-0-7636-5508-2

13 14 15 16 17 18 BVG 10 9 8 7 6 5 4 3 2 1

Printed in Berryville, VA, U.S.A.

This book was typeset in Sabon.

Candlewick Press
99 Dover Street
Somerville, Massachusetts 02144

visit us at www.candlewick.com

For my father,
for all his support and encouragement

PART ONE: *Spring*

I

Her father was dead, and all Grace could think about was pie.

Sure, it wasn't just any old pie—the box an early mourner had delivered was crisp and white, boasting the logo from the best patisserie in San Francisco—but even as she wondered what kind of filling was hidden inside (blueberry, maybe, or a fluffy lemon meringue), Grace was hit with a crushing sense of shame. Meditating on baked goods during her father's funeral made her a Truly Terrible Person.

"John was taken from us too soon," the priest murmured up front. Grace's older sister, Hallie, let out a wretched sob. For once, her hysterics weren't an overreaction—no, this time, Grace was the inappropriate one. She sank even lower in the hard wooden pew, as if everyone could see the visions of pastries dancing in her head.

She didn't even like pie! She hadn't had a sweet tooth since fourth grade, when her overzealous dentist warned her that sugar would make her teeth fall out. Grace had barely opened her mouth for two weeks, until her father noticed her trying to slurp mashed potato through tight lips and gently explained that her molars weren't about to scatter on the floor that very moment.

But that had been when he was around to explain things. When he'd been around at all.

". . . and it's this zest for life that he'll be remembered for—"

The priest was cut short by a piercing wail. In the front pew, baby Dash began to scream, red faced and shaking with rage. Her brother. Half brother, Hallie was always quick to snap, but Grace always thought that sounded even more useless. Like their father had only half left them, or half married someone else.

"Shh!" Grace's stepmother, Portia, bounced him, her black veil quivering, but Dash only screamed louder, his cries echoing in the cavernous church.

Behind her, someone tutted softly. "Poor thing, he'll never know his daddy."

Grace felt Hallie stiffen. "He's lucky," Hallie whispered. "He won't miss him at all! We're the ones they should be sorry for."

Grace said nothing. Dash screamed on, until finally, Portia thrust his flailing body at the waiting nanny. The poor Swedish girl fled with him down the aisle; Dash's wails receding until the main church doors closed behind them and there was quiet again.

Grace wished it could be so easy for her: the escape route, and the tears. She still hadn't cried yet, there hadn't been the time. Her mother had collapsed into bed when she heard, refusing to eat or drink anything until Grace called in their family physician to prescribe her something to sleep. Hallie had sobbed for days in such a fit that, in the end, Grace had crushed up a pill in her food as well, so that they might all get some peace. Then, she'd sat alone in the formal living room—the one they rarely used since her father left—with a stack of her mother's old address books, and made the calls. Third cousins, and old neighbors, and distant friends from college. The calls Portia wouldn't know to make, if she even cared to at all.

The priest cleared his throat. "Let's take a moment to share some of our happy thoughts and memories of dear John."

This was Grace's cue. She rose from the pew, her fingers curled around the poem she'd chosen, but before she was even two steps down the aisle, Portia slipped out of her pew and glided up the stairs to the lectern. She carefully lifted her veil, folding it back over her elegant chignon. "John and I were soul mates," Portia began, gazing out across the church with a wounded look.

Beside Grace, Hallie hissed with a sharp intake of breath. "She didn't!"

But she did. And she was.

Grace slid back into her seat as Portia clasped a lace-gloved hand to her chest. "I knew from the moment we met that we were meant to be together," she continued. "He was my destiny."

A destiny that was already married with children at the time, but now, as then, Portia seemed unconcerned with such trivial details. Grace looked anxiously to her mother, but her face was blank, as if she couldn't hear a word.

"He was the best man I'd ever known. Kind. Honorable. Loyal."

Hallie shot to her feet. Grace yanked her back down.

"Are you going to sit here and listen to this?" Hallie demanded. Her face, which had for days been drained and ashy, was now bright with outrage; eyes lit up with a fury Grace knew all too well signaled trouble. Very public kind of trouble.

"Please," Grace whispered, looking nervously around. "Just let it go."

"Let what go?" Hallie hissed. "The fact she stole him away, or that she's standing up there acting like we never existed?"

"All of it. Hallie, come on," Grace pleaded. There wasn't just the funeral to get through, but a reception after, too: hours of politely accepting condolences from people they'd never met. "She's allowed to be sad too, you know. He was her family."

It was the wrong thing to say.

"*We* were his family!" Hallie wrenched her arm free and clambered out of the pew, trampling on Grace's toes.

"Hallie!" Grace whispered desperately, but it was too late.

". . . said that he was happier than he'd ever been—" Portia stopped midsentence as she saw Hallie standing in the aisle. Their eyes met, and for a terrible moment, Grace waited for the explosion. But none came. Hallie shuddered and gave a desperate sob, then she turned and fled.

Grace exhaled with relief. She waited a moment for Portia to continue, then murmured in her mother's ear, "I'll go."

There was no response; her mom was still staring numbly ahead with the same vacant expression she'd had all week. Grace edged out of her row and scurried for the back door, head down to avoid the stares she was so sure followed her out.

Grace found her sister wandering the graveyard, dark hair tangling in the wind. Hallie had forgotten her coat, and her long black skirt billowed out around her, like a silhouette from a gothic novel. Grace sighed, trudging through the muddy grass toward her. Trust Hallie to pick pneumonia for the sake of a dramatic scene—she wouldn't be the one delivering cough syrup up two flights of stairs for the rest of the week.

"Look at this place." Hallie gestured wildly, her arms wide. "We shouldn't be here. *He* shouldn't be here!"

Grace wasn't sure if Hallie meant any graveyard, or just this one. The crumbling mausoleums and gleaming granite headstones marched around them in stiff rows marked with huge displays of roses and wilting lilies. Her father had always joked about cremation—that he wanted his remains scattered in the dugout at the Giants' stadium — but when Grace had tried to bring that up with Portia, she'd looked at Grace in horror. Of course John would be buried, and since her family plot was all the way back East in Connecticut, then only the best, most prestigious church in San Francisco would do.

Perhaps it was better this way. He hadn't taken Grace to a game in years, and at least here, she'd have a place to visit him.

"Come on, Hallie, let's go back inside."

"No! Leave me alone." Hallie turned away from her. She was shivering now, so Grace shrugged off her coat and put it around Hallie's shoulders. It draped, too big around her slight frame. People who didn't know them often thought that Grace was older. She'd caught up with Hallie height-wise two years ago, and then kept right on growing. This year, Grace's figure had filled out too, so at sixteen she was left feeling like a stranger in her own body: off balance from the inconvenient curves that made her already-poor gym class performance just plain embarrassing, and caused her pimply lab partners to stutter and stare.

"Mom will be worried," Grace tried reasoning. "We don't even have to sit through the rest of the service, we can just wait in the lobby until it's over."

"I don't understand you!" Hallie pressed her palms against her face, wiping the lonely streak of mascara on each cheek. "How can you even look at her and not want to rip her prissy head off? And him! All this bullshit about what a great guy he was. I would kill him again if he weren't already dead!" She collapsed into sobs again.

"You don't mean that." Grace patted her shoulder in what she hoped was a soothing fashion.

"I do! I hate him!" Hallie sniffled. "He ruined everything, and now he's not even around to blame anymore."

Grace stood, patiently waiting for the sobs to subside. Hallie's outbursts came like a tempest—flaring up at the slightest provocation, whether glee of landing the lead in the spring play, or desolate sobs over the season finale of her favorite TV medical drama—but she always wore herself out soon enough.

At last, Hallie seemed to calm, and Grace steered her back toward the church, glad she'd worn her thickest black tights under her stiff formal dress. It was May, but in San Francisco that only meant the slight possibility of sunshine escaping the thick, gray clouds above.

"Let's just get through today, OK?" she said, a pleading note in her voice. "Then Portia and everybody will be gone, and we can try to get back to normal."

"Normal?" Hallie gave her a scathing look. "How can you even say that? It's like you never loved him at all."

Grace froze. Hallie grabbed her hands. "I'm sorry! That was awful. I take it back!"

Grace tried to pull away, but Hallie held on tight. "I didn't mean it, Grace. I'm, like, the worst sister in the world! Forgive me. Please?"

"Hallie, it's OK." Grace was too tired for this. Only her sister could switch from wishing she'd killed their dad herself to blaming Grace for not loving him enough, all in a single breath.

"No, I mean it!" Hallie cried, wide-eyed. "I know

you cared, of course you do. I just don't understand how you can be like this. So, *calm.*"

Grace didn't reply. Hallie said "calm" like it was a dirty word, but Grace didn't see what choice she had. Anger wasn't getting Hallie anything, besides headaches and dehydration, and denial may suit her mom just fine, but Grace preferred to function in the real world. The world hadn't stopped when their father left them, and it wouldn't cease spinning now that he was dead. There were distant relatives to console, a chem paper to write for school by Monday, the search for a summer job.

They'd managed well enough with a part-time father these last two years. Grace suspected they'd manage just fine without him around at all.

II

Portia's penthouse was apparently besieged by renovations, so the reception was held back at their house. By the time Grace and Hallie arrived, the block was jammed with shiny cars parked inches apart on the perilous incline. The neighbors had all long since succumbed to big-money developers who put up luxury apartment complexes with wraparound decks; charging young professional types half a million dollars or more for a one-bedroom condo with a view all the way to the bay. But Grace's parents had always held fast. The ramshackle, three-story Victorian sat squarely at the top of the hill, surrounded by an overgrown garden plot that was equal parts wild roses and weeds, and spelled death to any mower that tried to tame it.

"I'm so sorry for your loss." Another well-wisher clasped Grace by the hand. "Is Valerie around?"

"In her studio, I think." Her mom had disappeared up to the attic as soon as they got home, and Hallie too, leaving Grace alone on the front line to handle the torrent of platitudes. "Thank you for coming."

"So brave." The middle-aged woman cupped Grace's cheek. Grace tried not to recoil from the touch. "Such a tragedy."

"Thank you," Grace repeated. "There's food set up in the living room, and drinks, if you want."

The woman finally moved off, and another mourner took her place. "What a terrible waste."

Grace nodded numbly. Out of church, it was easy to see the divide, between her father's old life, and his new one. Her stepmother's crowd was straight backed, adorned with hats and designer black mourning attire. They carried tiny dogs, and wore family jewelry, and probably did things like play golf, and yacht. And they were white. A sea of pale faces; Jewish at best, Grace noticed wryly; they were barely even tan. Their group—their mother's group—was a more motley crew: college professors, artists, activists. The people who had known and loved her father before. Before the long hours and corner office. Before the personal trainer and new suits. Before he'd made enough money to catch the eye of his East Coast event planner, and decided that he wanted an "after," after all.

"Grace, dear." She felt a tug on her sleeve, and turned to find Portia frowning at her. "Are those shrimp puffs on the buffet gluten-free?"

Grace blinked. "I don't know," she answered slowly. "You'd have to ask the caterer."

"I can't find her anywhere," Portia tutted. "And you know Dash has a wheat intolerance. I e-mailed you a list of his diet requirements." She looked at Grace expectantly, her skin stretched tight and luminous over the sharp angles of her cheekbones.

"There are vegetables too," Grace offered. "I think I saw crudités?"

"Yes, but Dash wants the shrimp puffs." Portia looked impatient. Grace sighed.

"I'm sorry," she said quietly. "I'll go find out for you."

"Please don't be long." Portia's tone belied the politeness of her words. "He gets so cranky when he's hungry." She saw somebody behind Grace and lit up. "Delilah! Darling!"

Grace watched her waft across the room. She was beautiful, there was no doubt about it, but to Grace it had always seemed a cool, precise kind of beauty: her hair smoothed back, her outfits always crisp and formfitting. Grace had met her around her father's office a couple of times before—well, before *it* happened—and remembered feeling intimidated by her glossy kind of perfection. Like Portia had read a memo on how to be a woman that Grace couldn't even decipher.

She'd never suspected for one moment what was to come.

The room was suddenly unbearably hot; her wool

tights prickling against her skin. Grace retreated to the kitchen, but there was no sign of the caterer.

"You must be one of the daughters." An older woman squinted at her through wire-rimmed spectacles. "Helena, isn't it?"

"That's my sister, I'm Grace," she corrected, but the woman was already beckoning over a group of proper-looking guests in starched shirts and high-necked blouses.

"This is one of them. You know, the girls from his first marriage." She said it with a hushed voice, like it was a scandal.

One of the men assessed her curiously. "You can't really see it, not like with Dashwood."

"Oh, I know!" the woman exclaimed. "That boy is the spitting image of his daddy. You have your mother's looks," she added, patting Grace absently on the arm.

They were wrong. Both girls looked like their father, he had always said so. Grace had his eyes and his laugh, and Hallie shared his smile. But Grace didn't bother correcting the group; to them, there was no way two black girls could look like their white father. They may not have been half as dark as their mother—second-generation Nigerian, by way of Philadelphia—but Grace had learned years ago that there were some people who would never look long enough to register the difference. Black was black, regardless of shade or hue.

"Such a tragedy. You at least had time with him," another woman told Grace. "And poor, poor Portia . . ."

"Poor Portia," they all echoed.

Grace tried to catch her breath. Her head was throbbing now, and the crowd seemed to close in on her, a mass of dark tailored clothing and insincerity. "Excuse me," she murmured, backing away, but the moment she stepped back into the living room, she was accosted by Portia's impatient call. "Grace? Grace, the puffs!"

Grace quickly turned to head the other direction, but bumped straight into another guest.

"Grace, sweetheart, I'm so sorry." The woman crushed Grace against her generous chest. She was an artist friend of her mother's, Grace remembered, a wild-haired woman with a penchant for spoken-word poetry and healing crystals. "You must be devastated. Wrecked!"

Grace struggled to breathe.

"Let it out, I always say. You have to let it all out!"

"I . . . I can't. . . ." Grace pulled away, gasping for air. "I'm sorry, I have to . . ." She turned and dashed toward the back kitchen door, the woman's words calling after her.

"Work through the pain, sugar!"

Outside, it had begun to rain, a misty drizzle that clung to Grace's face as she hurried across the overgrown lawn and into the thicket of elm trees at the back of the yard. The trees were wide and shady here, a natural hideaway out of view from the house.

Grace made straight for the largest tree and scrambled up the ladder nailed to the side of the gnarled bark. The tree house had been her father's pride and joy, the greatest achievement of a man who could barely replace a blown fuse. It was simple, sure—a sturdy floor lodged over the

V of two wide branches, planks hammered into uneven walls, a dripping roof—but it was hers. Grace had spent hours up here as a child, cataloging leaves and bugs into her notebooks, while Hallie danced around with the fairies below, and staged dramatic readings of *A Midsummer Night's Dream*. Later, her father had brought up a telescope, and shown Grace her first glimpse of the infinite possibility of the night sky: that the random scattering of stars was actually a precise moving equation, a million forces pinning the whole universe together.

Grace pulled an old blanket from the chest in the corner and settled cross-legged on the damp floor, looking out through the trees to the city below. From here, the world was shrouded in thick white mist, only the vague outline of the bridge visible in the distance. Grace shifted, and heard the rustle of paper in her pocket. Her poem.

She pulled it out, crumpled and creased, but didn't unfold it. She didn't need to.

"'When I am dead, my dearest,'" Grace began, her voice soft. "'Sing no sad songs for me.'"

She'd learned it in fourth grade, for an intramural speaking contest. Her father had helped her, drilling the lines every night with the promise of a dollar to spend at the bookstore for every time she made it through without an error. In the end, she'd lost the competition to a whey-faced girl reciting a limerick about her dog, but it didn't matter; Grace's father had presented her with a beautiful leather-bound guide to the night sky, illustrated with every constellation. Roxy Heatherington could keep her silly certificate; Grace had won the prize that really mattered.

" 'Plant thou no roses at my head, nor shady cypress tree.' " Her voice was stronger now, the lines spilling from her lips with barely a conscious thought. " 'Be the green grass above me, with showers and dewdrops wet, and if thou wilt, remember, and if thou wilt, forget. . . .' "

Grace paused, the words catching in her throat. She hadn't grasped it as a child. This was a poem about death. About what happened after we were gone—or didn't happen. Was her father dreaming through his twilight? Did he remember, or was there nothing left of him with which to even think? Hallie was the one who believed in spirits, in souls; Grace had always believed in science instead.

"Rossetti, right?" A voice came from below. Grace made a startled noise, and grabbed the door frame to stop herself from tumbling right out of the tree.

"Sorry! I didn't mean to scare you."

Grace caught her breath and peered down. A teenage boy was staring up at her. Hallie's age, maybe a little older, wearing a black jacket with something under his arm. He had square-rimmed glasses, his brown hair already tufting in the rain. "I always liked that one," he added. "The poem, I mean. And 'Do not stand at my grave and weep.' Mary Elizabeth Frye, I think."

Grace recovered. "Can I help you?" she asked, trying to sound polite.

"I was actually looking for a place to hide." The boy glanced back toward the house, then gave Grace a rueful smile. "It's pretty crowded in there, and my sister is being . . . let's just say, demanding."

He wanted to join her in the tree house, Grace realized with dismay. "I don't know if it'll take the weight."

"I have food." The boy offered up a box from under his arm with a hopeful expression. *The* box.

Pie.

Grace relented. "OK, but be careful, the ladder is kind of . . ." She trailed off as the boy expertly scrambled up the tree. "Weak," she finished as he collapsed on the floor beside her.

"Practice," he explained. "I climb rigging all the time out on the water."

"Oh," she said, disappointed. "You're one of *them*." He looked quizzical. "The people who yacht."

The boy laughed, then offered his hand. "I'm Theo."

Grace shook it carefully. "Grace."

"I know," he replied, easing open the pastry box. "We met before, at the christening."

Grace paused, assessing him again. But she had nothing. "I'm sorry, I don't remember. That day was kind of . . . a blur."

It was the only other time she'd stepped foot in that fancy church, exactly nine months after her father had left them. (The math was unavoidable.) Hallie had refused to go, of course, so it was left to Grace to stand politely in the front pew while baby Dash wailed so loudly even the pastor looked nervous to bless him. All Grace remembered was the reception afterward at some upscale hotel, and the fancy layer cake with chocolate frosting she'd eaten until she felt ill.

Faced with the pie there on the floor between them, Grace brightened. Maybe she wasn't a terrible person, after all; maybe that was just her mind's way of dealing with tragedy. In times of unbearable sadness, she thought about baked goods.

Theo must have seen her expression. "You like blueberry?" He pulled a fork and some napkins from his breast pocket and passed them over. "Go ahead."

Grace cut a couple of misshapen slices. "So how did you know my dad?" She passed a crumbling wedge to Theo. "You're one of Portia's crowd, aren't you?"

"You could say that." Theo took a bite, smearing blueberry filling across the side of his face. He laughed awkwardly, wiping his mouth. "She's my sister."

"Oh." Grace blinked. She'd known Portia had a younger brother, two of them, in fact, but had always pictured them just like her: perfectly coiffed hair and an elegant smile. Theo's tie was askew, his hair stuck out in wet tufts, and there was still a blueberry smudge on his chin. Still, there was something comforting about his haphazard appearance; she'd had just about all the fake perfection she could take.

"How is Portia doing?" Grace ventured at last, more because she felt she ought to than because she actually cared.

Theo gave a sad kind of smile. "She's holding up for now, but . . . she wasn't prepared for this."

"None of us were."

If Theo noticed the edge to Grace's voice, he was too polite to say. "I'll be sticking around for a while, to help out with Dash and . . . the arrangements."

He lived in New York, Grace remembered now. There were trust funds, and a town house on the Upper East Side, and a grandmother who ruled them all with an iron fist. Her father had explained about her new stepfamily, but Grace had done her best not to listen.

"My brother, Rex, is tied up with school in London at the moment." Theo added, "He sends his apologies."

"It's OK. Everyone's a blur to me," she admitted. "They all have the same look on their face, the same platitudes. 'I'm sorry for your loss.'" Grace sighed. "But I guess there's nothing else to say."

Theo swung his legs off the edge of the tree-house floor, back and forth. "Your dad talked about you all the time," he offered. "You and Hallie."

Grace looked over.

"Whenever I saw him at functions," Theo continued. "You know—Christmas, anniversaries." He made a wry face at that, then explained. "The Coates family is big on black-tie events. He said you were doing really well in school. Science, right?"

She nodded slowly. Grace never liked to think of her father off in his new life. It was easier, somehow, to leave it just a vague space, instead of imagining the realities of his day-to-day existence. Breakfast at someone else's table. Watching the nightly news, feet up on someone else's lap. But of course, he had a whole world, with people to talk to. About them.

"Astronomy," she said finally.

"And your sister's going to Juilliard." Theo smiled. "He was really proud of you both."

For the first time all week, Grace felt the sting of tears in the back of her throat. She quickly turned her face away. "I should get back," she said, swallowing them down. She scrambled to her feet, brushing the dust from her dress. "My mom, and Hallie . . ."

"Right. Of course, I'm sorry I kept you." Theo leaped up, but Grace waved him away.

"It's OK, you can stay."

"I shouldn't. This is your place." Theo gestured to the ladder. "After you."

Grace slithered back down the tree, and Theo followed. They lingered awkwardly for a moment.

"Thanks," Grace offered, forcing a tiny smile. "For the pie."

"No problem." Theo shoved his hands in his jacket pockets. "And, I know it doesn't mean anything, but . . . I'm sorry." His eyes met hers, quiet, sincere. "For your loss. For everyone's. He was a good man, and he loved you all so much."

Grace felt her control slipping. If she opened her mouth to say a single word, she knew she'd be powerless to stop the tears. She couldn't cry, not yet—not in front of Theo—so instead, she just nodded at him briskly, folding her arms tight around her, as if she could physically hold everything inside, and then hurried away, back to the house.

III

What do you mean, *nothing*?"

Grace flinched at Hallie's cry of disbelief. It was a week after the funeral, and they were sitting in the living room across from their dad's college friend Arthur. He was the executor of John's estate, he'd explained on the phone. He just needed a few minutes with their mom to discuss some legal details.

He'd neglected to mention that those details involved the complete ruin of the first Weston family.

"How can there be nothing?" Hallie demanded, as if Arthur were the one at fault, and not just the regretful messenger.

Arthur cleared his throat, a profoundly awkward look on his grizzled face. "Your, uh, father died intestate."

"No, he didn't," Hallie exclaimed. "He died in bed with that bitch!"

"Hallie . . ." Grace tugged her sister's sleeve—long and black, since Hallie had declared herself in official mourning and was recycling every outfit from her juvenile goth phase. "Let him finish."

"*Intestate* means without a will." Arthur coughed again, avoiding their gazes. "And in those cases where the deceased has no will, all assets pass directly to his nearest living kin." He coughed again. "His wife."

Hallie swore. Their mom sat silently on Grace's other side. By now, Grace knew not to expect a response from her. Her mom's fugue state had been replaced with wild-eyed nights spent painting in her studio; Grace had to physically drag her downstairs to meet Arthur, red paint still staining her fingertips like blood.

"But I don't understand," Grace said. "He had to have a will. He was all about paperwork, it was his thing." Bills, forms, official documents: those had been her father's forte. His filing system was a work of art, his study lined with banks of cabinets. "It's all in the details," he'd said, and winked, stowing away Grace's report card in her personal drawer. That was what made him such a financial whiz: he'd always take care of the fine print.

"I'm sorry." Arthur finally met their eyes. "There was one, but he and Portia had it voided, after the baby. . . . He always planned on making a new one, but things got busy, and . . . well, they never got around to it."

"How convenient," Hallie remarked, scathing. "Bitch."

• • •

Grace showed Arthur out, and then joined her mom and Hallie in the kitchen. It was still gray and damp out, but the kitchen had always been the warmest part of the house, painted yellow and snug with heat from the antique Aga cooker that took up half of one wall.

"We'll be fine," Hallie was saying, stabbing leftovers from a sympathy casserole straight from the dish. "We don't need anything from him, we never did."

Grace put the kettle on. "We can challenge it. The alimony he's been paying these last years, they have to keep that going. There'll be documents, some divorce judgment."

Their mom stayed silent. Grace looked over. "Mom? The alimony documents? Do you have them somewhere?"

She gave a faint shrug. "We never went to court. He offered more than enough, so we just kept it private."

Grace gaped. "You didn't have a lawyer?"

"He wanted it settled quickly, with the baby coming." Their mom looked drained. "I didn't see the point in fighting it. He was already gone."

"No, *now* he's gone." Grace set out teacups and a plate of cookies. The pie had only been the beginning: their cupboards were stocked full of sympathy baskets and bereavement baked goods. They'd be needing it, since apparently now they had no money to buy food.

"I don't get what you're so stressed about." Hallie pouted. "If he couldn't care enough to write a stupid will, then we're better off without him."

"Oh, yeah?" Grace shot back. "Who's going to support us now? Pay for heat, and electric bills, and all your trashy shows on cable?" She turned to their mom hopefully. "When was the last time you sold a painting?"

"Last month." Their mom paused, frowning. "No, wait. That was a gift, for Julianne. She gave me those lovely glazed urns in exchange." She smiled fondly at the row of hideous misshapen pottery.

So their mom's artistic endeavors wouldn't put food on the table. Hallie would be away at college soon, and Grace didn't think there were any businesses out there looking to hire a high-school student to work part-time for a full-time salary.

She slumped, the solution to their problems becoming painfully clear. "We'll have to sell the house."

Hallie gasped. "Grace!"

"What? It's our only option." She looked around, trying not to feel the clench of pain at the thought of leaving it and, instead, look at the cold, hard real-estate facts. Four bedrooms, two baths, a charming—if decrepit—attic studio . . .

"We can't leave. This is our home!" Hallie was still glaring at her as if Grace were the one who'd forgotten to leave a will.

"Which we can't afford on our own," Grace explained, trying to stay calm. She poured the tea and wished that, for once, Hallie could think logically. "But if we move somewhere smaller, we can live off the money from the sale. At least for a while." Grace put a teacup in front of their mom. "You should call a Realtor, start the whole process."

Their mom toyed with the delicate china cup. "I

can't, sweetie." She sighed. "The house is in his name too. Was."

Grace sat down with a thump. "What do you mean?" she whispered.

"Like I said, it was all so stressful. I didn't want to have to deal with the taxes, so we decided to just leave it in his name. So nothing would have to change."

"But it did!" Grace exclaimed. "It has! And now . . ." She trailed off, the terrible truth becoming clear.

"Don't worry, sweetheart." Her mom squeezed Grace's hand. "I'm sure it'll work out. It always does." She suddenly brightened. "Varnish!"

"What?"

"Varnish! I've been trying to get a glossy finish on this new piece I'm working on. Of course." Their mom got up from the table, finally animated. "Why didn't I think of it? Try not to disturb me, honey." She kissed Grace on the cheek. "I need total concentration." She wafted out.

Grace slumped until her chin was level with the table. Hallie pushed the casserole dish her way. "Don't be such a drama queen."

Grace's mouth dropped open, but Hallie didn't seem to grasp the irony. She rolled her eyes, unconcerned by their imminent poverty and destitution. "It's not like Portia's going to throw us out of our own home. We'll be fine."

Grace wanted to believe them, and for the next few weeks, it looked as if, perhaps, they might be right. She dug through the boxes of paperwork left in the study and found the statements for a forgotten savings account with enough money to pay their bills that month. Her mom was in talks with a new agent about a gallery show and a couple of potential commissions, and with school almost over, Grace could find a summer job. It wouldn't be much, she knew, but it might just be enough. Sure, there was still a hollow ache in her chest that Grace couldn't bear to think about—like staring into the sun—but every guide to grief and bereavement said that would ease, in time. Things were getting back to normal.

Then the letter arrived from Portia's lawyer.

"That . . . She's . . . Mmmph!" Hallie screamed in frustration, beyond words. She stormed out, leaving Grace clutching the crisp page.

Ownership of assets . . . Ms. Portia Weston's legal right . . . Vacate the property . . .

She lowered the letter, her hand shaking. "Mom?"

There was no reply.

"Mom?" she said, louder this time. Their mother was staring at a magazine cover, head tilted slightly as she gazed at some starlet posing in the ocean.

"Would you say that's an azure blue, or more of a cobalt?" she asked. "There are hints of aqua in the waves, but . . . No, it's definitely more cobalt."

Grace stifled a whimper. If there was any way of surviving this upheaval, it was down to her alone to find it.

IV

Grace waited across from school for the downtown bus the next day, trying to distract herself from the epic task ahead of her. She watched as students streamed through the gates: hipster, steampunk, Harajuku girl, goth, mathlete. Their mom had insisted on sending her and Hallie to an alternative charter school, the kind of place where Grace took mandatory personal empowerment classes along with her science and math immersion, and her fellow classmates were as likely to be tech wizards with Silicon Valley start-up funding as wide-eyed homeschoolers who were trying to integrate with society for the first time.

"Grace!" Hallie yelled from across the street, hanging with her group of cooler-than-thou graduating class—all red lipstick and weird vintage fashions that, to Grace, looked like something dragged from the back of their grandmother's closet. "Tell Mom I'm staying over at Mirabelle's tonight."

"Tell her yourself!" Grace yelled back.

Hallie looked exasperated. She detached herself from a guy wearing an ugly tweed jacket and a handlebar mustache, and sauntered across the street, not paying any mind to the traffic that had to screech to a halt in front of her. "Come on, Grace," she pleaded. "It's not like Mom even notices when I am there."

"She noticed enough to give you a midnight curfew," Grace replied, immune to Hallie's eyelash batting and pitiful puppy-dog stare. Hallie's helpless expression dropped; she glared at Grace with kohl-smudged eyes.

"You can be so immature, you know that?"

"And you can be back by midnight." Grace turned away as the bus shuddered to a stop in front of them. Hallie made a muffled scream of protest, and stormed back to her hipster friends, her long black skirts flaring out in her wake.

Grace swiped her pass and made her way to a free seat in the back. She was sick of being the one keeping tabs on her sister—Hallie was right, their mom was tuned out of the world right now: spending all day painting up in her studio, then surfacing out of nowhere at random hours to demand they eat their vegetables and get their homework done. But just because they could run around until dawn if they wanted, didn't mean they should. Hallie had been more of an erratic drama queen than ever since the funeral, and for all Grace knew, she was liable to wind up dead in a gutter outside some East Bay rock show at three a.m.

Or worse, hooking up with boys who thought Hitler was a role model when it came to facial hair.

Grace disembarked downtown and made her way past blocks of towering office buildings and chic storefronts to Portia's fancy apartment building. She and Grace's father had moved there only a few months ago: a prestigious address with brocade-trimmed doormen and views of the park. Grace stood a moment outside, staring up at the dark-green canopy as she steeled herself for what was to come. She'd never actually visited before; there had always been some excuse about Dash's nap routine, or renovation work. But now, with the pale sandstone towering above her, Grace felt like she was trespassing in a world to which she'd never been invited.

"Miss?"

Grace turned. The doorman was holding the polished glass door open, waiting. "Sorry," she murmured quickly, ducking past him.

Inside, it was more of the same: marble floors and glossy mirrors, and everything gleaming like it would smudge if she so much as looked twice at it. Grace crossed the lobby, nervous. "I'm here to see Portia Coates," she told the man behind the vast reception desk.

He stared at her blankly for a moment, then his expression cleared. "You mean Mrs. Weston?"

Grace swallowed. "Right. Her."

"Let me call up for you."

Grace waited while the man murmured into his phone, struck by the sudden fear that Portia would refuse to see her. They didn't have the kind of faux friendship she knew other friends managed with their stepparents, and although Grace had always been relieved by the distance between them, now she wished they'd at least pretended to be close. Maybe then Portia might feel some sense of duty to her stepdaughters, instead of having her lawyers treat them like squatters.

"You can go up," the man finally said, nodding toward the elevators. "Fifteenth floor. Penthouse."

When Grace emerged from the elevator, Portia was waiting in the cream carpeted hallway, wearing a pale silky dress and expression of wide-eyed delight. "Grace, darling, what a surprise!" She beckoned Grace closer and enfolded her in a brief, bony excuse for a hug. "How are you? How is your poor mother holding up? You poor dears."

Grace pulled back. "We're fine," she managed, thrown by the outpouring of enthusiasm. "I wanted to talk to you—"

"Of course, come in, come in! I'm afraid Dash is out with his uncle right now, but let's sit down and have some tea."

Grace followed her into the apartment. "Shoes." Portia pointed to the neat row by the door. Grace awkwardly kicked off her sneakers. There was a pause; Portia was still waiting expectantly, so Grace bent to straighten them in place. "Do you want a tour? We just finished the guest suite." Portia added, "The designer is a genius, I swear."

"Umm, sure." As much as Grace wanted to get this over with, she had to admit, she was curious about the place her father had called home. It looked like something out of a foreign design magazine, all-white sectional furniture with bulbous silver lamps swinging from the ceiling.

"So, these are the bedrooms," Portia began, striding briskly down a hallway. "Master, second, guest, Dash's room, the nanny's quarters . . ."

Grace peered through doorways as they passed, but they all looked the same: an expanse of white linens and pale carpet and austere abstract art. *Where did they put all their stuff?* Grace wondered. Clothes, and books, and last week's newspapers, and next week's projects. There had never been even the suggestion that she and Hallie would have a room here, and looking around, it was finally clear why. God forbid the girls ruin all this spotless perfection with their messy teenage lives.

"And here we are, back to the beginning!" Portia led her to the open living area, and sat on the very edge of one of those square white couches. "Please, sit," she told Grace. "Greta!"

Grace carefully took a seat as the Swedish nanny appeared, placing a tray of tea on the glass-topped coffee table before disappearing without a word. "Thanks!" Grace called after her, before the kitchen door swung shut and there was silence again.

"So." Portia poured her a dainty china cup of herbal

tea, then fixed Grace with an expectant look. "What's on your mind?"

Grace tried to organize her thoughts—to sound mature, and calm, and not sixteen. "We got a letter from your lawyer," she began. To her dismay, her voice came out shaking. "About the house."

"Mmm." Portia slowly stirred her tea, but didn't say anything else.

"They say we have to move out."

Portia gave her a patronizing smile. "Why don't we just leave that to the adults? How's school going? Are you looking forward to summer?"

Grace blinked. "No, you don't understand," she managed. "We can't leave, it's our home!"

"Now, Grace." Portia's tone was chiding. "Don't be so sentimental, you're not a little girl anymore. Home is wherever you make it." She tapped her teaspoon once on the edge of the cup; the ring of china echoing.

"But couldn't you let us stay?" Grace tried. "Just until Mom sells a few paintings, and we have some money saved?"

"Of course." Portia smiled at her again. "I told the lawyers, I'd be happy to work something out, provided your mother paid the going market rental."

Grace deflated. "But we can't afford to pay rent, not right now!"

Portia leaned forward. "You're looking at this all wrong, Grace. It's an opportunity for you all: a fresh start. Imagine how much happier you'll be when you're not rattling around that big old place. You know, I swear I smelled damp there," she added, "maybe even mold. Who knows what would happen to you if you stayed in that death trap? It's a blessing, you'll see."

"A blessing?" Grace's control slipped. "Don't you get it? We can't afford a new apartment, we can't afford anything! Without Dad, there's nothing!"

Portia folded her hands in her lap. "Now, your mother's financial life is not my responsibility. I'm sure there are savings, work she can do . . ."

"But this isn't what he would have wanted!"

Portia flinched.

"I'm sorry." Grace swallowed back her frustration, fighting to keep her voice even. "But you have to see, he never meant for this to happen."

Portia gave a little shrug, as if she were helpless. "Grace, dear, I'm a single mother now, I have to put poor Dashwood first. Do you have any idea what it costs to raise a child these days?"

Grace shook her head slowly.

"The nannies!" Portia exclaimed, aghast. "And then there's baby yoga, and mini-Mozart classes, and ante-pre-preschools to moderate his social adjustment. His child nutritionist alone runs three hundred dollars an hour, and that's not even accounting for private-school fees, or summer camp, or the Ivy League . . ." She shook her head, as if overwhelmed just by the thought of it. "I'm sorry, but you can see, my hands are tied."

Portia sipped her tea. Silence.

"But . . . what are we supposed to do?" Grace looked

at her, horror dawning. She really wasn't going to budge; Portia was going to take their home. "You can't just throw us out on the streets."

Portia widened her eyes and let out a mellifluous laugh. "Dear girl, what do you take me for—some kind of monster?"

Grace exhaled in relief.

"No, I'm giving you until the end of the month to move out." Portia beamed. "That should be plenty of time."

V

Grace managed to hold back the panic long enough to murmur a polite good-bye and make it down to the lobby, but no farther. As she stumbled out of the silent, polished bubble and into the noise and bustle of the street, she was overwhelmed with helplessness, so fierce she could barely breathe. What could they do now? Where were they going to go?

The tears were stinging in her throat again, but this time, Grace had no strength left to swallow them down. She pulled on her parka and hurried blindly down the sidewalk, her chest shuddered with the first traitorous sob.

"Grace!"

She was halfway down the block before the sound of her own name filtered through her distress. Grace turned to find Theo behind her: dressed in preppy khakis and a parka, tugging Dash in a stroller.

"Grace?" His face changed as he took in her expression. "Are you OK? What happened?"

She tried to tell him everything was fine, but her voice choked in her throat.

Theo looked around at the rush-hour crowds, jostling past them with impatient expressions. "Come on."

He ushered her across the street, pushing the stroller with his free hand. Grace was powerless to resist; it took everything she had to swallow back the sobs. She was mortified. Weeping in the middle of the street like she was some pitiful basket case. Like she was Hallie!

Theo steered them into the park across the street, depositing her on a bench. "Do you need me to call someone?" he asked, digging through the diaper bag until he found a packet of tissues for her. "Your mom, maybe?"

"I'm fine!" Plastering on a smile, she wiped the tears from her cheeks. "Nothing's wrong. It's just . . . my allergies," she covered. "You know, hay fever."

The excuse sounded weak, even to her. "You sure you don't need anything?" Theo kept pulling items from the bag. "Juice box? Pacifier? Mr. Wiggums?" He waved a stuffed elephant. Grace took the juice with a faint smile.

"Thanks."

She sipped through the tiny straw, focusing on taking one deep breath, and then another. The park around them was shady and green; kids playing on a distant set of monkey bars. The comforting hum of the city surrounded them, a world away from the icy silence of Portia's apartment. Slowly, she felt herself calm.

Grace could feel Theo studying her, so she turned to the stroller—which was less a stroller than an off-road vehicle, swathed with sun-netting protection and safety straps. "How's Dash?" she asked brightly. "Have you guys been having fun?"

"If by 'fun' you mean intellectually stimulating structured playtime, then yes." Theo grinned. He reached into the stroller, lifted Dash out, and before she could protest, gently placed him in Grace's arms.

"Hey, you." Grace held him awkwardly. "What's up?" He had blue eyes, and tufts of dark hair, like her dad—their dad—and was swathed in a tiny white sailor's suit. He blinked at her, gurgling. Grace blinked back. "I don't think I've ever seen him so calm," she told Theo, surprised. "He's always . . . you know."

"A brat?" Theo laughed. "It's all the fussing Portia does, it gets him wound up. I tell her that he just wants to eat and sleep, but she's convinced he needs all those classes." He shrugged. "But what do I know? I just get to be the cool uncle, I'm not the one getting up in the middle of the night."

Nor, Grace suspected, was Portia, but she didn't say so. That awful sympathetic look was gone from Theo's face, and she felt less like a wretched mess. "What about you?" she asked, slurping her juice. "How have you been?"

"OK. I mean . . ." Theo paused. "I heard, about the

will." He looked awkward. "I wanted to say something before, but—"

"It's fine!" Grace interrupted. "I mean, it's out of our hands. There's nothing we can do about it."

"I tried to reason with her," Theo offered, looking miserable. "I mean, you're family. Sort of. But she wouldn't—"

"Can we not talk about it?" Grace cut him off again. "Please. I can't . . ." She swallowed. "I just want to forget about it, OK?"

"OK." Theo nodded. He opened his mouth to speak, and Grace was afraid he'd ask something more about her father—about the grief, or the money, or any one of the things she knew would prompt a whole new wave of "hay fever" tears. But instead, he offered a grin. "Want to go show Dash the ducks?"

"Sure." Grace exhaled in relief. "That sounds perfect."

They found a dry spot near the pond. Theo produced a blanket from the depths of the stroller and spread it on the grass. They settled on either side, letting Dash crawl around between them.

"So what's Hallie up to?" Theo asked, leaning back on his elbows. "I think I heard something about a street-drama project . . . ?"

"Oh, God." Grace rolled her eyes. "That was last month. She and some of her theater friends decided to perform scenes out on the street, like a flash mob, but with theater? Anyway, it would have been fine, except they decided to do the murder scenes from *Macbeth*. In downtown Oakland. With fake blood and prop swords."

Theo laughed.

"It wasn't so funny trying to get her home from the police precinct," Grace told him. "She nearly got charged with public disturbance, ranting about freedom of creative expression and the fascist police state."

"She's certainly . . . interesting," Theo said, lips twisting as he tried not to grin.

"That's one way of putting it." Grace watched Dash pick up a leaf and start chewing. "Should we . . . ?"

Theo shrugged. "It's organic, right?"

Grace laughed, the last of her tension draining away. "What about you? How come you're done with school already?"

"I had enough credits to graduate early." Theo pulled his jacket sleeves over his hands. "I was at boarding school," he explained, "so I didn't really feel like sticking around. And then when Portia called . . . I figured she could use the help."

"That's really nice of you." Grace frowned. He caught the expression.

"What?"

"Nothing. I just . . . You're not at all alike." As soon as the words were out, Grace realized how that sounded. "I didn't mean, you know . . . Just . . ." She sighed, defeated. "You're different, that's all."

"Too different," Theo murmured. Dash tried to crawl off into the pond, but Theo caught him by the suspenders on his sailor suit and yanked him back. "Not so fast, kid."

"What do you mean, 'too different'?" Grace shifted so she was sitting cross-legged.

"I'm kind of the black sheep of the family."

"You?" Grace laughed. Theo was kind, polite, and didn't seem to mind toting his baby nephew around for the day. In her book, that made him some kind of saint among teen boys. "What, are you hiding some secret addiction, or criminal record or something?"

"Ha, that would be fine," Theo told her. "Uncle Emmett is doing two years for tax evasion, and my grandma . . . Let's just say, she likes her brandy." He gave a rueful grin. "Nope, I'm the real scandal. Chronic lack of ambition."

Grace blinked. "You're eighteen. Are you even supposed to have ambition yet?"

"Oh, yes." Theo nodded. "I'm supposed to be on track for law school, or finance. I wanted to take time off before college, you know, travel. Volunteer, maybe, but the way they flipped out . . ." He exhaled in a long sigh. "I don't know what they'll say when I declare my major."

"Fashion," Grace guessed, teasing. "Modern dance. Nineteenth-century Romantic poetry."

"Close," he said, laughing. "No, I want to study philosophy."

"How is that weird?" Grace exclaimed, baffled.

"I know, it's crazy," Theo agreed. "To hear them go on about it, you'd think I was going to wind up stripping in some dive bar in Pensacola."

Grace laughed. "With an Ivy League education, you could make it to Miami at least. Someplace classy."

Theo laughed with her. "The Coates family . . . it's a weird beast, that's all. Normal rules don't really apply. But I guess every family is strange, in its own way."

"Yup." Grace nodded slowly, thinking of her mom—still locked in the attic, far from reality—and Hallie, probably out getting arrested even as they spoke. Theo winced.

"I'm sorry. Going on about college, and family—that's, like, nothing, compared to you and—"

"No!" Grace cut him off. "No talking about that. We had a deal."

Theo paused. "OK."

They were interrupted by his cell phone. Grace paused. "Is that . . . the *Addams Family* theme?"

"What? No. Never." Theo snatched the phone up. "Hey, Portia. . . . No, we'll be right up."

He hung up, looking apologetic. "I have to get back. It's time for his language immersion hour."

Grace stared. "His what?"

"Portia likes to play French language tapes at him while he naps," Theo explained, getting to his feet. "It's supposed to acclimatize them to the sound."

"Wow." Grace looked at Dash, now happily sucking on Theo's shoelace. "When I was a kid, I just had Disney movies and My Little Ponies."

"You had Disney?" Theo clutched his chest. "I'm jealous. We just had PBS." She laughed, helping him fold up the blanket and strap Dash back into the stroller.

"Hey, are you doing anything later?" Theo asked as they headed back across the park. "I was thinking about seeing a movie. If you're free, I mean."

Grace paused. Did he think he had to babysit her, like Dash?

"It's just, I don't really know anyone in town, and I really need a break from family. Not you," he added quickly. "You're not—well, you know what I mean."

"OK," Grace replied slowly. "I mean, sure, that sounds fun."

"Great." He grinned. "I'll call you later."

Theo's phone rang again, with the same familiar booming chords. He picked up. "Yes, Portia, I'm literally across the street." He rolled his eyes at Grace. "We'll be right there." He hung up, sighing. "Duty calls."

"Au revoir."

VI

Grace went to the movies with Theo that night, more to escape the thought of her imminent homelessness than for the gross-out comedy they wound up seeing. But Theo proved a good distraction: regaling her with horror stories of his family, and the hell that was boarding school, and never once mentioning Grace's father or the crisis what was left of her own family now faced. To her surprise, it was fun, and Grace was glad of the friendly face and the chance to put the real world on hold, just for a few hours. Soon they fell into a regular routine: meeting after Grace got out of school to go take Dash to the park, or the zoo, until that familiar *Addams Family* theme started up and Portia summoned Theo home again.

"How's Theodore?" Hallie asked with a mischievous smile at the end of the next week. It was dinnertime, or at least what passed for dinner those days: Grace throwing cheese and toppings on some store-bought pizza bases while Hallie dumped a couple of bags of salad into a bowl.

"He's fine." Grace shrugged, doling out the pepperoni slices. Hallie reached over to grab a handful of chopped olives. "Hey!"

Hallie danced back, tossing the olives in the air and catching them in her mouth. "You guys have been spending a ton of time together . . ."

"Sure. I guess." Grace didn't want to tell her that it was better than sitting around the house all evening, waiting for Hallie to saunter home or their mom to finally emerge from her attic studio, too distracted to hold a conversation. "He's fun, once you get to know him."

"You know, he could be kind of cute," Hallie mused, "if he lost those preppy shirts . . . and changed his hair . . . and did something about those glasses . . ."

"What, you mean, got a pair of those stupid big hipster frames and grew a mustache?" Grace replied, laughing. "Sure, like that's cute."

"You need to move past this generic standard of hotness you've been indoctrinated with," Hallie told her airily. "The whole Abercrombie dumb jock thing is so over."

"Theo isn't a dumb jock!"

"Aha!" Hallie grinned. "So you *do* like him."

"I never said I didn't." Grace finished assembling the pizzas and carefully slid them into the oven. "He's nice. You should come hang out with us sometime."

"I wouldn't want to intrude."

"On what?" Grace turned, and found Hallie wiggling her eyebrows suggestively. "No!" Grace yelped. "You don't think . . . ? Hallie, that's ridiculous!" She hurled a tea towel at her, but couldn't keep from blushing furiously.

Hallie ducked, laughing. "You *like* him," she teased, singsong. "You want to *kiss* him!"

"He's our stepbrother! Or stepuncle," Grace managed, stumbling for words. Her, and Theo . . . ? "Whatever he is, he's related!"

"Not by blood." Hallie grinned.

"You're crazy," Grace said firmly as their mom wafted in. She was still wearing pajamas, braids splattered with a gruesome pattern of red paint.

"Who's crazy?" She blinked at them, as if they were slowly coming into focus from very far away.

"Nothing," Grace replied quickly. "Hallie, can you help at all? Set the table, or something."

"Grace's got a crush on Theo," Hallie said, collapsing at the table, so Grace was left to set out silverware and dishes alone.

"I do not!"

"Do too." Hallie stuck her tongue out.

"Real mature."

Their mom joined Hallie at the table. "Theo, Theo . . ." she mused, as if trying to place him. Then she brightened. "Oh, yes, he's a sweet boy. Very polite. You two would be good together."

"Mom!" Grace cried.

Hallie giggled. "She's right, you do match: you're both as boring as each other. You'd just sit around apologizing: 'No, you go first.' 'No, you,'" she mimicked. "Be still my heart."

"Now, sweetie, don't say that," their mom chided her. "I'm sure Grace and Theo have a sweet little romance."

Grace ignored them. Arguing was futile once Hallie got a notion in her head, so instead, she pulled out the real-estate section she'd marked earlier, and deposited it on the table.

"We only have a couple of weeks left," she reminded them. "I circled some apartments to check out. You can call the Realtor tomorrow."

Hallie glanced at the first page. "Oakland? Emeryville? Grace, you can't be serious!"

"We can't afford to stay around here." Grace sighed, for what felt like the hundredth time.

"But these places . . ." Hallie screwed her face up as she scanned the page. "Above a Chinese restaurant . . . Fourth-floor walk-up . . . Two bedrooms?" She gasped. "I need my own room!"

"You need a pull-out bed for when you're home from college," Grace corrected her.

"But what about my studio?" Their mom frowned. "I need good light, and space too. Maybe we can find somewhere with an annex in the garden. . . ." She flipped through the listings. "Ooh, this one sounds nice: three-bedroom cottage, wood floors, a conservatory out back . . ."

Grace looked over her shoulder as she passed. "Gee, and only four thousand dollars a month."

"That's not too bad." Their mom circled it with a pen.

"We can't afford that!" Grace cried, but it was as if she'd never spoken.

"And what about this one?" Hallie bent her head closer to their mom's, pointing out a new listing. "Charming Victorian, wraparound porch, original fireplaces . . ."

Grace stifled a groan. "Please, be serious . . ."

"Oh, go call Theo." Hallie rolled her eyes. "Maybe a few hours making out with him will get you to lighten up."

"For the last time," Grace cried, "there's nothing going on!"

"Sure there isn't, sweetie." Their mom patted Grace's arm absently. "But be careful. Use protection."

Grace tried to forget Hallie's teasing. For years, her sister had been on a diet of weighty Russian literature and heartbroken poetry; obsessed with the idea of true love. She was forever seeing secret romances where there were none to see: Mrs. Martinez (their aging housekeeper) and Kingston (neighbor, midforties, gay); their (happily married) principal at school and the barely out of college math teacher; and now, it seemed, Grace and Theo.

But she couldn't shake it. Toting Dash around Fisherman's Wharf with Theo the next afternoon, Grace couldn't help but wonder: if Hallie thought Grace had a crush on him, did that mean other people did too? And—oh, God—what about Theo himself?

"You want me to take him?" Theo interrupted her

panicked thoughts. "You're looking kind of flushed. He gets heavy, I know."

"Oh, right, sure." Grace passed Dash over, and took possession of the empty stroller in return. Theo settled the baby easily on one hip.

"Time to stop wearing Auntie Grace out," he told Dash. "You're too chunky."

"Just chunky enough," Grace corrected quickly, opening a granola bar snack. "We don't want him growing up with an eating disorder."

Theo laughed. "This kid? No way. He'll be sneaking candy behind Portia's back as soon as he's old enough to walk."

They paused by a guardrail overlooking the bay. A middle-aged tourist couple was taking photos with Alcatraz in the background, and stopped to coo over Dash; neon fanny packs strapped around their waists. "Your son is adorable!" The woman beamed.

Grace choked on her granola bar.

"Thanks," Theo replied, straight-faced. "We're very proud of him."

The couple moved off; Grace smacked his arm. "Why did you say that?" she cried, flushing. "They probably think I'm some kind of teen mom!"

He grinned. "Hey, that's not a bad career move. You could get a reality TV show, get in some magazines . . ." Theo stopped, seeing Grace's expression. "I'm sorry. I figured it was the easiest way to brush them off, you know? If we'd said he wasn't ours, they'd have asked where his parents were. . . ."

"No, you're right." Grace tried to relax. She shouldn't overreact, just because Hallie had been teasing her. And what was it they said about protesting too much? "It was just weird. I mean, us, together!" She gave an awkward laugh.

As they strolled back toward the street, Grace's gaze slid over to Theo. Hallie was wrong about his hair. It was cute the way it always stuck out slightly, as if he'd absently run his hand over it in the wrong direction; better than those boys in school with their side-swept bangs they were constantly brushing across, like they were trying to be a teen pop superstar. And his glasses weren't that dorky either, she decided: plain gold wire rims that framed his brown eyes, a kind of absentminded professor look. She could picture him in twenty years in a patched tweed jacket, hiding out in a book-lined study grading papers.

"How's the apartment hunt?" Theo ventured. Grace had shared some of her frustrations when it came to her family and their rose-tinted view on reality, but the topic was still edged with tension; Portia always lurking, unspoken, at the back of every conversation. "Have you found anywhere you like yet?"

"No." Grace sighed. "I don't know what Mom and Hallie expect to happen: that some fairy godmother's going to conjure a place out of nowhere. I've started packing up our stuff," she added. "It's such a big house, I don't want to leave it to the last minute."

"I could help," Theo offered immediately. "I'm a master

packer. Trust me, I was the envy of the whole school come the end of the year. Advanced special awareness."

"Fancy!" Grace bit her lip, thinking. "There is a lot to do. I'm not even halfway through the lounge yet. . . ."

"Then I'm in," Theo declared. "I'll come by on the weekend, bring some takeout. Make a party of it."

"Either you've been to some lame parties, or Portia won't let processed foods in the house." Theo looked bashful. "Knew it!" Grace laughed.

"It's all organic, raw stuff. I'm wasting away!"

"Then fine," Grace agreed. "But you'll need to earn it. Bring duct tape."

When Grace returned home, she found Hallie in the middle of one of her fits: clutching a letter on the stairs, while their mom tried in vain to calm her.

"It'll be OK, sweetie."

"It won't! He's ruined everything!" Hallie screamed. "I hate him, I hate you all!" She turned and stormed upstairs in a whirl of black, her door slamming a moment later.

Grace shrugged off her jacket. "What is it this time?"

Their mom looked drained. "Juilliard. They can't hold her place without the next tuition installment."

"But . . . Dad set up college funds for us!" Grace gasped, "Portia can't take that too!"

"Your father had investment accounts," her mom corrected. "Portia's lawyers say he could have meant that money for anything."

Grace felt a surge of rage, and fought to keep it back. Getting mad wouldn't solve anything. It was done. "Can she apply for financial aid? Scholarships?"

"Not for this year. And with her grades . . ."

They shared a look. Hallie may have excelled when it came to theatrics, but as for regular math and science? Not so stellar. "Poor Hallie," Grace said. "She was so happy to get in."

Their dad had been happy too: taking them out for a fancy dinner at Hallie's favorite French restaurant, and boasting to every waiter who'd listen about his brilliant daughters and what amazing colleges they'd attend.

Portia had been otherwise engaged that night.

The phone began to ring down the hall. "I'll get it," her mom said quickly. "You go see if she's OK." She hurried away before Grace could object—as if parenting were a simple matter of claiming "Not it!" first.

Grace climbed the stairs and tapped awkwardly on Hallie's door. There was no reply, so she pushed it open. The room was dim, light barely filtering through the thick velvet curtains onto dark walls pinned with pages from fashion magazines and framed art deco advertisements. Hallie was crumpled in a heap on her bed, sobbing loudly.

"Hey," Grace began, carefully picking her way through the clothing and magazines strewn across the floor. "Mom told me. I'm really sorry."

Hallie lifted her head, eyes smeared with running mascara. "How could he do this to me?"

"He didn't mean to," Grace murmured, perching on the edge of the bed. "It's not his fault."

"Would you stop it!" Hallie cried, bolting upright. "God, I'm so sick of you making excuses for him. Can't you just be angry for once?"

Grace sighed. "Why?"

"Because he left!" Hallie's voice cracked. "He turned around and left, and didn't even care what would happen to us—"

"Hallie, you know that's not true."

"Is it?" Hallie glared at her, defiant. "If you care about someone, you look out for them. You write a freaking will!"

This was useless. Grace stood. "I'll go make you some tea. We can talk about it when you calm down."

"There you go again!" Hallie leaped up. "'Calm down,' 'he didn't mean it,'" she mimicked. "When will you just admit you hate him too?"

"I don't," Grace told her firmly.

"Right," Hallie said, her voice scathing. "And Portia's just doing what she thinks is best, and Mom will get her act together soon, and you aren't sitting around all day pining over your precious Theo."

Grace hardened. "So what do you want me to do—throw tantrums like you?" she shot back. "Use up all my energy weeping and wailing, like that's going to make a difference?"

It was the wrong thing to say. "You always do this!" Hallie clenched her fists. "Make me feel like I'm crazy for having feelings. It's not fair! I'm allowed to grieve!"

"Grief is one thing," Grace told her, patience finally

worn out. She'd been indulging Hallie for too long. "Wallowing in denial doesn't solve anything."

"It's not supposed to!" Hallie yelled. Her voice was hoarse now. "It's about *expressing! How! I! Feel!*" Hallie punctuated every word by hurling something at Grace: a handy magazine, a pair of pants, a vase from her nightstand.

Grace ducked. The vase smashed against the door. "You're insane!"

"And you're a robot with no heart!"

"Well, which is it?" Grace yelled. "Either I have no feelings, or I'm repressing them!"

Hallie threw herself down on the bed again and screamed into her pillow.

"See? This is why I have to keep it together," Grace told her, furious. "Someone has to be the grown-up in this family, and apparently, I'm the only one left!"

She whirled around to leave, but their mom appeared, blocking the door. Grace flushed, guilty. "Sorry."

Her mom blinked. "For what?"

"She started it!" Hallie's voice was still muffled, face-down in her comforter.

But before Grace could even begin to explain, their mom continued. "Everything's going to be all right," she said, her expression brighter than Grace had seen in weeks. "I found a place for us to live!"

VII

The house—well, guesthouse—belonged to Auggie Jennings, a cousin of their mother's in Los Angeles who had made a name for himself producing scandalous true-crime TV movies, and now wanted nothing more than to offer his riches and real estate to his poor, impoverished family.

"Apparently, he's rattling around some huge mansion with his *twenty-two-year-old* wife," Grace told Theo as they transferred the contents of the lounge into packing crates.

"Twenty-two isn't so young," Theo argued. "My parents got married right out of high school."

Grace fixed him with a look. "He's in his fifties."

"Ah." Theo laughed. "OK, that is kind of weird."

"Not as weird as packing up and moving to a whole new city to live with a man we've never met." Grace's relief at the answer to all their prayers was dampened by what she didn't know about their new favorite "Uncle." Namely, almost everything.

"Of course you've met him," her mom insisted, breezing in. "He came to your birthday party, when he was in town one year. The one with the cowboy theme."

"I was four!"

"And clearly, you made a great impression." Her mom beamed. She'd been wafting around on a cloud of joy ever since Uncle Auggie (as he insisted they call him) had been in touch, thrilled by the thought of a dedicated studio and all that Southern Californian light. "Or maybe it was the portrait. I painted his dogs for Christmas last year," she explained to Theo. "Matching shih tzus. So cute!" She sailed out.

Grace sighed.

"Maybe it won't be so bad," Theo offered. "A fresh start. Or it could just be temporary, until you figure something else out . . ." He trailed off with a guilty look. "I'm sorry. I know I keep saying this, and it doesn't make a difference, but . . . I'm sorry. I never thought Portia would take it this far."

So far, in fact, that Portia had already sold the house to one of those condo developers. The demolition was scheduled for next week; Grace was glad she wouldn't be around to witness that, at least.

"I know," Grace reassured him. "It's not your fault. It's just the way things are."

She surveyed the half-packed room, full of crumpled newspaper and the objects that had, for so long, made up the background fabric of her life. Generous as Auggie's offer was, there wouldn't be room for the Westons plus all their worldly belongings; half the house was going into storage, and thanks to Hallie and her mom's inability to part with so much as a used ticket stub, it was down to Grace to decide which half.

"Come on," she said, trying for a brighter tone. "I've got a ton of old textbooks that need to go to Goodwill. You can break your back as penance for Portia's sins."

Theo laughed. "I don't love her that much. A muscle strain, maybe."

"I'll take it."

They spent the rest of the morning dismantling her bedroom; Grace trying to ignore the pangs of loss with every photo she peeled from the wall, and every book she stashed away in the "storage" pile. She should be grateful. Hallie's fairy godmother had appeared in the form of a balding distant cousin with a mysterious sense of family loyalty. Without him, she knew, she'd still be wrangling her mom and Hallie into a fifth-floor walk-up on the other side of the bay. But Grace couldn't help the apprehension that bubbled up every time she thought about leaving town. Beverly Hills may be only six hours away on the freeway, but it seemed like a world away from home, her school, her friends . . .

And Theo.

Not that he was staying, Grace reminded herself firmly. He was heading back to the East Coast next week, to start his summer job teaching sailing in the Hamptons.

"That sounds fun. Preppy, but fun," Grace had teased when he'd told her about his plans.

"Tell that to my grandma. Coates men don't soil the family name with manual labor." Theo's voice had been light, but Grace could tell there was tension there.

"Right," she'd agreed. "Because yachting is up there with coal mining and lumberjacking. Oh, the shame!"

"Is lumberjacking even a word?" Theo had grinned, and just like that, the tension was broken.

"Here, catch," Grace said, tossing a canvas bag down at Theo. He caught it deftly, peering inside.

"What is this stuff?" Theo pulled out a miniature blowtorch and a handful of metal pins.

"Design elective last year," she explained. "I had to do an art project, so I picked the most scientific one I could."

Theo pulled out one of her finished pieces: a pendant in the shape of a periodic element, pins welded together as electrons and neutrons. "You made this? It's great." He looked at it a moment, then laughed.

"What?"

"Nothing, it's just . . . it's the sign for gold, and you made it out of silver." Theo turned it over in his hands. "That's cool."

"You're the first person to get that." Grace smiled. Their eyes met for a moment, and she turned away, awkward. "Science geeks, we be crazy!"

"So which box?" Theo asked. "Keep?"

Grace wavered. "Storage," she decided. "No, wait, trash."

Theo put the bag in the storage box. "Maybe you'll want it one day," he told her with a smile. Grace sighed. "At this rate, we'll need ten lockers! And that's not even counting Hallie's collection of *Vogue*s."

"What are you saying about me now?" Hallie's voice came from down the hall.

"Nothing!" Grace yelled back. "Be careful," she whispered to Theo as footsteps came closer. "She's been kind of . . . emotional, since Juilliard."

He nodded, arranging his face into a cautiously sympathetic expression, but when the door swung wider, Hallie danced in. The black mourning garb was gone: in its place was a floaty vintage print dress and fifties starlet lipstick. She was humming an indie rock song, as carefree as if the past month of tantrums had never happened. "Hey, Theo!" Hallie held out her hand. "Up high."

Theo slowly high-fived her, sending Grace a confused look. Hallie waltzed over to the storage pile. "Oh, our old teddy bears, cute!"

"Umm, Hallie," Grace asked carefully. "How are you feeling?"

"Great!" She beamed.

"Did you take some of Mom's pills?" Grace checked. "Because you know the doctor says to be careful—"

"Relax!" Hallie grinned. "I'm not high."

"OK." Grace was still suspicious. "Drunk?"

"Grace! I'm fine. Even better than fine." Hallie beamed. "We're moving to Hollywood!"

"Beverly Hills isn't technically Hollywood," Grace corrected, but Hallie just rolled her eyes.

"It's close enough. Don't you see?" she declared. "I wanted to be an actress, and now I will be! I don't need stupid Juilliard, I can get all the experience and contacts I need in L.A. Train with the greats, go to auditions . . ." She struck a pose, knocking into Grace's stack of old school reports. Theo leaped up to keep them from tumbling down. "It's perfect."

"Uh-huh," Grace murmured. Hallie narrowed her eyes.

"It wouldn't kill you to be more supportive. I thought you wanted me to move on, embrace the change. So I'm embracing it!"

"That's great," Grace said quickly. "I'm really happy for you. Have you started packing yet?"

"Packing can wait!" Hallie danced back across the room. "I'm going to go celebrate. Mirabelle and the gang are dying of jealousy!" She paused, looking back and forth between Grace and Theo. "You should do something too." She gave Grace a suggestive look. "Go out. Get crazy." She winked, slamming the door behind her.

"Wow." Theo blinked. "Where does she find the energy for all those mood swings? I'm exhausted just looking at her."

"I think it's like photosynthesis," Grace replied, going back to packing. "She absorbs drama and conflict from the universe, and turns it into pure emotion."

"Still, I think she's right about one thing." Grace looked up. "Going out," Theo explained. He stuck his hands in his pockets, suddenly looking awkward. "I was thinking tomorrow night? As a good-bye. I'll be leaving next week, and you need to give the city a send-off. . . ."

"But there's so much to do!"

"It can wait," he reassured her.

"I guess . . ." Grace suddenly realized: he'd said "tomorrow *night*." Aside from that first movie, all their hanging out had been in daylight hours: museums, parks, usually with baby Dash around as chaperone. This would be different.

"Come on," Theo insisted. "Hallie shouldn't be the only one to have some fun."

He looked at her across the room, brown eyes warm behind his glasses, and despite herself, Grace felt her resolve slip. She had so little time left, she shouldn't spend it all with boxes and packing tape. This wasn't about Theo, she decided, it was about the city—her home. She deserved a good-bye. "OK," Grace finally agreed. Theo grinned.

"It's a date."

Grace knew that Theo hadn't meant "date" like *date*. But still, she felt a flutter of nerves when she opened the door to find Theo wearing a dress shirt and tie, his hair smoothed back into something resembling a neat style.

"Fancy," she teased, hiding her dismay. She'd picked a skirt and sweater almost exactly like the half dozen other skirt-and-sweater outfits Theo had already seen her in. After all, there wasn't anything to get dressed up for; they were just hanging out, like normal.

Right?

Theo coughed, looking awkward. "You look great."

Grace felt herself start to blush. "Thanks."

There was a pause.

"You, umm, ready to go?"

"Sure!" Grace startled. "Let me just grab my coat."

Grace hurried down the hall and ducked into the mudroom, scrambling for the lip gloss she knew Hallie always kept in her coat pocket. Was it too late to put her hair up? Grace wondered, smearing on the pink balm. She caught sight of her reflection, and immediately wiped it all off again. No, she was overreacting again. Theo was just a nice guy who had been raised to wear something other than a ratty T-shirt from time to time. Tonight was nothing special.

She grabbed her coat and hurried back, hoping to get Theo out of the house before Hallie could—

"Hey, Theodore."

Too late. Grace returned to find Hallie sizing Theo up with a careful stare. "Where are you kids going?"

"Out," Grace answered shortly. She pulled on her parka and turned to Theo. "Ready?"

But Theo was nothing if not well mannered. "How's it going?" he asked Hallie.

"You mean, besides moving across the state because your sister is a thieving selfish bitch?"

Grace gasped. "Hallie!"

"What?" She shrugged, apparently unconcerned. "We all know the truth, there's no point dancing around it."

Theo looked amused. "I'll tell her you said hi."

Hallie turned to Grace. "Don't stay out too late," she said with a smirk. "I'd tell you to be good, but you don't know how to be anything different."

Grace glared, and hustled Theo out the door. "I am so sorry!" she told him, the minute they were outside.

Theo gave her a grin. "How is it we spend most of our time apologizing for our sisters?"

"Because they're insane?" Grace suggested, then stopped. "I didn't mean—"

"Oh, you did, and she is." Theo laughed. "You know, she's got Dash seeing a child psychologist?"

"What?" Grace stopped. "He can't even talk!"

"She's worried he's traumatized by all the change," Theo explained. "So now some guy comes for an hour every night to watch him play and make notes about his sociability."

"OK," Grace agreed. "You're right. Our sisters *are* crazy."

VIII

Theo had planned a whistle-stop farewell tour of the city: trying to cram a visit to every major tourist spot into just a few hours. They took a cable car up to Chinatown, browsed the used bookstores along Little Italy, and tossed pennies in the Japanese fountains in Golden Gate Park. By the time they climbed the cliff staircase at Ocean Beach, Grace felt as if her feet were about to give way, but as Theo led her out to the cliff-top lookout point, her exhaustion disappeared.

"God, I love this view." Grace walked to the very edge of the observation deck and clutched the stone balustrades. The bay was chilled and windswept before them, sun just sinking in the distance. Grace knew they had beaches in Southern California—golden sands, gentle waves—but she would miss the coastline here the most.

The waves shifted, dark and stormy even on the clearest days, and the cliffs cast shadows over the water below.

"Dad brought me up all the time as a kid," she told Theo, smiling at the memories. "Hallie would have a theater class over in the Presidio, so we'd come here. There used to be a museum right here at the top," she added, "full of old arcade games. I would make the fortune-teller keep spitting out new futures until I got the one I liked."

"What did it predict for you?"

"Fame, fortune, eternal happiness. You know, the usual." Grace remembered the way her father would always follow the same routine: first the arcade, then a bracing walk across the beach—heads down against the winds, wrapped in their warmest winter gear—then finally a hot dog from the stand up by the cliffs, before meeting Hallie with ketchup stains on their fingers and mustard on their shirts. But soon enough, Hallie quit the theater group over some fight, and their dad started spending weekends at the office, and their Saturday rituals became a thing of the past.

The moments they'd shared, she'd never get back. Grace shivered.

"Hungry?" Theo's voice brought her back to the windy cliff top. For a moment, she'd forgotten he was even there.

"Always." Grace turned away from the ocean, trying to smile. "Where to?"

"Right here." Theo nodded behind them, to the white building where the ramshackle museum had once stood.

"Oh." Grace paused, taking in the sleek cars parked

out front, and the uniformed guy loitering at the valet stand. She swallowed, feeling that flutter of nerves return. "Sure," she exclaimed brightly. "Looks great!"

Inside, the restaurant was all bleached wood and wrap-around views of the ocean, filled with the low hum of adult conversation and the dignified ring of silverware on expensive china. Grace carefully placed the heavy linen napkin on her lap and gave Theo a nervous smile over the arrangement of lilies between them on the table.

This was way out of her comfort zone.

At least Theo looked as awkward as she felt: Grace could see him flushing slightly. He reached for the bread basket, and knocked his water glass—righting it just before it spilled.

"Phew." Theo made an exaggerated expression. "Close one."

"Yup."

Silence.

Grace sank in her seat, hiding behind her menu. Why couldn't they have just grabbed sushi from their usual hole-in-the-wall, and eaten off paper plates on her living room floor? Sure, it wasn't exactly atmospheric, but right now, Grace would happily take half-packed boxes and the distant sound of Hallie's arty rock playlists than this stifled, awkward silence.

"So . . . what are you getting?" Theo asked. Was it her imagination, or did he sound nervous?

"Umm." Grace hadn't even glanced at the neat calligraphy. She quickly scanned the list, trying to decide what—

She yelped. "Thirty dollars, for pasta?"

"Don't worry about it," Theo reassured her. "It's my treat. Get whatever you want."

But Grace couldn't let him do that. Theo might have a trust fund waiting for him when he turned twenty-one, but she knew he wasn't the kind to coast on family money a day before then. This meal would be paid for with part-time tutoring earnings, and the last of his summer-job savings—and Grace could never stand for that. "Theo, I can't let you do this!"

"It's fine, really."

"But we could get, like, our body weight in hot dogs for what they're charging." Grace looked back at the menu. "Fifty-dollar lobster plate? Does it come with a side of solid gold?"

A mischievous smile curled the corner of Theo's lips. "What if I told you it wasn't technically my treat?"

Grace paused. "What do you mean?"

He looked around, and then leaned closer, sliding a credit card across the table. Grace turned it over. "Portia Weston?"

Theo shrugged. "I figured she should give you a farewell dinner, at the very least."

Grace's mouth dropped open. "You didn't!"

He grinned back. "I won't tell if you don't."

Grace laughed. Her tension slipped away, and in its place, she felt a delirious kind of relief. He was still the Theo she knew, even in a dress shirt, surrounded by middle-aged diners murmuring over overpriced fish courses. Everything was OK.

"Well, then," she said with mock seriousness, picking up her menu. "We can't turn down her generosity. That would just be rude."

"So rude," Theo agreed, beckoning to the waiter. "Do you want to go first?"

"Sure." Grace turned to the waiter, trying not to laugh. "Maybe you can help. I can't decide between the lobster and the truffled filet mignon. . . ."

"Why decide?" Theo asked. "Get both!"

"I'm never eating again!" Grace groaned three hours later, when they clambered off the bus and headed up the street toward her house. It was after midnight, and the street was silent; bright with the glow from condo windows and the streetlamps that they passed. "I'm serious, just lay me down and roll me home."

Theo put both hands on her shoulders and pushed her from behind, step-by-step. "But it was worth it. Those chocolates . . ."

Grace moaned at the memory. "Now I get why you rich people are always throwing parties. You just want the food!"

"We give good catering," Theo agreed. He was toting two bags with their leftovers, boxed up neatly with foil swan twists alongside. "I call dibs on the salmon."

"No!" Grace wailed in protest. "The salmon and I have a connection. We're destined to be together!"

Theo laughed, pushing her in a meandering path up the middle of the street. Grace let him, the feel of his hands solid against her shoulders even through her padded jacket. For a moment she wished it were warmer, that she didn't have a jacket on at all, that his hands were touching her—

Grace caught herself. She'd never been drunk, but she wondered if this was what it felt like: loose-limbed and easy, like her careful voice of consequence and self-control was dozing in a corner somewhere. Grace wasn't used to feeling so relaxed, so reckless. If she wasn't careful . . .

"We leave Monday," she said instead. Monday. That was just three days until her life would change completely.

Theo dropped his hands to fall into step beside her. "How do you feel about it?"

"How am I supposed to feel?"

"That wasn't an answer."

"Maybe it wasn't supposed to be," Grace shot back.

Theo looked at her sideways with a curious kind of smile. "You're a tough girl to read, Grace Weston."

"Well, you'll just have to try harder, Theodore Coates." Grace giggled. They were outside Grace's house at the top of the hill now, the city spread behind them in a blanket of lights. She stopped, turning to stare. She could pick out streets, and the winding passage of traffic; the far glow of the Golden Gate Bridge. "I'm going to miss this view."

Theo pulled out his phone. He held it up to take a photo, then scrolled through his contacts list. "Now you can take it with you." He smiled at her. A second later, Grace felt her phone buzz in her pocket with the text.

"Can I get one with you?" Grace asked, suddenly feeling bold. She wanted something to take with her; a reminder of him, here, like this.

Theo gestured for her to join him, and she scrunched in close; backs to the city. He held up the phone. "Say 'chocolate truffles'!'"

Grace laughed. He clicked to take the shot, then showed it to her. "No, wait, I look like I'm possessed." Grace laughed.

"You look fine!"

"For a demon. Take another," Grace insisted.

"Girls." Theo sighed. He put an arm around her shoulder to pull Grace in closer, then held up his phone. "Three, two, one . . ."

The flash went.

"Let's see," Grace demanded. Theo scrolled to the photo. "You weren't looking!" Grace cried. She was smiling at the camera, caught midlaugh, but Theo's head was turned toward her.

"I was." He shrugged. "I was just looking at you."

Their eyes met, and suddenly Grace felt just how close he was: his arm, still around her shoulder, his face, just inches away. His eyes were dark in the shadow of the streetlight, but something in them made Grace's pulse skip.

"I, umm, should . . ." Grace blinked, but she didn't leave.

"Right," Theo agreed. But he didn't step away either.

The city hummed below them. Somewhere in the distance, Grace could hear the grind of a garbage truck—brakes squealing—but to her, it seemed like she and Theo were the only people in the world.

She could kiss him.

The thought bubbled into Grace's mind, and in a split second, she could see it. The possibility. She could kiss him: just move in those last few inches between them, press her lips to his, reach out to touch his face . . .

She reeled back. "I should go!" she exclaimed, face burning. What if he could tell what she'd been thinking? What if he *knew*? "But, thanks. For tonight. It was fun!"

"Sure." Theo seemed thrown. "I . . . Will I see you again, before you leave?"

"Maybe?" Grace gulped. "I don't know. I mean, we'll be busy. But . . . take care!"

Theo blinked. "Uh, you too."

There was another pause.

"OK, then!" Grace backed away. "Bye!"

She turned and fled up the front path. What was she doing? Why did she have to go and ruin everything? This was good-bye; it was supposed to matter.

"Theo?" Grace turned, but he was already walking away, a silhouette against the city lights.

Her heart fell. It was over.

She let herself into the house.

PART TWO: *Summer*

I

Hallie didn't understand her sister. There they were: delivered from poverty to the land of fame, fortune, and twenty-four seven valet service, and Grace was moping around like someone had just died.

Which, OK, someone had, but as far as Hallie was now concerned, dropping dead of a heart attack was the best thing their lying, cheating disgrace of a father had done in a long while.

"Will you just relax?" Hallie emerged from her new bedroom to find Grace heaving boxes up the guesthouse stairs; her face set in that mousy little frown she'd been wearing ever since their U-Haul had left San Francisco city limits. Hallie had been tired enough of it after the first hour, but now, three weeks into summer, it was seriously threatening her good mood. "We're not in a prison camp somewhere," she reminded Grace. "Let someone else do the heavy lifting."

"Like who?" Grace stubbornly shoved the box down the hall.

"I don't know." Hallie shrugged. "The housekeeper, maybe, or the gardener. . . ."

"They're Uncle Auggie's staff, not ours," Grace reminded her. Hallie just rolled her eyes. Details!

"Hasn't he told us, like, a hundred times? What's his is ours—and that includes Julio. You're looking at this all wrong." She grabbed Grace's arm and steered her to the window. "See?"

Grace tried to tug away. "Hallie . . ."

"No, look!" Hallie insisted, opening the window out onto the courtyard below. "How can you not be happy right now? This is heaven!"

It was. Pure paradise. Uncle Auggie's mansion was in the style of an English country estate, all crumbling red bricks and billowing clouds of white roses. It struck Hallie as kind of ridiculous—given that they were five thousand miles and at least a hundred years away from Victorian England—but she guessed that when you were that rich, the usual rules of taste and decency didn't apply. And what her newly beloved uncle lacked in substance, he certainly made up for in style. The back of the house was all folding glass partition: opening out onto a patio area large enough to entertain two dozen of his closest friends on the white calico-covered couches. Beyond that, immaculate green lawn stretched down to the pool area, a perfect rectangle of gleaming tile and sandstone, with canopied sun loungers and a dining area.

Their guesthouse was at the back of the property: a sweet cottage adorned with a thatched roof and white shutters, overlooking a tiny paved courtyard filled with ceramic cherub statues. Hallie breathed in the faint scent of roses and felt utterly content. "Everything's going to be OK now." She beamed at Grace. "I told you everything would work out, and it has!"

"Sure, except for how we're going to support ourselves," Grace replied, in her familiar depressing refrain. "And if Mom's going to be able to get a job, or if we can—"

"La, la, la!" Hallie covered her ears. "I'm not listening!"

She went back into her room to collect her sunglasses and her well-worn copy of Sarah Bernhardt's memoirs. Leaving San Francisco had been heart wrenching, but it had taken only a few days of poolside reflection for Hallie to realize that L.A. was her destiny. There had to be a reason for all the misery she'd been through this last year. Her father, Portia, Juilliard . . . Hallie sometimes felt like she was the princess in a cruel fairy tale—suffering one needless punishment after another, as if the universe had conspired against her and the Fates were laughing at her pain.

But no more. The heartache was over; her evil stepmother was far away, and Hallie was finally right where she was supposed to be.

Hollywood.

Sure, it had taken her a while to come around. Los Angeles was, as all her friends agreed, a cultural wasteland: the domain of fake boobs and even faker smiles. Everybody knew that to become a real actress, you had to go to New York. Chicago, maybe, in a pinch. But L.A?

Never!

Hallie had despaired. How was she supposed to embrace her destiny as a true *artiste* in such a shallow, superficial place? This was where people came to become (and she shuddered at the word) *famous*—not serious actors, dedicated to their craft. Here, people read tabloid magazines, and thinly veiled celebrity "novels," if they read at all! Here, women starved themselves half to death and injected bacteria into their faces, as if their wrinkles were something to be ashamed of, and not the canvas upon which great works of theater could be painted! Here—

"Girls!" A voice echoed up from the backyard, all honeyed tones. "Come join us for breakfast!"

Hallie sighed, and started down the stairs. "'Girls,'" she mimicked as Grace followed behind. "She's only three years older than me!"

"Don't be like that," Grace scolded. "You should give her a chance. She's nice, really."

"Sure she is."

Hallie wasn't convinced. The one downside of Uncle Auggie's generosity was that it came complete with his new bride, Amber—a former soap actress turned trophy wife who was a walking, talking, bleached, manicured testament to Los Angeles's inferior cultural legacy. As they emerged from the guesthouse, the child bride was sauntering across the lawn in a gauzy white wrap—hair in a perky ponytail, lips glossed bright pink. The sturdy Mexican housekeeper followed behind with a tray of food.

Amber waved them over to the dining area. "You've got to try some juice—fresh squeezed! It does wonders for your digestion!"

Hallie forced a smile. Amber had been overflowing with advice and "helpful" tips since the moment they'd walked through the door. So far, she'd offered to "hook Hallie up" with her dermatologist, cosmetologist, and dietician. Hallie had asked where the nearest bookstore was, but Amber had just blinked at her in confusion, and then recommended a salon that she swore gave the best bikini waxes on the West Coast—complete with Swarovski crystal bejazzling.

Hallie couldn't even.

"How are you girls settling in?" Amber asked as they joined her at the table.

"Great, thanks," Grace answered. Hallie gave a vague smile and tried to shoo away the matching shih tzus yapping at her ankles.

"Marilyn! Monroe! Come to Mama!" Amber called them over and scooped one onto her lap. Whether it was Marilyn or Monroe, Hallie couldn't say. "You know, I'm from out of town too," she told them, nuzzling the dog's nose. "Mayfield, Wisconsin. Middle of nowhere. Nothing but hogs and hay bales for miles, we used to say!" She giggled. "There was no way I was sticking around waiting tables the rest of my life, so the day I turned eighteen, I was out of there. Hello, Hollywood!"

Hallie didn't want to encourage her, but part of her was burning with fascination. "How did you meet Uncle Auggie?"

"On set," she declared, a note of pride in her voice. "You know the Lifetime movie *A Small, Distant Scream: The Kayla Bates Story*?"

"About the girl who got kidnapped and sold into white slavery?" Hallie perked up. Trashy movies of the week were her secret guilty pleasure; she'd seen more of the posters framed in Uncle Auggie's study than she'd ever care to admit to her thespian friends.

"Yes!" Amber beamed.

"You were in that?" Hallie frowned, trying to place her.

"I played Social Worker Number Two," Amber said proudly. "Anyway, Auggie dropped by to oversee production, our eyes met across the soundstage . . . and that was it. Love!"

Grace smiled at her. "That's so sweet."

"Uh-huh," Hallie murmured politely. Love, and the chance to escape from nonspeaking, background roles. "Do you still act?"

"Oh, no." Amber shook her head. "I don't have the time now. Life is so crazy!" She popped a fresh strawberry between glossed lips and put on a pair of huge designer sunglasses. Crazy indeed.

"How are my favorite girls today?" Uncle Auggie's

voice boomed, startling Hallie. He crossed the lawn toward them, resplendent in white pants and a bright-orange polo shirt—unbuttoned down his neck to reveal a swath of wiry chest hair peeping through. His dark skin was weathered, hair balding on top, but from the way Amber leaped up and cooingly kissed his cheek, Hallie would have guessed it was Adonis himself come to eat with them. "Remember, *mi casa* is *su casa,*" he said, taking a cup of coffee from Rosa's waiting hands. "You need anything, you just let me know!"

"And be sure to put lotion on, both of you," Amber added. "You're not used to the sun down here, you don't want to burn!" She thrust a tiny tube at Hallie. "It's like my mama always said, 'Lotion, lotion, lotion!' And that goes for moisturizer too."

"Listen to the woman," Auggie chortled. "I swear her mama doesn't look a day over thirty-five!" The couple laughed together, then Uncle Auggie noticed his plate: half a grapefruit and a dry slice of toast. "Sweetie, what is this? Where's my omelet?"

"Baby, you know you're supposed to watch your cholesterol," Amber cooed, squeezing his arm.

Auggie turned to Grace and Hallie. "Isn't she a princess? Always looking out for me."

"That's because I love you, honey." They snuggled together, cooing. Auggie tickled her under the chin, Amber fed him a grape, and Hallie finally broke.

"You know, I better get going," she told them, standing.

"Awww!" Amber cried. "Stay, eat."

“I can’t,” Hallie insisted, already edging away. Another ten minutes of *Inappropriate Age Gaps: The Live Show* and her breakfast could well make a reappearance. “I’ve got a ton of stuff to do.”

Grace raised an eyebrow. “More tanning and pool time?”

“No,” Hallie told her with an icy glare. So, maybe she had spent the last weeks in a lazy rotation between sun lounger, pool mattress, and couch, but it wasn’t like Grace had been off curing cancer or anything. “I have plans,” she informed them dramatically. “Important plans!”

II

Hallie changed into a vintage nineties print dress and her favorite Victorian boots, and struck out from the shaded confines of the compound. People who said you can't get around L.A. without a car clearly didn't live in Beverly Hills, she decided. Uncle Auggie lived just north of Rodeo Drive, in a leafy, quiet area that could almost be called suburban, if the suburbs were made up of a parade of huge mansions on every block. Their English country manor turned out to be almost dignified compared to the neighbors': as Hallie strolled, she counted two Tuscan villas, three stucco mansions adorned with Greek columns, and one modern monstrosity—looking like someone had tossed huge cubes in a random heap.

When she made it big, Hallie would show some restraint. A rambling Spanish estate up in the hills, maybe, or a small mansion somewhere. Something that showed a little class. . . . Hallie daydreamed, happily anticipating the change of fortune that was surely just around the corner. Some of her theater-class friends used to argue that to be a true disciple of your craft, you had to cast off material possessions, and devote yourself to your art—body and soul. Hallie thought that was being kind of hasty. There was no reason why she couldn't become a serious actress *and* have pretty things. Jodie Foster. Halle Berry. Tilda Swinton. They played worthy, demanding roles, and still got to waltz down the red carpet in fabulous designer gowns.

It didn't have to be *either/or,* Hallie would argue right back. They could pick *and.*

That was when she finally saw the light and realized that Hollywood wasn't the end of all her dreams: it could be the beginning of them. There were plenty of respected teachers in town, and what better way to learn her craft than to actually get out there and *act*! Theater groups, indie movies . . . Hallie could get more experience on stages and sets than she ever would cooped up in a classroom in college. She even felt sorry for her friends: they would be trapped by the chains of textbooks and term papers, while she would roam free to be her true creative self—

A car horn blasted, and Hallie leaped back just in time to avoid the low bronze sports car cruising past. "Hey!" she called after it. "That was my light!"

A slim arm slipped out of the tinted window, and the driver flipped Hallie off with a perfectly manicured hand. Charming.

Hallie looked around. She was out of the neighborhood now, onto Rodeo Drive with its spotless sidewalks and gleaming storefronts; the sheen of light reflecting off polished windows seemed to make everything look brighter, sharper. Sports cars rolled slowly down the street, and inside every boutique, a silent doorman waited so that customers wouldn't even have to demean themselves by pushing inside. Hallie had seen wealth, of course—San Francisco was hardly some truck-stop backwater—but under the blazing bright sun, this still seemed like another world, of glamour, and success, and infinite sunshine.

A world where she belonged. Yes, this was exactly where Hallie was supposed to be, and she was going to prove it. Starting today.

Hallie checked the address on her printed map, then gazed up at the towering office building. As well as having designer stores and cute cafés, the neighborhood had five major talent agencies, home to the very best actors in town—and Hallie's future. She took a deep breath and strode inside, across the plush lobby.

"Hi." Hallie beamed at the receptionist. He was in his twenties, sharp-suited and marooned behind the desk in the middle of a vast marble lobby. "I have a delivery for Marshall Gates."

The man barely looked at her. "No, he said the car would be here at noon." He had a headset on, stabbing at buttons on the console in front of him with dizzying speed. "Please hold. No, you need the fifth floor. This is Dynamic, how can I direct your call?"

"Hello?" Hallie tried again. "If I can just leave this . . ."

The man held up one finger. "Noon. I don't care, just get it here!" Finally, the receptionist flickered a gaze at Hallie. "Yes?"

"I have a package, for Marshall Gates." She slid a manila envelope across the desk, neatly addressed and containing her headshot, résumé, and a DVD of her assorted acting highlights. Hallie had stayed up all night editing the best clips together. Her Desdemona—performed by her flash theater troupe in the parking lot during an Oakland Raiders game—was a personal best, she felt, with a death scene so convincing three passersby had called an ambulance.

The receptionist slid the envelope back. "We don't accept unsolicited materials." He tapped his headset again. "Dynamic, please hold."

"You don't understand," Hallie tried again, making her smile even brighter. "I just want him to take a look. When he sees my test reel, he'll thank you!"

"You and five thousand other girls." He gave her a withering stare.

Hallie's smile faded. "Can't you make an exception, just this once? Just slip it in with his other mail."

The man smirked. "Mail comes from the mail room. Does this look like the mail room?"

"No." Hallie swallowed. "Can't you say it's a delivery? Or even let me take it up myself? I won't say anything, I promise!"

"Let you in here?" he snorted. "It's company policy,

there's nothing I can do. No. Unsolicited. Materials." The man used his index finger to push the envelope back, a few inches with every word.

Hallie decided it was time to change tactics. "If those are the rules, then how do I get solicited?"

He smirked.

"I didn't mean . . ." Hallie blushed, realizing her double entendre. Her confidence was crumbling in the face of such disdain. "Just, tell me, please. What does it take for them to take a look?"

"Have your manager submit it." He looked bored, already stabbing at the console again. "Get scouted by a casting agent. Perform in a showcase. Jesus, did you just step off the bus today?"

"A few weeks ago." Hallie's voice was small.

"Welcome to Hollywood, sweetie." His voice was scathing. "Now, are you going to leave me alone, or do I need to call security?"

It was the same at all the other agencies. Hallie tried her best smiles, her most charming tone—even buying a bouquet of balloons and trying to masquerade as a PR girl with a special gift delivery—but it made no difference. The receptionists barely looked up long enough to sneer at her with polished condescension, before pushing her portfolio back across the desk, or—worse even—sliding it straight into the trash.

She stood in line at the Coffee Bean, seething with frustration. It wasn't as if she'd expected Hollywood to welcome her with open arms, but this was impossible! To have an agent even take a look at her photo, Hallie would have to have a manager submit it, but to get a manager, she had to have interest from an agent. What was she supposed to do?

"Can I help you?"

"I'll have a large vanilla ice-blended with extra espresso." Hallie eyed the blond barista's perfectly toned arms. Maybe she should take Amber up on that gym recommendation. "Can I get that light?" she added.

"Sure. That'll be five twelve."

Hallie opened her wallet. Two lone dollar bills stared back. Her heart sank. Her bank account was empty, and her credit card was maxed out from that spree last week to buy all her "moving to L.A." essentials. (New wardrobe, audition monologue books, a fabulous new bathing suit with a genuine 1950s vintage cover-up . . .)

"It's OK. I can, uh, get that."

A guy in line behind her moved to the register, his wallet already out. He was in his early twenties, maybe, with a burnished-copper tan and stubble. His clothes were scruffy—a rumpled navy shirt, jeans that were clearly not designer—and when he turned back from the cashier toward her, Hallie saw an ugly scar snaking up from the neckline of his shirt, the red puckered skin cutting up the side of his neck.

"No, thanks," she told him, edging away.

"It's fine." He shrugged, looking awkwardly at the floor. "I mean, I was already—"

Hallie turned back to the barista. "You know what? I'm detoxing. An iced green tea would be great."

She peeled off the dollar bills and then took her place waiting by the counter. The scarred guy loitered nearby, so Hallie pretended to click through her cell phone. You couldn't give them any encouragement, that's what they'd learned in fifth-period Women's Empowerment classes: firm declarative statements, and, at last resort, a quick blast of pepper spray. Hallie had left her travel-size canister in her other purse, but she wouldn't let it get that far; the minute her tea was ready, she hurried out, despairing over her bad luck.

Couldn't it have been some gorgeous actor looking to save her, instead of some drugged-out surfer dude? They would have struck up a conversation over the condiment station, and by the time their drinks were ready (espresso for him: strong, bold, masculine), he would have been begging her to star opposite him in his new indie film—something harrowing that would make the perfect entrée to the Hollywood elite. Long hours on set together, their overwhelming natural chemistry . . . Hallie would have an A-list boyfriend *and* an Oscar nomination all sewn up by the end of the year—without needing her material solicited by anyone!

But no, instead she had Mr. Crazypants back there with his creepy serial-killer stubble. Hallie ducked into the nearest store, and then peered out the front window, just to be safe.

"Can I help you?" A polished clerk who reminded Hallie of Portia—all severe haircut and pencil skirt—hovered nearby.

"Just browsing," Hallie replied, but the woman stared

at her with suspicion until Hallie drifted deeper into the store. It was an upscale boutique, full of gauzy dresses and perfect slouchy tanks hung casually from empty rails as if they were works of art. Hallie checked the price tag of a cute dress and winced. Three hundred dollars!

God, she missed having money.

It wasn't that they'd been rich exactly . . . Well, no, Hallie had to admit: they had been. She'd had a clothing allowance, and money to go out with her friends, and had never once even considered an after-school job—not when she had so many acting commitments to fill her time. Even after their father had left, she'd never worried about money, not when he was lavishing them with guilty gifts, and slipping fifty-dollar bills into her purse every time they had coffee.

But now . . .

Now she couldn't even afford the basic necessities, like ice-blended coffees, let alone a cute new dress.

"Oh, my God, that is so fierce."

A voice from the back of the store made Hallie look up. A girl had emerged from the dressing room and was assessing herself in the mirrors; her blond friend sprawled on the couch, tapping at her phone.

"You think?" The girl turned slowly, examining her reflection. She had glossy dark hair that fell in a perfect cascade over the skintight black minidress. "Maybe it's too classy. I mean, he's into rock-chick girls—tattoos and leather and stuff."

"So what?" Another girl looked up from the jewelry she was browsing; beachy and boho in a long patchwork skirt and cropped tank. "Are you going to go pierce something for him?"

"No way." The dark-haired girl grinned. "We all know how that turned out. Brie."

The blonde looked up from her phone. "Hey! That was one little tongue stud, and I took it right out!"

"Only after an infection and antibiotic shots!" The girls laughed together, piling onto the couch in a tangle of limbs and necklaces and glossy leather bags.

Hallie watched, struck with a sudden pang. All her friends were back in San Francisco, and although she'd tried to keep up with the latest news—texting, calling, and checking in via Skype—she could feel the distance between them grow: a gaping canyon that used to be filled with after-school hangouts, and nights sharing dim sum in Chinatown, but that now only had voice-mail messages and the occasional afterthought of a chat. Part of the reason Hallie had been so glued to that pool lounger these past weeks was that she didn't have the first clue how to make friends here in L.A. Was she supposed to join a club? Take classes? Grace didn't seem to mind her solitude, but to Hallie, the empty space was loneliness: a hollow ache in her chest.

One of the girls saw her staring at them, and raised an eyebrow. Hallie quickly turned and hurried out of the store. For all her talk of belonging, the sad truth was she didn't.

Not yet.

III

The sting of rejection still fresh, Hallie regressed to poolside lounging for the rest of the week. She needed a vacation, she told herself, restlessly flipping through plays she knew by heart. She was in recovery, recharging her batteries before her next grand assault on Hollywood. But for all her reasoning, Hallie knew the truth: she didn't really know *what* to do next. Plan A had crashed and burned, and she was suddenly completely adrift in her own life, with no schedule or school or social plans to fill her days. Instead of seeming like a marvelous vacation, it felt, to her shame, like failure.

This was why people went to college, she thought mournfully. Not for knowledge, or partying, but four more blissful years of structure and routine.

Hallie wandered into the main house, and found Amber idling in the vast marble wonderland of the kitchen: flipping through magazines with one of the dogs cradled in her arms. Now, there was a woman who didn't mind a life of utter leisure.

"Hey, sweetie!" She lit up. "How are your mysterious plans working out?"

"They're not." Hallie slumped, too dejected even to muster horror at Amber's matching pink velour sweats. "I can't get anyone to even look at my headshots."

"Awww, you poor thing!" Amber put down the dog and enveloped her in a lavender-scented hug. "I know exactly what you're going through. Trying to get that first break is just a nightmare, but you can't give up."

"I won't." Hallie may be dejected, but she was also determined. Unlike Amber, she had no intention of finding herself a balding producer and giving up her craft for a life of yogalates and tanning. She would survive! She would endure!

But, she would also need some cash.

"The problem is, I'm broke," she explained. "I need a job if I'm going to pay for acting classes, and going out, and stuff."

"Job?" Amber frowned, as if she'd never heard of the word. "What kind of job?"

"I don't know. Retail maybe? Except, I don't have any experience," Hallie admitted. "And office work is out. I can't really type, and spending too long in front of a computer makes my head hurt."

"Hmmm," Amber mused. "If you were over twenty-one, I know a ton of hosting gigs you could get . . ." She brightened. "How about dogs?"

Hallie stared at her blankly.

"Marilyn and Monroe need walking twice a day," Amber explained. "We pay a boy to come take them, but you could do it instead. They're darling, no trouble at all, and you'd get tons of exercise!"

Hallie paused, reluctant. "I guess . . ."

"And it's flexible, so you have all that time for your acting things!" Amber seemed convinced. She headed for the door, phone in hand. "I'll go call, say we've found someone else. Yay!"

"Yay," Hallie echoed faintly. Dog walking and universal rejection—was this what her shining future had come to? She opened the huge fridge and gazed listlessly at the rows of bottled water and no-fat yogurt. All her excitement from earlier in the week had drained away, and now Hallie just felt tired and—

"AAAAAAAAAAAARRRRRGHHHHHHH HHHHH!"

She let out an almighty scream. A strange man was standing five feet away from her. No, worse than that, she realized with a dawning horror. The crazy guy from the coffee shop!

Hallie screamed again, reeling back behind the kitchen island. "What are you doing? Get away from me!"

"Whoa, calm down!" The guy had his hands up. "You've made a mistake."

"No, you did!" Hallie yelled, scrabbling in her purse. "I have Mace!"

Except she didn't. Wrong purse.

She lunged for the butcher block and grabbed a seven-inch carving knife, waving it at him. He leaped back. "Get away from me! Security!" she screamed. "Security!"

"I'm telling you, I'm Brandon," the guy insisted, flustered. "I live next door. I'm not a—"

"SECURITY!"

Amber came racing back into the room, just as Uncle Auggie and her mom burst through the patio doors. "What's going on?"

Hallie jabbed the knife toward the intruder. "He's stalking me!" Hallie cried. "He must have followed me back from town the other day. He's trying to kill me! Or worse!"

There was a pause, then Auggie began to laugh.

"It's not funny!" Hallie was shaking. This was how *Nightline* specials went: the beautiful young woman, the deranged stalker . . . "He broke in! He was trying to attack me!"

"He has a key," Auggie explained, still chuckling. "He lives next door."

Hallie caught her breath, trying to process the situation. "He's not a crazy stalker?" she ventured in a small voice.

"Nope."

"And you didn't follow me back?" she asked Brandon.

He shook his head. "I'm sorry I scared you."

Hallie glared at him, the knife still clenched in her hand, just in case. Sure, they said he was safe, but wasn't that what they all said about serial killers. "Oh, yes, he lived next door, perfectly normal until that day he snapped and cut her up into five dozen pieces."

"Really," Brandon insisted. "It's OK." He approached slowly, hands open, as if she were a wild animal. Closer, closer . . . He carefully took the knife from her shaking hand and laid it on the counter.

It seemed to Hallie that the entire room exhaled. Brandon gave her a nervous smile. "I guess I should have used the main bell."

Hallie looked around. Adrenaline was still pumping through her, her whole body paralyzed with fear. "I thought I was going to die!" she cried, and burst into tears.

Hallie had to retire to the lounge to calm down; stretched on the velvet chaise with her mom and Brandon clustered around. She pressed a cold compress to her forehead, and let out another moan.

"Are you sure I can't get you anything?" Brandon looked anxious. Hallie carefully shifted away from him. Psycho killer or not, he still creeped her out, with his two-day stubble and wavy brown hair in dire need of a cut falling over that scar. Freakier than the poor personal grooming, and those baggy cargo pants, however, was the stoic kind of silent vibe he radiated, like he was watching every move she made.

"I'm fine." Hallie's voice quivered bravely. "Just a little faint." She dreaded to think what would have happened if it had been a real killer hunting her down. Uncle

Auggie would probably have made a movie of the week *(Lock All the Doors: The Hallie Weston Story),* and Hallie would have been doomed to be immortalized by a failed sitcom actress who couldn't emote.

"There, there." Hallie's mom patted her absently, before turning back to Brandon. "Come, sit down. What did you say your name was?"

"Brandon Mitchell, ma'am. Like I said, we live next door, and Auggie lets me drop by to use his darkroom. I really am sorry," he told Hallie again, looking shameful.

She managed a brave shrug. "I'll be OK. . . . Eventually."

"I was actually looking for you and your sister," Brandon continued, his gaze fixed on Hallie. "To, um, invite you to this pool party, in Malibu. But, I guess, you're not really in a mood to go out," he added quickly.

A party? With him? "No, thanks," Hallie replied, at the same time as her mom exclaimed, "What a great idea!"

"Mom!" Hallie glared. "I'm *recovering*!"

"Shh, you said it yourself, you'll be fine. And I'm sure Grace would be happy to get out of the house." Valerie beamed at Brandon. "They'd love to come. What time is it?"

"Uh, I can come by and pick you up around eight?" Brandon looked to Hallie. She sighed, and lifted her shoulders in the faintest of shrugs. "OK! Great! I'll see you then. You and your sister, I mean," he added, before bolting from the room.

The moment he was gone, Hallie turned on her mom. "Why did you do that? He's . . . weird!"

"Don't be silly." Valerie patted her again. "He's just a little shy, that's all. And Amber said, his father is very successful. Apparently, he owns a law firm that has all the A-list clients."

"So? I'm not going to this party with his dad." Hallie sulked.

"It'll be good for you to get out, start making friends," her mom insisted. "Now, go tell your sister. I think she's reading by the pool."

Hallie rolled her eyes and pulled herself off the chaise, but instead of finding Grace, she hid away in the guesthouse: taking an extra-long bath, and hoping that by the time she emerged, her mom would be distracted by painting again and forget all about her orders for Hallie to socialize with Brandon and his weird surfer friends.

But she was out of luck. When Hallie finally headed back to the main house for dinner, Brandon and his visit were the only topics of conversation at the table.

"Such a polite young man," her mom cooed, over a spread of roasted chicken.

Amber nodded in agreement. "I heard they paid three million for that house."

"And he seemed plenty taken with you," Auggie added, giving Hallie a wink. "You could have yourself a new beau there."

"Ugh! No way. He was just being polite," she said quickly, but Auggie was not to be dissuaded.

"Trust me, I can see these things," he insisted.

"He does," Amber agreed. "Like a little cupid, aren't you, sweetie?"

Grace gave Hallie a smug grin. "Hallie and Brandon, sitting in a tree . . ."

"Grace!" She kicked her under the table.

"Oww!"

"He'd be good for you," Auggie mused. "Solid, dependable. Bit quiet, I'll give you that, but you can talk enough for the both of you!"

"Look, she's blushing." Amber giggled. "Maybe we've got a match on our hands."

"No," Hallie tried again. They were like some kind of wretched double act, chirping and gossiping away! She thought quickly for a diversion. "Anyway, Grace is the one you should talk to about boyfriends."

As predicted, Amber and Auggie lit up. "Who?"

"Nobody," Grace said, glaring at Hallie. "I don't have anyone."

"She's just being shy." Hallie smiled serenely. "But I'll tell you, his name begins with the letter *T*."

"T!" Amber exclaimed. "Hmmm, Tristan, or Tyler . . ."

"Toby," Auggie offered. "Teddy."

"Todd!"

Grace shot her a murderous look. Hallie just grinned. Served her right. Grace's tryst with Theo was the worst-kept secret ever, but Hallie didn't know what Grace saw in him. Sure, he was nice enough—if by "nice," you meant boring, and lifeless, and bound with blood to their mortal enemy—but Hallie would never bring herself to settle for that.

Nice! No, Hallie wanted passion, adventure, spirit. A Heathcliff! A Romeo! (Except not quite so slow on the uptake when it came to life-or-death planning.) Sure, she'd dated a little back home, but it had never lasted. The guys she knew all just wanted to hang around in windowless basements, watching movies, talking about politics, and attempting to slip her clothes off without her noticing. (As if Hallie would be so distracted by the evils of late-stage capitalism that she'd somehow lose all track of her underwear.) Even the college boys were a bore: acting as if a messy dorm room and half a semester of literary theory made them kings of the known universe.

She didn't want to fool around in a drunken haze, or hold hands at the movies like every other pedestrian teen couple. Let Grace simper at Theo all she liked; Hallie wanted *more*. She was looking for a Great Love: something epic, and sweeping, that would shake the very foundations of her soul. A love that would affect her, open the world to her; something mysterious and magnificent, the kind of grand affair that would be written about one day, by hushed scholars in a dusty library. A Burton to her Taylor. A Fitzgerald to her Zelda. A Brad to her Angelina.

She wanted (and Hallie sighed at this, with no small measure of longing) a *man*.

IV

Grace agreed to come to the party—more to escape Auggie and Amber's relentless questioning than because she wanted to go, she told Hallie with a scowl—and soon they were piled into Brandon's shiny new Jeep and headed for the coast.

"How are you feeling?" he asked Hallie, looking over from the driver's side.

Hallie softened, appreciating his concern. "Better, now. Thanks."

She studied him thoughtfully. He radiated an intense kind of quietness, and he hadn't bothered to shave or even change for the party: still wearing the same rumpled shirt and two-day stubble from that afternoon. She would have thought being mistaken for a crazy psychopath might have inspired some adventures in basic hygiene, at the very least.

"So, what's your deal?" she asked curiously. If his family lived in the sprawling Greco-Roman abomination next door, he must be rich, so perhaps this scruffy beach-bum look was the Californian equivalent of the whole East Coast disheveled wealth thing—where they dressed in moth-eaten cashmere and scuffed Italian leather shoes to prove just how ancient and stuffy the family fortune was. That must be it, Hallie decided: kind of like, "I'm too busy surfing to need a real job. Or a shower."

"What do you mean?" Brandon asked.

"What do you *do*?" Hallie pressed. "Are you home from college, or dropped out, or what?"

"I never went to college." Brandon kept his eyes on the road. "And, I'm not really doing anything right now."

"Hmmm." Maybe he had issues, Hallie decided. Smoked too much pot and dropped out of regular life, like Kenny Mathers from her theater group. One day, he was all set for a sound-design course in Florida; the next, he's locked up in his room playing first-person shooter games for twenty hours a day and subsisting only on cheez-based snack foods. Now that Hallie thought about it, Brandon's eyes did seem kind of bloodshot. . . .

Her gaze drifted to the puckered line of red skin on his neck. "What's the story with your scar?"

"Hallie!" There Grace was again with the wail of protest.

Hallie twisted around and glared at her. "What? I'm just asking."

"No, it's OK." Brandon coughed. "I, uh, was in Iraq."

Hallie stared.

"Like, the army?"

"Yup." Brandon rubbed his neck absently. "I served a couple of years."

Hallie blinked in surprise. She'd never met anyone who actually joined; most of her friends were the ones staging antiwar sit-ins and campaigning about the hypocrisy of American imperialism. "So what happened?" she asked.

Hallie felt a sharp kick in the back of her seat. "You don't have to answer that," Grace spoke up quickly.

"No, it's cool." Brandon drummed his fingers on the steering wheel. "There was an ambush, I got hit by shrapnel." He shrugged. "I was lucky. Some of the other guys . . . they weren't so lucky."

"Sorry," Grace murmured from the backseat.

Brandon shrugged again. "It happens."

Silence lingered in the car until Brandon turned the radio up, and they drove the rest of the way without any more awkward conversation. Hallie stared out the window, guilty—and embarrassed for feeling guilty. It wasn't her fault! She'd been expecting a story about a bad surf wipeout, or a crazy stunt with his buddies, and instead, Brandon was, like, Captain America. Protecting and Serving. No wonder he was so awkward and withdrawn: the guy was probably wracked with post-traumatic stress, or survivor's guilt, or something like that.

But as they turned off the freeway, all of Hallie's unease melted away. "Grace, look!" she cried, gazing at the ocean: clear and blue under the fading sunset sky. The road wound along the very edge of the beach, rocky shoreline and pale sand falling away on their left as they headed up the coast.

"Pretty special, huh?" Brandon smiled over at her, but Hallie was too busy drinking it all in to respond. The horizon stretched, limitless, in the distance, a world away from the stormy San Francisco skies that always hung so low with fog. She craned around to see as they passed north into Malibu, past houses squeezed together on the side of the road—jutting out over the beach on spindly stilts.

"Imagine waking up every day to that view," Hallie breathed. She made a new promise: screw that Spanish compound in the hills. When she made it big, she'd buy a place here, with the ocean right on her doorstep.

They followed the winding highway along the shore until Brandon eased off to the side of the road, opposite one of the modern houses: stacked cubes, all chrome and glass. "Here we are," Brandon said. "The famous de Santos compound." His voice seemed to have an edge to it; a faint curl to his lip.

"Who is this guy?" Hallie asked, climbing out of the Jeep.

"Girl. Her name's Ana Lucia." Brandon waited for them to grab their stuff, and then led them across the busy highway. "She was a couple of years below me in school. So, your age."

"Awesome!" Hallie strode on ahead. "I can't wait to meet everyone."

Inside, the music seemed to shake the very foundation

of the house with a heavy bass; the party spilling in from outside as girls in bikinis scampered through the hallways, and guys wearing expensive shades poured cocktails from a kitchen countertop covered in bottles of liquor. Hallie drank it in, glad she'd already perfected her nonchalant stare.

"Everyone's so . . . shiny," Grace murmured beside her. "It's like we walked into the middle of a magazine shoot."

She was right. The kids around them were all glowing with a Hollywood gloss that seemed to Hallie to be equal parts orthodontics and golden tan. "We did." Hallie grinned. "Look."

Over in the lounge area, two girls were bouncing on a white leather couch as an older guy photographed them with an old-school camera. They clutched their chests to keep their bikini tops in place, shrieking with laughter.

"Watch out for him." Brandon paused to glare over at the photographer. "He's a total perv. Has this website, Friday Night—"

"United?" Hallie finished excitedly. "I read it all the time! He does the best party pics!"

Grace screwed up her face. "All those girls collapsed in the bathroom with glitter all over them? Eww."

Hallie ignored Grace, and filed the photographer's face away for future reference. One of the last big stars of his site now modeled for Prada and Gucci, and had a column in some style magazine about her international jet-setting adventures with the fashion elite. Not bad for a girl whose main claim to fame was wearing a lion hood—and not much else—in a series of gritty club-hopping snaps.

"The guys are probably out back." Brandon nodded ahead. The whole rear of the house was sliding glass panels, pushed back to reveal a multilevel deck crowded with people. "I can introduce you around."

Hallie felt a flutter of nerves. "Just a sec." She stopped at a mirror in the hall and quickly touched up her lipstick. New city, new scene to conquer. And conquer it, she would.

She made to follow Brandon out, but Grace caught her arm. "Please don't drink too much, or go off with strange guys, or do anything stupid."

Hallie gave her a withering stare. "What do you take me for?"

"You," Grace replied.

Hallie pulled free. "I'll be fine. You're the one who needs to not embarrass *me.*" She caught up with Brandon as he stepped outside. The deck was even more crowded: kids lounging in groups, splashing in the hot tub, and clustered in front of a makeshift stage area as a group of guys set up speakers and sound gear. A rickety wooden staircase led down from the deck onto the beach, where more people were partying on the sand; a volleyball game in progress.

"So these are your friends?" Hallie asked, following Brandon through the crowd. It looked like she was wrong about his beach-bum look: the guys here all wore designer polo shirts, or skinny denim, or were bare-chested over board shorts.

"Not exactly," he replied. Hallie barely had time to wonder what that meant before Brandon stopped by a group in the corner. It was the prime spot, Hallie quickly noticed: loungers and canopies, with a full view of the rest of the party. Two shirtless guys with artfully mussed hair were trying to rouse a trio of girls clicking at their cell phones with matching distracted expressions.

"Hey." Brandon approached, low-key. There was a beat, then one of the guys laughed.

"Brandon Mitchell, what the hell?" He enveloped Brandon in a backslapping hug. "We haven't seen you in forever! Thought you'd run off to Mexico, or, like, rehab or something."

"Nope. Still here." Brandon had his hands bunched in the front pockets of his pants. He turned to Hallie. "This is Hallie, she and her sister just moved to town. They're Auggie Jennings's nieces, or cousins . . . ?"

"Something like that." Hallie switched on her brightest smile. "Hey!"

"Hellooo . . ." one of the guys drawled, waggling his eyebrows lasciviously. The girls looked up from their phones, and Hallie realized suddenly that they were the ones from the boutique in town. The dark-haired girl beside him smacked his stomach.

"Ignore him. Welcome to L.A." She flashed a warm smile. She was wearing bright-pink lipstick, and a high-fashion swimsuit constructed from so many straps and cutouts and metallic rings that Hallie wondered how exactly it was held up at all.

"I'm Ana Lucia," she introduced herself, moving

close enough to give Hallie a faint air-kiss on each cheek. "And that's Tai, Carter, Brie, and Meredith." She nodded to each person in turn.

Hallie smiled back. "It's great to meet you all."

Carter turned to Brandon. "We were just heading out for a game." He jerked his head toward the beach. "You in?"

Brandon looked toward Hallie, almost as if he were asking permission. "Go ahead," she said quickly. "Please, I'm good here."

"We'll take care of her." Ana Lucia laughed. "Come, sit." She patted the lounger beside her.

"See?" Hallie took a seat. Brandon still looked reluctant, so she shooed him away. "I don't need babysitting. Have fun!"

He nodded, still looking reluctant. "I guess I'll see you later."

The guys hustled off, Carter and Tai charging down the staircase with Brandon following slowly behind. Hallie settled back, feeling relieved she'd had such a warm welcome so far. The shiny TV shows had lied: nobody was throwing her into the pool and telling her, "Welcome to Malibu, bitch."

"So, tell us about you." Ana Lucia turned to Hallie with an inquisitive smile. She pushed a handful of hair back from her face; it slowly slithered over one shoulder in a move Hallie made a mental note to practice herself. "Where did you move from?"

"San Francisco," Hallie replied, making herself

comfortable. "We're living with my mom's cousin, Auggie Jennings, over in Beverly Hills."

"He's a producer, right?" Ana Lucia paused, brow furrowed.

"Yup. He makes movies."

"TV movies," the blonde called Brie corrected. She had a face that was all narrow angles, and she was wearing one of the designer dresses from Hallie's red-carpet fantasy list—damp and crumpled over her bikini like it was a cheap cover-up.

"Oh." Ana Lucia's nose wrinkled, just a bit. "And your parents, what do they do?"

"My mom's an artist," Hallie answered carefully. "And, my dad is a stockbroker. Was," she added dramatically. "He just died."

"Oh, my God, I'm so sorry." Ana Lucia gasped. There was a chorus of agreement from the other girls.

"That's awful."

"You must be wrecked," Meredith added, eyes wide with sympathy.

"It's been hard." Hallie had, by now, perfected her "so brave, and yet so vulnerable" look. She gave a courageous smile. "But, it's behind us now. I'm looking forward to making a fresh start out here."

"That's great." Ana Lucia squeezed her hand. "So will you be BHH-ing it?"

Hallie stared blankly.

"Beverly Hills High," Meredith explained. She was dressed the most casually of the girls, her hair caught up in a beachy braid, with a Missoni-style print bikini and long draped skirt.

"Oh, no," Hallie said quickly. "I graduated in May."

"Nice! Me too," Meredith said. "Brie's a year ahead, she just dropped out of UCLA—"

"I'm taking time out," Brie corrected her. "I'll go back soon."

"Uh-huh." Meredith shook her head slightly at Hallie. "Sure you will. Anyways, I start at USC in the fall, and Ana Lucia is a sophomore at Harvard."

"Only because Daddy insisted." Ana Lucia rolled her eyes. "He says I need a backup plan, in case acting doesn't work out."

"You're an actress?" Hallie brightened. "Me too! You'll have to tell me everything, I want to know all about the audition scene."

"For sure!" Ana Lucia agreed. "Who's your rep?"

Hallie was confused.

"Representation," Ana Lucia explained slowly. "Agent? Manager?"

"Oh, I don't have anyone yet." Hallie shrugged. "Like I said, we just got here."

"Huh." Ana Lucia's smile dimmed slightly. "Any credits?"

"Tons," Hallie said quickly. "Theater mainly, but also some short films, TV . . ." Hallie didn't add that the films were all shot by her friends, and the television spot had been more accidental than anything, but still, appearing in the back of a live news broadcast totally counted! "Why, do you have . . . reps?"

"Of course." Ana Lucia flipped her hair back. "I'm with WME," she said, naming the biggest and glossiest of all the agencies as if it were nothing. Their security hadn't even let Hallie past the door when she tried to deliver her portfolio.

"Wow." Hallie blinked. "That's amazing."

Ana Lucia shrugged. "I don't know, I'm thinking about moving. They don't seem to get my brand, you know?"

Hallie didn't, but before she could reply, Ana Lucia saw someone across the party and suddenly brightened. "Oh, my God, they came!" she squealed, suddenly sounding like a starstruck teenager.

"Who? What? Ooh." Brie exhaled.

Hallie turned. A group of guys had arrived on the other side of the deck: a mess of skinny jeans and leather jackets and artful rocker facial hair. Ana Lucia scrambled up, adjusting her many swimsuit straps for optimum cleavage display.

"I got, like, this close to talking to Reed at their show last week," she said, breathless. "Come on."

"You go ahead." Meredith yawned, but Brie obediently followed her across the deck. Hallie watched as Ana Lucia tried to insert herself into the group—leaning in close to one of the tattooed rocker guys and bursting out with laughter. Interestingly, the guy seemed unconcerned; barely paying any attention to her, no matter how often she pressed up against him and flipped her hair around.

"Take Fountain," Meredith explained. "They're, like,

this close to a major label deal. Ana Lucia's been stalking them ever since they said no to playing her last birthday."

"She's not used to being turned down?" Hallie watched as the guys sauntered into the house—and Ana Lucia followed eagerly behind.

Meredith laughed. "Not at all. Oh, and don't worry about the agent thing," she added, getting up. "Ana Lucia forgets to mention that her dad is one of the execs over at Universal. Every agent in town would represent his dog if they thought it would help them set up a deal."

"Oh." Hallie felt relieved. The way Ana Lucia had been acting, it was like Hallie was a failure for not already having an agent, manager, and publicist lined up. "Thanks."

"No problem." Meredith gave her a conspiratorial smile. "This scene can be kind of crazy. My dad's a writer—he dragged us out here from New York my junior year of high school, and I swear, I thought I'd dropped into a reality show." She looked around the party. "I'm going to go say hi to some people. Want to come along?"

"Sure." Hallie bounced up. "That would be great."

V

By the time Meredith had introduced her to the five hundredth person, Hallie's cheeks ached from smiling so long and telling the same familiar "San Francisco/dead father/actress" refrain. To her surprise, Ana Lucia's question about reps seemed standard, so Hallie quickly adjusted her answer to say that she had some meetings lined up, rather than face the same knowing looks. She couldn't blame them for thinking she was just another wannabe, fresh off the bus, but Hallie knew she was different. She *would* make it—it was just a matter of time.

"Want to come hang?" Meredith asked. It was louder now: kids drinking and dancing in every available space. She pointed to corner of the lounge where a group of surfer guys was lighting up what was most definitely not a cigarette.

"I'm good, thanks." Hallie looked around, the room feeling cramped and too noisy. "I think I'm going to go take a look at the ocean."

"Cool." Meredith pulled her into a hug/double-air-kiss. "I'll call you tomorrow. We'll brunch!"

Hallie headed back outside and down the rickety stairs to the beach, kicking off her sandals so the sand was cool between her toes. The beach was empty, save a few amorous shadows in the distance; the ocean crashing in a soothing hum. She breathed in the night air and felt herself finally relax. Hallie usually thrived in crowds, but that was when she'd been at the center of them; tonight she was hanging on the edge of every group, trying to make an impression. Barely registering at all.

For now.

Hallie headed for the water's edge, shaking off her loneliness. This was all just the introduction in her story, the struggles she'd look back on fondly, during her interviews, as building character and grit. "Sure, it was hard," she'd tell the magazine journalists, "being an outsider. But I knew if I just focused on my craft, everything would work out for me."

And it would.

She reached the ocean, squealing as the cold surf swirled around her feet. The horizon stretched in front of her, an inky shadow, and suddenly, Hallie was overcome with a wash of possibility. She was exactly where she was supposed to be; at the dawn of a new chapter in her life.

She could be anyone she wanted to be; create the life she was destined for!

Hallie stripped off her cover-up and tossed it behind her onto the sand. She waded deeper into the dark ocean. This would be her baptism: washing away the old world in the cold waters of the Pacific; emerging her shining new self. Yes!

The water was freezing, but Hallie kept going, ducking under a breaking wave so she was completely submerged, and then swimming deeper. Out past the breaking point, the water shifted and rolled, and she flipped on her back to float, gazing at the sky. It seemed to stretch forever, dark and still, dotted with the faint pinprick of stars. Her sister was always droning on about the science of the universe, the mathematics and order and history, or whatever, but Hallie thought the great mysteries of the world should remain just that: mysterious. Who cared about physics when there was poetry to be had, art and emotion rather than facts and figures?

Hallie bobbed upright again. The beach looked far away now; lights from the houses disappearing with every new swell of waves. She shivered. Her skin was puckering, and the chill of the ocean had finally numbed her enthusiasm for the grand gesture. Time to get back to Uncle Auggie's, and the miracle of the heated whirlpool tub. Hallie struck out back for shore, half hoping there were some people on the beach to watch her emerge, mermaid-style, from the water. Now, that would make a first impression!

She swam hard, but the shore didn't seem to be any

closer. Instead, it almost looked as if it were farther away. The tide pulled at her legs, and although she kicked, her limbs felt heavy and slow. For the first time, Hallie realized she was alone, at sea, in the dark. Nobody knew she was out here.

She tried not to panic.

"Hello?" she called. Her voice seemed thin, and disappeared on the breeze. "Is anyone there?"

Hallie kicked again, but her body felt like lead. It was going to be OK, she told herself. She wasn't going to drown—she couldn't. She was destined for great things! She was going to—

A wave broke over her, and for a moment, she was pulled under. Hallie flailed, gasping as she broke the surface. She coughed, terror gripping her fast. "Help!" she called. "Somebody, help me!"

The water was inky black, nothing but the rolling swells surrounding her. "Somebody!" she cried again. She thought she saw something in the water—a shadow, maybe—before another wave broke hard overhead. This time, she spun underwater for what seemed like hours, until her lungs burned and she wasn't sure if she was kicking toward the surface or even farther down.

Then there were arms locked tight around her, and a warm body dragging her to the surface. Hallie spluttered, gasping for air, dizzy. She flailed, but her rescuer held on tight.

"It's OK," he told her, already kicking back toward the shore with powerful strokes. "I've got you now. Everything's going to be OK."

Hallie caught a glimpse of dark eyes, and sharp-angled cheekbones. He was beautiful. An angel, she thought faintly. A saint, come to rescue her from certain death.

And then everything was black.

VI

His name was Dakota. Dakota Kane. He was nineteen years old, a musician and a poet, and by the time the ER doctor had cleared Hallie with nothing more than a case of mild hypothermia, she knew with utter certainty—he was the man she'd been waiting for her whole life.

"You saved me," Hallie breathed, wincing slightly as a nurse pulled out her IV. "I would have drowned!"

"Don't think like that." Dakota squeezed her hand. His hair hung damp in long dark strands almost level with his chin, shirt clinging to his torso under his leather jacket. And those eyes. . . . Hallie gazed at him happily. God, he was beautiful.

"Are you sure she's OK to leave?" Dakota asked the nurse. "Is there anything we need to do?"

We. Hallie thrilled at the word.

"Just take it easy for a few days, keep warm." The nurse gave Hallie a thin-lipped look. "No more midnight swimming."

"I promise!" Hallie clasped her hands fervently. "I'm so sorry for all the trouble!"

The nurse moved off. Dakota turned to Hallie with concern. "How are you feeling?" he asked gently. "Do you need me to get you anything?"

"I'm OK," she said, shivering slightly. They'd taken her wet clothes, and given her baggy hospital scrubs to wear. She just hoped she looked good in aqua.

Dakota whipped off his jacket and slung it around her shoulders. "Is there anyone you need to call?"

Hallie blinked. "Oh, my God, Grace!" She'd been so caught up in the romance of her dramatic rescue that she'd forgotten all about the people waiting for her, back at the party. "My sister," she explained hurriedly. "She won't know where I am."

Dakota offered her his cell phone. Hallie dialed, then hesitated. "She'll be really mad. . . ."

"I'll handle it, don't worry." Dakota took the phone back. "Hey, is this Grace?" He gave Hallie a reassuring smile, and then retreated to the hallway to talk.

Hallie waited until he was out of sight and then leaped up, dashing to the tiny bathroom. Dear Lord. She blinked in horror at her bedraggled reflection. This was her destiny out there, and she was looking like a drowned stray cat! She spun into action: finger-combing her no-longer-so-relaxed hair and swiping under her eyes to clear the streaks of mascara.

"Hallie?"

She gave her hair a final pat with the paper towels and reemerged. "I told her what happened," Dakota said, tucking his phone away. "I said I'd take you home."

"Thank you. I mean, for everything. If you hadn't been there . . ." The thought of those cruel, insistent waves, and how close she'd come to death, was overwhelming. She felt her legs buckle. In an instant, Dakota was by her side.

"Everything's going to be OK," he promised, holding her upright. "I've got you."

Hallie sank against him, banishing the dark thoughts to the very back of her mind. It was over now, the darkness before the dawn. Her pain had served its purpose, and brought him into her life.

Destiny.

"So I've got to ask," Dakota said as they headed toward the exit—Hallie leaning close against the warmth of his body. "What were you doing out there?"

"You'll think I'm crazy." Hallie blushed.

"Never. Go on, tell me." His face was open, curious, and in that moment, Hallie was flooded with a strange sense of reassurance—like she could tell him anything and he'd understand.

"I was doing a kind of ritual," Hallie explained. "Like a baptism, to start my new life here."

She waited for the laugh of derision, but instead, Dakota gave her a conspiratorial smile. "Venus rising from the ocean . . ."

"Exactly!"

Dakota led her through the main doors, then paused a moment on the asphalt, as if he were deciding something. "I burned it," he told her finally. "I drove cross-country, moving out here, and when I reached the ocean, I burned the map."

"Because it didn't matter how you got here," Hallie said, understanding completely.

"A fresh start," Dakota finished. Their eyes met. The fluorescent lights overhead cast sharp shadows across the angle of his cheekbones; his hair dried in a halo of dark curls. Hallie had to stifle a sigh of pure longing.

"I better get you home," Dakota said, and Hallie could almost convince herself that was regret she heard in his voice. "Come on."

She followed him to his beat-up Camry. She would have followed him anywhere. It was past two a.m. by the time Dakota pulled up in front of Uncle Auggie's. Inside, every light was blazing. "I'm sorry." Hallie braced herself for what was to come.

"For what?" Dakota helped her out of the car.

"You'll see."

They hadn't even stepped more than a foot inside before Hallie's mom raced out to meet them in the front hall; Amber hurrying behind.

"My baby!" Her mom clutched her in a frenzied hug. "What happened? Are you OK? If I lost you too . . ."

"Grace called and said you were missing," Amber added, wide-eyed. She was wearing a tiny pink negligee, her curves barely concealed under a sheer white robe. "We didn't know what to think. Auggie's on the phone with the police now. He was about to have them send divers out!"

"You should have told someone before you wandered off." Grace's voice came from behind them. She was loitering at the back of the hall with Brandon, glaring at Hallie accusingly. "Didn't you stop to think for one moment we would worry?"

"Are you OK?" Brandon asked, moving to her side. He looked at her with bloodshot eyes, clearly exhausted. "We searched the party for hours."

"She's fine," Dakota told them as Hallie detached herself from the anxious hugs. "The doctor checked her out, everything's OK. She just needs rest and recovery."

They all turned.

"This is Dakota," Hallie announced, beaming. "He saved me."

Dakota gave a self-deprecating shrug. "Anyone would have helped, it was just lucky I heard her—"

"Nonsense!" Uncle Auggie came bursting through the crowd. He clasped Dakota in a hug, slapping his back enthusiastically. "You're the hero of the hour! We owe you."

"No, really, it's nothing." Dakota turned to look at Hallie. "It's enough that she's OK."

Hallie felt her legs buckle again. This time, it had nothing to do with her ordeal, and everything to do with the intensity of his expression. "Do you want to stay?" Hallie asked hopefully. "Have some coffee, maybe, or—"

"It's been a long night," he cut her off, with a gentle smile. "You should get some rest."

Her mom must have seen Hallie's disappointment, because she blocked Dakota's path to the exit. "Tomorrow, then," Valerie declared. "She'll be rested then. You can come by anytime."

For once, Hallie didn't care about her mom's interference, because Dakota smiled at Hallie. "Definitely." He turned to the rest of them with a polite nod. "Good night."

The door closed behind him. There was a pause, and then Hallie was smothered in an avalanche of voices.

"My poor baby!"

"Isn't he cute?"

"God, could you be any more self-centered? We were all worried sick!"

Hallie ignored them all, gazing after Dakota. "I'm going to bed," she said dreamily. His jacket was still draped around her shoulders, smelling faintly of smoke and spices and *him*. "See you all in the morning."

"Hallie!" Grace squawked in annoyance.

"The doctor said I need to rest." She wandered back through the house, leaving the crowd of chatter behind. Let them be dramatic and have their big scene, she had more important things to think about.

Like the new love of her life.

As promised, Dakota dropped by to see her the next morning, and found Hallie reclining on a shaded lounge chair by the pool in her best sundress, her hair painstakingly straightened into a glossy sheet. She'd been there since nine, just to be safe—arranged at what she hoped was a pretty angle, clutching her copy of *Another Bullshit Night in Suck City,* but too excited to focus on a single sentence. Every time the gate clattered open, she couldn't help but whip her head around to check. Since it was Julio's day to prune the roses, Hallie's neck ached by the time Dakota finally strolled up the garden path, but just the sight of him—black jeans and a V-neck shirt, hair ruffled in windswept curls—made her forget even the minor tendon ache.

"He's here!" she breathed. Grace—seated beside her, stealing mango from her restorative fruit platter—rolled her eyes.

"You don't say."

Hallie ignored her. "Hi!" she called as he sauntered closer. "I completely forgot you were coming over."

Grace snorted. Hallie shot her a warning look.

"Hey." Dakota leaned down to kiss her cheek—the L.A. way, as Hallie was learning—and then presented her with a small posy of flowers. "I picked these. And for you, too," Dakota added, passing another posy to Grace.

Grace's expression softened in surprise. "Oh. Thanks."

"Grace can't stay," Hallie said quickly, sending her a pleading look. "She's busy, right?"

Grace glanced back and forth between Hallie and Dakota, before finally giving Hallie a begrudging smile. "Right." She got up. "But thanks for these."

"That was sweet," Hallie told him as Grace headed back into the guesthouse. "I bet she's never gotten flowers before."

“I know they’re not fancy or anything . . .” Dakota trailed off, eyes going to the excessive display of orchids Brandon had brought over earlier, perched in a cut-glass bowl in the middle of the table.

“No, I love them!” Hallie exclaimed. “Wild flowers are better than stuffy florist bouquets, they’re so pretty. Natural.” She yanked Brandon’s flowers out of the water and tossed them aside, arranging Dakota’s posy in their place. “There.”

Dakota folded himself onto the lounger next to hers and picked up Hallie’s book. “He’s one of my favorites,” Hallie explained quickly. She’d almost picked out Kerouac, but figured Dakota would be more of a modern, edgy guy.

She was right. Dakota’s smile got wider. “Me too!” He flipped through the dog-eared pages. “I read this years ago, but I lost my copy.” He passed it back to her. “Maybe I could borrow it when you’re done?”

“Take it now,” Hallie insisted. “I’ve read it tons of times.”

“You sure?”

“Absolutely.” Hallie pushed it into his hands. “Then you can tell me what you think.”

“Our own private book club,” Dakota suggested with another heart-stopping grin, and Hallie had to stifle a sigh.

He was still perfect.

She’d known he would be, of course she had, but in the two hours she’d been waiting there, a tiny niggle of doubt had crept into Hallie’s mind. What if she’d been suffering some post-traumatic stress episode brought on via saltwater inhalation—built him up in her mind to unfathomable heights—and in the cold harsh light of day he turned out to be nothing more than a wannabe rock star with a taste for dirty denim?

But he was there, beside her now, just as magnificent as she'd remembered. More so, even, because her memory couldn't contain the intensity that radiated from him, or the dark mischief in his eyes. . . .

"Yooo-hooo!" Amber's high-pitched voice echoed across the lawn. She was on the back patio, phone to her ear. "Don't you two move," she called. "I'll be right out!" She waved, then disappeared back inside.

Hallie gulped. "You know, I'm feeling kind of restless." She turned to Dakota. "And I should really take the dogs out." He didn't miss a beat.

"How about a walk?" he suggested, a knowing smile tugging the edge of his lips.

They strolled the leafy streets for hours: Marilyn and Monroe scampering at their heels, Hallie's hand tucked in the crook of Dakota's arm like they were an old-fashioned couple. They talked about everything she could think of—words tumbling out in an excited stream. She couldn't help herself, she needed to know everything about him.

"High school," Hallie demanded.

Dakota made a face. "Endless. Frustrating. Limited. Done."

She laughed. "Me too."

"No way," he told her. "You were the most popular girl in school, I can tell. Homecoming queen. Most likely to succeed, all that stuff."

"No!" Hallie protested. He gave her a dubious look. "Well, OK, maybe I was popular," she admitted, "but that didn't mean it mattered to me. I always felt . . . different. Like the things I wanted, they'd never understand."

"Like what?" Dakota turned.

She exhaled. "To . . . matter. To have people know my name. To leave a mark on the world!" She stopped, self-conscious. "It sounds, conceited, I know, but it's not like that. I just mean, we're all so *small,* and life is so fleeting; I don't want to just be gone, and have there be nothing left of me, you know?"

"I do." Dakota smiled slowly. "It's why I write. So somebody out there can know I exist. So I can reach them."

"I mean, imagine twenty years from now, someone watching a movie with me in it, or listening to one of your songs. Not even here," Hallie added excitedly, "but in England, or China, or somewhere. That they would know who we are, that we existed! Instead of just . . ."

"Fading away," Dakota finished. "My parents think it's crazy, to just move out here and try to be, what, a rock star?"

"But it's not!" Hallie insisted. "I think it's crazy to just sit around, and not try to make your dreams happen. Think about spending your whole life wondering, *What if?*"

"They don't get it!" he agreed. "My dad works a

factory gig, just slaving away ten hours a day, and for what? A paycheck that's gone by the end of the month? I want more than that."

"You *are* more than that," Hallie told him, breathless. He understood. He understood *her.* "We both are."

He stopped walking, and with a flash of disappointment, Hallie realized they were back outside Uncle Auggie's mansion. The dogs yapped, impatient. "I'm really glad I met you," Dakota said, almost shyly. "Not that you nearly drowned," he added quickly. "But, you know."

Hallie nodded, not trusting herself to speak.

"Me and the guys are playing a gig Friday night, over in Hollywood." Dakota looked hopeful. "I can put you on the list if you feel up to coming?"

"I'd love to!" Hallie exclaimed. "But . . ."

Dakota waited. "What?"

"It's just . . . Friday is a long way away." She felt her cheeks flush. But she couldn't help it! The thought of a whole week passing before she could see him again? Unfathomable!

Dakota must have agreed, because he grinned. "You'll need to build your strength back up, like the doctor said. How about another walk? Tomorrow?"

"Perfect." Hallie sighed with happiness. And he was.

VII

Dakota came to visit the next day, and every day that week, bringing Hallie a new gift each afternoon. A copy of his last demo CD; a ripe peach; a single blush-pink peony. Hallie lined them up on her bedroom windowsill like trophies—evidence that their time together was real, that *he* was real, and not conjured out of her imagination after a lifetime of idle daydreaming and sheer longing.

Because he was so right for her. Sensitive, thoughtful, artistic, intense . . . Since the night he pulled her from the cruel ocean—so brave! so heroic!—she'd been in a constant state of nervous anticipation, adrenaline jittering through her system at the mere thought of him. And when they were together . . . Hallie would have sworn that the world disappeared. This was what love felt like, she was sure of it.

"Hallie!" Grace yelled from downstairs. "Brandon's here!"

"Just a minute!" Hallie called back. It was Friday night, the band's big show, and Hallie was venturing up into Hollywood to go see him play. Without a driver's license, or money for a cab, she'd found the perfect solution: Brandon, and his Jeep. Hallie quickly pulled on her boots and Dakota's leather jacket, then smudged on another layer of dark eyeliner. Grace's footsteps thundered on the staircase, and a moment later, she was in the doorway.

"What do you think?" Hallie twirled around, breathless. "Will he like it?"

"Brandon?"

"Ugh, no! Dakota!"

Grace rolled her eyes. "You look fine. You always look fine—when you're not dolled up like you traveled here from nineteen fifty-two, I mean."

Hallie gave her a look, collecting a tiny cross-body bag and her lip balm. "I just want to be perfect for him."

Grace bit her lip.

"What?" Hallie sighed.

"Nothing," Grace said, still reluctant. "It's just . . . You shouldn't rush into anything. I mean, you've only known him four days."

"Five," Hallie corrected quickly. "And time doesn't matter. We transcend time!"

Grace didn't seem impressed. "Just . . . don't rush into anything. You haven't seen a single other person since we got here: all you do is sit around waiting on him, and go on those walks."

"Because I've been in recovery, after my near-death experience, or are you forgetting that?" Hallie protested. "And, hello, you aren't exactly a social butterfly either!" She didn't add that her friend requests and super-casual texts to Ana Lucia and Meredith had gone unanswered; their breezy party friendship failing to materialize into anything more solid. "I know plenty about him," she argued, focusing on the real thing that mattered. The only thing. "We have talked, you know. What else do you think we've been doing all this time?"

There was a pause. Grace looked awkward. "But, you will be *careful,* right?"

It took Hallie a moment to realize what she meant. "Grace!"

Her sister looked equally disturbed. "He's older, OK! And you've been glued together all week. I'm just saying . . ."

"Well, don't!" Hallie pushed past her. "Never say anything about my sex life ever again!"

Hallie hurried downstairs. She'd never admit it to her sister, but the truth was, she and Dakota hadn't even kissed, let alone . . . anything else. They'd talked for hours, exchanged a lifetime's worth of deep, intense looks, and even, on one occasion, his hand had brushed against hers and stayed touching for a full three seconds. But beyond that? Nothing.

It was romantic. It was courtly. It was driving Hallie insane. And she was determined for it to end, tonight.

• • •

Brandon found parking along Sunset Boulevard, and walked with Hallie toward the club entrance, already marked with a snaking line of insouciant hipsters in plaid shirts and gaggles of eager teenage girls. "Thanks for the ride, but are you sure you want to stay?" Hallie checked. He'd been his usual introverted self on the drive over—all awkward abrupt statements, and nervous tapping—and somehow, he didn't strike her as the über-cool rock-show type.

"I can check out a couple of songs." Brandon jammed his hands into the pockets of his bulky khaki jacket. His Unabomber jacket, Hallie had secretly christened it. "Anyway, won't you need a ride home after?"

"Dakota will take me," Hallie told him, smoothing back her hair. "He would have given me the ride here too, but he had to be here early to do the sound check, and set up with the guys."

"Oh." Brandon paused. "I mean, sure, that makes sense. Listen"—he paused again—"I was thinking . . ."

"Uh-huh?" Hallie was already distracted, scanning the crowd. The club was tucked away between a neon-fronted hotel and a grimy liquor store, the lights glowing all the way down the block.

"You were talking earlier about trying to be an actress—"

"I *am* an actress," Hallie corrected.

"Right, anyway, I was thinking you'll need new head-shots, and all of that stuff, and, well, I've been doing some photography . . ." Brandon trailed off. "I could help you out. If you want."

Hallie turned and assessed him quickly. He didn't look like a star photographer, but who knew—perhaps there was a visual genius lurking beneath that scraggly beard. "Maybe. Drop by with a portfolio or something, and I'll take a look."

"Great, I could come by tomorrow, or—"

"Ana Lucia!" Hallie called, spotting a familiar cascade of dark hair. She turned to Brandon. "See you later!" she told him quickly, then hurried over to where Ana Lucia was waiting with Meredith and Brie, the trio outfitted in an array of skinny denim and perfectly draped tank tops. "Hey!" she cried, excited to see familiar faces. "How are you guys?"

"Don't even ask." Ana Lucia scowled. She crossed her arms, metallic bracelets jangling against her chest.

"They're saying the show's sold out," Meredith added, giving Hallie air-kisses on each cheek. Brie looked up from her phone, flickered a wave in Hallie's direction, then resumed her tapping.

"The idiot on the door won't even call the manager to get me in!" Ana Lucia exclaimed. "And I promised Reed I'd come. He'll think I blew him off!" She craned her neck to see ahead of them in line, standing on the tiptoes of her dangerous-looking studded boots.

"Why don't you guys just come in with me?" Hallie suggested. "I'm on the list."

Three heads whipped around in unison. "What? You? How?" Ana Lucia exclaimed. "Sorry, I mean, I thought you just got into town?"

"I met Dakota at that party last week," Hallie replied.

"And, well . . ." She couldn't keep the smile from spreading across her face. Ana Lucia gasped.

"No!"

"Yes." Hallie gave a shrug, the perfect kind of nonchalant "sure, I'm dating the gorgeous rock star, no big deal" shrug that she figured this kind of situation demanded.

"You don't wait around!" Meredith grinned, and even Brie looked up from her phone again to offer Hallie a nod of approval.

"This is perfect!" Ana Lucia linked arms with Hallie and marched them toward the head of the line. "I was going to call you to hang out anyway, but now we can get to know each other some more. You with Dakota, and me with Reed!" Ana Lucia's face suddenly brightened with a new thought. "You can get us backstage, right?"

The band was great, but with Dakota up there, how could they not be? Jagged chords, wild, infectious melodies—the crowd adored them, yelling along to the lyrics as the guys attacked their instruments and struck their rock-star poses. They were ramshackle, sure, but all the more irresistible for it—an unpolished, wild fervor behind every song.

"Aren't they beyond?" Ana Lucia yelled as the audience whooped and hollered. Hallie nodded, wordless. There was no "they" to her, only *him,* because as far as she was concerned, Dakota was alone on that stage.

"We're going to take it down a moment," he said, gesturing for quiet. His shirt was wet through with sweat, hair plastered against his scalp, but there was an undeniable energy radiating from him; a shimmering aura of confidence in the way he swaggered across the tiny stage. "This one is new. We hope you like it."

Reed strummed out a few chords, and then the beat kicked in—slower, seductive. Dakota stepped back to the microphone, and began.

"I saw you in my dreams, so many years before . . ."

Hallie forgot how to breathe.

It was a ballad, plaintive and heartfelt. Dakota stood, lit by a single spotlight; guitar slung across his chest. He seemed larger-than-life, somehow; not entirely real. To Hallie, it was as if there were a great distance between them, a huge divide between him—up there—and her, lost in the mass of people below.

And then his eyes caught hers in the crowd.

"It was you, only you, everything I waited for . . ."

The distance disappeared; it was only her, and him, and nobody else. She could have sworn he sang the rest of the song to her, and her alone. She was so lost in the sight of him that she barely even noticed when the song was done, and the band sauntered offstage to the plaintive cries of every girl in the audience.

"Oh, my God." Ana Lucia clutched Hallie's arm, wide-eyed. "He totally sang that to you."

Hallie tried to maintain her nonchalance, but failed. She let out an excited squeal. "Wasn't he amazing?"

"And did you see how hot Reed looks?" Ana Lucia matched her glee. "Come on, let's go say hi!"

They headed for the grimy back hallway, fighting through the crowd of adoring teen girls already clustered by the dressing room door.

"Sorry, off-limits." A burly guy blocked their way.

"We're with the band," Ana Lucia insisted. The man didn't move. "Hallie?" she turned.

"Just a second." Hallie quickly texted Dakota, and, moments later, he appeared.

"They're good, Al," he told the bouncer, who stood aside to let them through. The girls sashayed past with a chorus of greeting, heading back to the dressing room, but Hallie held back, suddenly shy.

"That was incredible," she told Dakota softly.

"You think?" Dakota was still sweaty and glowing, practically vibrating with energy. He grinned at her, pushing back a swoop of hair. "I can't tell. It's like, I come offstage, and get instant amnesia. It's all a blank to me."

"You were great," she insisted. "Everyone was going crazy. I can't believe you haven't been signed yet."

Dakota made a "what can you do?" gesture. "Come and meet the guys," he said, and led her down the hallway to the tiny, graffiti-covered dressing room where the guys were enthusiastically recapping the show, surrounded by a jumble of speakers, instruments, and power cords.

"Dude, you screwed me on the count for 'Liar's Game'!"

"No, you screwed me with that solo, you went three beats too long!"

Ana Lucia, Brie, and Meredith were squeezed onto an ancient, peeling couch in the corner, and another couple of girls loitered nearby, trying to look as if they didn't care they had nowhere to sit.

"Reed, McCoy, and AJ." Dakota pointed to each in turn. "Guys, this is Hallie."

"So this is the girl." Reed gave Hallie a long look. He was dirty blond in a leather vest and jeans, tattoos creeping down his arms. "Tell us the truth, he didn't really pull you out of the ocean, right?"

"No, that happened." Hallie and Dakota exchanged a private look.

Reed groaned. "He hasn't shut up about it all week. The grand rescue!"

Hallie tried not to show her excitement. He was talking about her! He was *thinking* about her!

Dakota shoved the stocky drummer, McCoy, aside to make room for them on the couch, and soon, the guys were loudly arguing about the set list again, and whether their song order needed switching. "I'm just saying," AJ argued, from behind a curtain of dark hair, "if they're dancing, we don't want to bring them down!"

Dakota shifted closer to Hallie. "I'm really glad you came," he murmured, lips brushing her ear. He slipped an arm around her shoulders, and Hallie could have sworn her heart leaped right out of her chest.

"Me too," she whispered back.

The conversation meandered, but Hallie only noticed the warmth of Dakota's body against hers, until Ana Lucia cleared her throat and fixed Reed with a dazzling smile. "Who's up for an after-party? I can get us into Soho House. Some of us," she added, glancing at the other girls.

"Sure, sounds good." There was a chorus of nonchalant agreement from the band. They headed outside, but once they were all on the sidewalk, Dakota hung back.

"Maybe I should get this one home. Since you're still in recovery." He squeezed Hallie's hand, and although she was dying to discover the classy members-only club she'd read about in all the magazines, she was dying to spend some time alone with Dakota even more.

"He's right!" Hallie exclaimed. She tucked her arm through Dakota's, and leaned against him, adopting a tired expression. "You guys go ahead, have fun."

"Call tomorrow?" Ana Lucia gave her an extravagant hug. "We'll do brunch."

"Fab!"

Hallie watched them pile into a pair of cabs and drive away. "So, where to now?" she asked.

Dakota grinned. "I said I was taking you home."

"Sure, that's what you said . . ." Hallie grinned back. The sidewalk was bathed in neon; billboards and streetlights glowing above them. It was beautiful: the buzz of the city vibrating, and she was there, in the heart of it all. With him.

Dakota paused, twisting his fingers through hers. "There is this one place I want to show you. . . ."

Dakota took her up to Mulholland; driving the narrow, twisted road through the canyon, until they crested the top of the Hollywood Hills, the valley sprawling out below them. He parked off the side of the road, and helped Hallie up beside him on the hood of his car.

"This is my favorite place in the whole city," he told her, gazing out at the blanket of lights: a sprawl of city blocks, the rush of red and white on the freeway, snaking out into the distance. It seemed to Hallie like the whole world was spread before them.

"So many people," she said softly, trying to imagine the individual lives marked by each tiny flicker of light.

"Sometimes it's daunting, you know—like, everyone down there has their dreams, and I'm just another kid. Insignificant." Dakota's expression was open, almost hungry. Hallie watched him, watching the world. "But then, I think, I'm up here; I made it this far. I can be that one, in a hundred—a million. We both can," he added with a smile. "Together."

Hallie's breath caught as Dakota turned to her; reached to gently touch her cheek. The moment stretched: eyes locked, the very air between them alive with electricity. And then he was leaning in, breath soft on her lips. Closer. Closer.

There.

She closed her eyes, falling into his kiss like it was

gravity, like she was drowning all over again. And this time, again, he was the one to hold her up. A hand pressed against the back of her head; her fingers clutching his shirt. Hallie held on as if for dear life, but she knew, it was too late.

She was falling in love with him, and there was no saving her now.

PART THREE: *Fall*

I

She should have kissed him.

It had been four months now since Grace had shared that *almost* kiss with Theo on the dark street overlooking San Francisco; four long months in a new town with little else to do but go to school, work weekends at a fancy macaroon store in Beverly Hills, and pull that night apart in her mind to ponder every tiny detail. The streetlights bathing them in neon, his lips so close to hers. She could remember that flutter of possibility in her veins, the invisible force that had seemed to draw her closer, closer . . .

But whatever angle she studied it from, no matter what excuses and justifications she designed—Grace came up with exactly the same answer:

She should have kissed him.

It had been her one shot, her parting Hail Mary pass. And who knew? Maybe if she'd been impulsive, or reckless, or bold, then she would have done it: just blocked out all the reasons why she couldn't, and kept reaching for him, the way she longed to. But the moment had passed—no, not passed, she'd fled from it!—leaving Grace to face the miserable truth: she wasn't that girl. She didn't kiss boys, let alone ones who had never indicated anything more than platonic (or, worse still, perhaps even brotherly) concern. She couldn't throw herself at someone, never minding the potential ruin to their friendship. She couldn't be so brave.

Now, when Grace thought back to that night—whenever she caught a glimpse of the photo Theo had taken of them, now pinned above her dresser; or saw Hallie and Dakota snuggling together; or felt her phone vibrate with what might be a text from him—her regret wasn't so much that she hadn't kissed him; more, that she wasn't the kind of girl who ever would. Aside from the fact that he was older, and disarmingly cute, and technically related to her (even if by marriage, not birth), he was, well, *Theo*. The idea of having the right to press her lips to his, or slip her fingers through his tufts of brown hair, or simply slide her arm around his waist and nestle in the crook of his arm . . . it was ludicrous. She may as well decide to kiss the Hollywood superstar who lined up ahead of her in Whole Foods, for all the chance she had.

No, the whole thing had been madness; a fever-dream. And, as far as Grace was concerned, madness was no excuse for very nearly humiliating herself and wrecking a valuable friendship.

It was clear, there was only one path open to her now: complete and utter denial.

There had been no swooning eye contact, no leaning in, and certainly no awkward fleeing into the house—in her official version of events, those ten seconds no longer existed and to her relief, Theo seemed to be doing the same. He sent her casual e-mail updates throughout the summer, and the occasional text, and continued their ongoing library of adorable animal video links, but not once did he ever refer to Those Ten Seconds. Hell, for all she knew, he wasn't even pretending. To him, nothing might have actually happened at all, and Grace was spending her time analyzing a moment that never even existed!

Still, a rebellious voice kept whispering in her mind: she should have kissed him.

"Grace. Earth to Grace?"

She looked up from her blank notebook. Her lab partner, Harry, was looking at her with a puzzled expression.

"What's up?" She gave an absent smile. "Do you need more iodine?"

"We're done. Didn't you hear the bell?"

Grace glanced around. The lab was emptying fast, students rushing to be done for the day, and outside, she could hear the babble and chatter of kids spilling out onto the front quad. She blushed. "Sorry. Thanks."

She started packing up, but Harry lingered, tugging

at the strap of his messenger bag. It was covered in Wite-Out and marker scribbles: tiny cartoons marching across the flap. "I was thinking we should get together, to go over chapter six," he suggested as Grace pulled on her backpack and headed for the door. "McLaren said there would be a quiz Monday."

"It's OK, I've covered it," Grace told him. "I did most of this stuff last semester at my old school."

"Oh." Harry looked downcast. "Sure. OK."

Grace felt guilty. As lab partners went, he was one of the good ones: actually doing the assignment, instead of slacking off, or fooling around like so many of the other guys in her class. The least she could do was make sure he didn't fail.

"I could take you through the material, if you want?" she offered. "Sunday afternoon, maybe, at the library?"

"Great!" Harry brightened. "Let me give you my number. You know, in case."

They exchanged details on the grand front steps. Unlike Grace's old school, with its cramped buildings stacked haphazardly in the middle of a city block, her new school radiated out from a grassy central quad: neat white stucco buildings fringed with trees, and seating areas set back from the main pathways. In the month since school had begun, Grace often marveled at the spotless grounds: there was no graffiti or litter or any sign that this was, in fact, a school and not some serene spa.

A car horn sounded behind them, loud and insistent. Grace turned to see Dakota's beat-up old Camry cruise into the parking lot; Hallie waving from the passenger side. "I better go," she told Harry, stuffing her notebook into her bag. The horn sounded again. Grace gave an apologetic smile. "My sister waits for no man."

Harry gave Grace a salute. "See you Sunday."

Hallie and Dakota were making out when Grace reached the car, hungrily intertwined the way they had been all summer. After months of walking in on them kissing in the hallway, out by the pool, and, one time, in Uncle Auggie's walk-in pantry (canned goods clearly proving an unlikely aphrodisiac) Grace barely noticed anymore. Except when things got . . . intimate.

Right on cue, Dakota's hand wandered lower. Grace banged on the window. "PG-13! Children present."

Hallie laughed, scooting forward so Grace could slide in the backseat. "No complaints! I'm the one doing the good deed here, picking you up."

"Why *are* you here?" Grace pushed aside Dakota's guitar case, and a stack of fast-food wrappers. "Not that I don't appreciate it," she added. "But I would have come quicker if I'd known."

"It's cool," Dakota said, yanking the car into gear. "You were busy with your new friend." He waggled his eyebrows at Grace in the rearview mirror. She kicked the back of his seat good-naturedly.

"What are you, a matchmaker now?"

"I think he's cute." Hallie joined the teasing. "All ruffled and skater-boy." Grace glowered at her. Hallie sighed. "I forgot, your heart belongs to another!"

Grace changed the subject. "What about you guys, what have you been up to?"

Dakota grinned. "Tell her."

"Tell me what?"

Hallie twisted in her seat, beaming. "I got a callback, on the soda ad!"

Grace gasped. "That's amazing!"

"I know! It's down to me and three other girls," Hallie added, "but I saw them in the waiting room, and I'm way more photogenic."

"And modest too." Grace laughed.

Hallie stuck her tongue out. "Just wait. Once I land this gig, I'll be able to get an agent, and then things will finally start happening!"

"I'm glad," Grace told her, sincere. "This is really great for you."

"And it's all thanks to this one." Hallie leaned over and kissed Dakota loudly on the cheek. "He's the one who found out about the job in the first place."

"The things you hear in line at Trader Joe's," Dakota agreed. He took Hallie's hand and kissed it, not taking his eyes from the road. It was an automatic gesture, an afterthought, even, but something about the warm familiarity made Grace's chest clench, deep behind her rib cage.

It wasn't that she begrudged Hallie her happiness. She was glad her sister was in love, she truly was, especially since that love had transformed Hallie from a tempestuous brat into an even-tempered delight, but their obvious intimacy still pained Grace. It wasn't so much a hurt as a wistful ache for a world she'd never known, only glimpsed from the outside looking in.

"So how's school?" Hallie demanded as they turned into their neighborhood. Fall was tinting the leaves orange and red, shady over the wide streets. "Are you making any new friends—besides the cute skater-boy, I mean?"

Grace shrugged.

"Grace! Come on, you need to try. You're a month into the semester already, and you haven't hung out with anyone!"

"Hey," Dakota said. "Ease up. It's hard settling in. Grace's doing fine, we can't all be social butterflies."

"I'm not a butterfly, I'm more . . . a hummingbird," Hallie declared. "Rare, delicate—"

"Arrogant," Grace added.

"Exhausting," Dakota finished, with a grin.

Grace laughed.

"Don't listen to Hallie," Dakota told Grace, meeting her eyes in the mirror again. "High school is hell on earth. As far as I'm concerned, if you make it through the day without wanting to slit your wrists, you're winning."

"Yeah, I'm not quite at the *Bell Jar* phase just yet." Grace smiled. "It's just, hard, that's all. They've all known each other forever, and everyone is so . . ."

"Spoiled? Rich? Bitchy?" Dakota offered.

"Pretty much."

Hallie sighed. "I've told you, Ana Lucia's little sister is a senior, and Tai's cousin is in your English class. Hang out with them!"

Grace didn't reply. Those kids were the über-popular crowd, all glossy haired and stylish, and although Hallie might have waltzed into their platinum-credit-card world—meeting her new, shiny friends for brunches, and shopping, and cocktail nights sneaking into the Roosevelt Hotel—Grace knew she didn't belong. One lunchtime spent lingering on the edge of their crowd as they planned a lavish birthday dinner, and weekend trip to Catalina ("because, like, who stays at home to celebrate anyway?") was enough to prove for certain that they occupied entirely different realities.

"I'll be fine," she insisted. "I'm a lone wolf, remember?"

"A-roooo!" Dakota howled. Hallie giggled, and nestled up against him; auburn curls spilling over his leather jacket.

Grace felt that pang again. "Actually, guys, could you just drop me here?"

"You sure?" Dakota checked. "It's no trouble."

"It's just a couple of blocks," Grace said. "I could use the walk."

He pulled over. She grabbed her bag, and clambered out.

"Tell Mom I'll be back late!" Hallie called.

"Are you kidding?" Grace sighed. "She started a new portrait series. You could elope to Vermont, and she wouldn't notice."

Grace's tone must have revealed something, because Hallie paused, leaning out the car window. "Maybe we could hang tomorrow," she suggested brightly. "Go to a movie, or something."

"Sounds good to me," Dakota added. "Maybe if you

come along, we'll outvote her, and I'll get to see something that doesn't involve tragic deaths due to consumption."

Grace gave them a faint smile. "It's OK, I don't need babysitting."

Hallie rolled her eyes. "Duh. I'm just saying, someone needs to get you out of the house."

"It's OK," Grace insisted. "Anyway, I have work. Thanks for the ride!"

Grace wandered slowly back to the Jennings estate. Or, as she couldn't bring herself to think of it yet, home. If there was anything worse than Hallie's relentless remarks about Grace's supposed secret love affair with Theo, it was the pity invites to tag along with her and Dakota. Grace knew that Hallie meant well, but she would far prefer to sit at home, alone, instead of be the third wheel as they gazed into each other's eyes, and murmured sweet nothings through the night.

Her phone buzzed with a new text. Theo.

Catalyst: 32 points. Bow at my erudite majesty, peon!

She should be glad, that nothing had changed, and part of her was. But the other part, the part that wistfully longed for something more. . . .

I bow to no one, she texted back. *The peasants shall rise and defeat you yet.*

A car slowed nearby.

"And on your left is the Carson estate, site of the Hollywood Hell murders of nineteen fifty-two."

Grace looked up. Their neighborhood saw a steady

stream of tourists on the star tour trail—strapped into open-top buses, clicking their cameras in unison—but this seemed unlike the others: five Japanese tourists clustered around an old pink convertible, with a blond girl on her hands and knees, trying to change a flat tire.

"Three of the Carson daughters burned to death in a fire," the girl continued loudly, heaving at the jack. She was wearing tweed city shorts and a white shirt that was crumpled and smeared with dust. "It was rumored to be a mob hit, but nobody was ever arrested for the crime."

She looked up, and saw Grace staring at them. "Look! One of the Carson granddaughters!" She pointed at Grace. "They're famous recluses. Photos, everyone!"

The tourists turned, and began snapping. Grace instinctively covered her face. "What's going on?" She moved closer to the car. "I'm not a Carson!"

"Shh! They don't know that!" the girl hissed. "I need to give them something, or they'll start asking for their money back!" She rocked back on her heels, wiping her forehead—and leaving a trail of dirt.

"You've got, um . . ." Grace pulled a tissue from her bag, then paused, looking at the girl again. "You go to my school, don't you? We have gym together."

"Right!" The girl brightened. "You were the one who hit Cassidy in the face with the volleyball."

Grace cringed. "I really didn't mean to."

"Are you kidding? That was, like, the highlight of my entire week. She'd only just gotten the bandages off from her nose job! I mean, 'deviated septum surgery,'" the girl corrected, with a grin. "Oh, I'm Palmer." She offered a hand to shake, then stopped. It was covered in grease.

"Grace," Grace replied. "Do you, umm, need any help with that?"

"Would you?" Palmer brightened. "I've seen this done, like, a million times, but I can't seem to make all the pieces fit." She hauled herself up, and turned to the tourists. "The next house up is where Brad Pitt once mowed the lawn in nineteen ninety-two, when he was working as a yard boy to pay rent!"

The tourists aah-ed, and obediently went to snap photos.

"Did he?" Grace asked.

Palmer shrugged. "He could have. Why ruin their happiness?"

Grace laughed, taking the pieces of the wrench and fitting them together. "Why didn't you call someone?" she asked. The car was old, but it was in gleaming new condition, and Palmer's clothes were clearly designer beneath the mud stains.

"And wipe out my profits? No way. Besides, aren't they always saying we need to learn this stuff—female empowerment, or whatever?"

"Feminism is all well and good, but I'm afraid you're missing a piece." Grace held up the jack. "This car isn't getting any higher."

Palmer swore, and hit the side of the convertible. "What am I going to do now?"

"Sorry." Grace began packing up the pieces, but when

she looked up, Palmer was gazing at her with an unreadable expression. "What? Do I have some on my face?"

"No, I was just thinking . . ." Palmer grinned. "Do you have a car?"

"Sure. I mean, my mom does."

"How many does it seat?"

"Oh, no." Grace caught on. "Sorry, but, I'm not into this kind of thing."

"You mean, making money?" Palmer beamed, fluttering her eyelashes the way Hallie always did when she wanted something. "Come on, you drive, I guide, we'll have them back at their hotel in an hour! I'll split the fee with you," she added.

Now it was Grace's turn to pause. "How much?"

"Twenty bucks a head, between us."

Grace turned to the group, calculating. That was . . . more than she'd make selling overpriced macaroons at the store tomorrow.

"You get a free hat!" Palmer added, producing a baseball cap from a bag in the backseat: bright blue and emblazoned with a replica of the Hollywood sign. She modeled it, striking a pose. "Fresh from the runways of Paris, the envy of every fashionista in town!"

Grace couldn't help but laugh. Palmer seemed nice—if a little insane—and besides, what else did she have planned other than her ever-thrilling routine of homework, reading, and studiously not checking her e-mail?

"OK," she agreed, feeling almost cheerful. "I'm in. But on one condition: you keep the hat."

Palmer grinned. "Deal!"

II

Helping Palmer with her alternative star tour earned Grace not just a healthy bump to her savings account, but also a new friend—and with it, a place to sit at lunch, someone to do homework with over coffee, and the hope that, perhaps, there were some relatively normal kids in the 90210 zip code, after all.

If Palmer could ever qualify as normal, that was. The result of a high-powered attorney's brief, misguided liaison with an NFL star (Palmer's own words), Grace soon discovered that Palmer was a force of nature with an unrivaled collection of vintage hats. Grace suspected that she could rule the school's social scene if she chose, but Palmer preferred to spend her time on madcap entrepreneurial projects that would build her a business empire by the time she was twenty.

Popularity was fleeting, she told Grace with the bitter smile of somebody who had seen, firsthand, the damage believing otherwise could do. Self-sufficiency would last forever. Grace, still pining for her old home that was, by now, nothing but a construction site, knew exactly what she meant.

"Here's your cut." Palmer grinned, counting out bills the next weekend, after their early-morning tour. Strike while the competition was still snoozing, that was Palmer's philosophy—and while jet lag still reigned supreme. "Don't you just love the British?" She sighed happily. "They have no idea how to tip, so they just keep thrusting money at you out of sheer politeness!"

Grace gave her a knowing smile. "I think it's more how you stand there, looking offended, so they think they're committing a grave cultural faux pas."

Palmer shrugged. *"You say 'potato,'"* she sang, *"I say 'exchange rate.'* Anyway, want to grab some breakfast with our entirely legit gains?"

"Thanks, but I've got a family brunch thing." Grace drew up outside Palmer's house, a sprawling ranch-style property just a few streets over from Uncle Auggie's. "Mom likes us all to get together once a week, it makes her feel like she's actually involved in our lives."

"Hey, you're lucky." Palmer passed over the wedge of bills, and jammed her trilby hat on at a jaunty angle. "My mom requires daily status updates and hourly check-ins. Or at least, her assistant does." She climbed down from the van. "See you later for a movie? I'll text."

• • •

Back at the compound, Grace found Dakota helping to set the outdoor table for breakfast—swatting away Rosita's protests as he ferried fruit bowls and clean silverware from the kitchen.

"You're up early," Grace remarked, stealing a strip of bacon from one of the serving plates. Yum.

Dakota murmured noncommittally, as Hallie breezed out from the guesthouse. "Where have you been?" Hallie exclaimed, collapsing into a seat. "Don't tell me you've started jogging, or whatever it is Amber does to stay so skinny."

"Jog? Ha!" Grace joined her at the table. "I was just hanging out with Palmer, this girl from school."

"Way to go!" Dakota cheered. "Making friends, getting out there. Soon you'll be the Queen Bee of Beverly Hills!"

Grace rolled her eyes, but she couldn't help feeling a small sense of achievement. Was it pathetic that making one lone friend counted as such an accomplishment, she wondered, or was that canceled out by the fact that someone, somewhere, didn't think she was a complete loser?

Hallie reached for the toast. "Shouldn't we wait for Auggie and Amber?" Grace asked.

"They're at the salon," Hallie replied, pouring juice. "Amber said something about having his back waxed?" She shuddered. "Can you imagine? I wouldn't go near a guy's back hair, not even if he was a *billionaire*."

Grace coughed.

"I know, I'm sorry," Hallie told her, not at all apologetic. "We must not speak ill of the trophy wife!"

Grace gave her another stern look. She didn't know why Hallie insisted on holding her grudge against Amber—to Grace, it was like holding a grudge against those adorable yappy dogs: sure, they could be annoying sometimes, but they were just so eager and cute, you would have to be heartless to cast them aside.

Grace had to admit, she'd been dubious at first. The age gap, and Amber's penchant for pink Lycra workout gear had indicated a gold digger of the most basic kind, but after watching her and Uncle Auggie together for months, it was clear: the connection between them was genuine, however unconventional a love affair. Amber showered Auggie with affection, he adored her unconditionally right back, and together, they gossiped and laughed and mercilessly teased everyone all the day through.

It may not be Hallie's idea of wedded bliss, but Grace figured there were worse ways to build a marriage. After all, her parents' union had seemed rock solid, but still crumbled when her father decided he wanted a faster, glossier life, with overpriced sushi restaurants instead of her mom's one-pot roasts; opera and gala balls instead of nights in, playing Monopoly. Amber and Auggie at least seemed to value the same things in life, even if those things were salacious gossip and expensive spa treatments.

"Darlings." Their mom wafted down the path from her studio annex, draped in a long skirt and blousy orange tunic. She'd taken up yoga now, at a studio Amber swore Oprah used, and left books about Transcendental Meditation and the power of *The Secret* littered around the guesthouse. Grace hoped this wasn't simply a stop on the one-way train to Scientology. Valerie kissed Grace and Hallie on the forehead, and offered Dakota a hug. "Look at you, up and over here so early."

Dakota caught Hallie's eye across the table, and the two of them shared the tiniest of smiles. Grace froze, bacon halfway to her mouth.

Had Dakota spent the night?

Their mom took a seat, oblivious. "Isn't this nice? All of us together?"

They began to eat, but despite the lure of bacon, Grace was distracted, sneaking looks at Hallie. Was that a womanly glow, or just a new brand of bronzer? And were the looks between her and Dakota their usual swooning affection, or something more loaded with meaning? A morning-after kind of meaning.

"When did you get in last night?" Grace asked Hallie casually.

She shrugged. "Late."

"How late? I didn't hear you come in."

Hallie gave her a look. "Then you must have drifted off early."

"Mrs. Weston," Dakota interrupted, turning to their mom.

She tutted. "Valerie, please!"

"Valerie." Dakota fixed her with a charming smile. "I was wondering if it would be OK to go away with Hallie for a few days. We're planning a road trip, maybe over to Vegas and up to San Francisco."

Grace choked on her juice. "Vegas?"

Hallie ignored her, turning to their mom with a wheedling tone. "Please, Mom? I can visit everyone back home, maybe even video the whole trip like a documentary short!"

"But how will you afford it?" Grace asked. She knew walking the dogs kept Hallie in coffees and acting classes, but a road trip?"

"Don't worry, Dakota's got it all figured out."

He nodded. "We'll stay in cheap motels, and crash with friends. A guy I know works entertainment for a hotel in Vegas. He can hook us up with cheap rooms."

There it was again. Vegas. City of casinos, tacky stage shows—and drive-through weddings. Grace felt an ominous shiver. Sure, Hallie was a fan of big romantic gestures, but she wouldn't go that far, would she?

"I'm not sure." Their mom frowned absently. "A big trip like that, it could be dangerous. What if you broke down, or got in an accident?"

"I'll look after her, I promise." Dakota gave Hallie an adoring smile.

"Still, I don't know. . . ."

"Will you at least think about it?" Hallie pleaded. "We were hoping maybe in November. There's tons of time."

Valerie sighed, then gave a small nod. "I'll think about it."

Hallie leaped up, squealing. "Thanks, Mom!" She flew around the table and hugged their mother tightly.

"But no promises!" Valerie added as if anyone at the table didn't already know she'd agree. Chances were, she'd get so wrapped up in her painting and positive visualizations that she wouldn't even remember the question, let alone notice when Hallie was gone.

Grace finished her breakfast in silence, but the minute Hallie went inside to fetch her beach things, Grace trailed her up the stairs.

"Vegas?" she asked, loitering in the doorway of Hallie's bedroom. "You're not going to do anything stupid, are you?"

"Like what?" Hallie smoothed her hair in front of the mirror, and slicked on some lip gloss.

"I don't know . . ." Grace paused. "Elope?"

Hallie spun around. "What?"

Grace blushed. "I know, it sounds crazy, but crazy is kind of your thing! I'm serious!" she protested as Hallie burst out laughing. "I've seen the way you look at Dakota, and now that he's spending the night . . ."

"Shh!" Hallie hissed, quickly moving to close the door. "What do you know about that?"

"Only that Dakota sleeps until ten, and lives forty minutes away." Grace fixed Hallie with a meaningful stare. "I can do the math."

Hallie exhaled. "It's none of your business."

"I know! I just don't want to see you get hurt," Grace said. "Not after everything this year. . . ."

"This is different!" Hallie said fiercely. "Dakota's not like Dad. He would never do anything to hurt me." She took a deep breath. "I know you can't understand," Hallie told Grace, moving to the closet. "You've never been in love before, you can't know what it's like. But trust me, I know what I'm doing."

Grace wasn't convinced. Love wasn't any reason to lose your mind. "I like Dakota, you know I do." She tried being reasonable. "But, you've only known him a few months. Don't you think you should slow down?"

"For what?" Hallie threw her arms out expressively. "You keep saying that: 'be careful,' 'slow down,'" she mimicked. "But why? I love him! What's the point in pretending, and holding back, when I know we're meant to be together? Always!"

Grace gulped. "But you just said—"

"I know what I said." Hallie shrugged carelessly. "And you can relax, OK? We haven't planned anything. But . . . it's going to happen, sooner or later." She sighed, starry-eyed. "This is for real. Forever."

Hallie scooped up her bag. "We're heading to the beach, and then meeting everyone at Ana Lucia's. Don't wait up!" She winked, then flew out of the room and down the stairs.

Grace watched from the window as Hallie raced over to where Dakota was waiting on the front lawn. She threw her arms around his neck, and he spun them in a circle before depositing her gently back on the ground. They kissed, long and passionate, before piling in his car and driving away, music blasting.

Was Hallie right? Grace turned the question over in her mind for the rest of the day, as she breezed through the rest of her homework; curled on a calico couch on the back patio. Was love like that: mindless, and headlong, like hurling yourself off a tall building? Grace had always thought she was sensible to be so careful when it came to her heart, but there Hallie was: careless to the core, but spinning in some boy's arms all the same.

Perhaps Grace was the fool, for always holding back.

III

With Hallie swept up in Dakota and their grand plans for a road trip, Grace tried to focus on her own life for once: spending the next weeks hanging out with Palmer, and surrendering to Harry's frequent requests for study sessions; even though, it seemed, studying was the last thing he wanted to do.

"So how are you finding it here?" Harry abandoned his textbooks for the fifth time that hour, sitting with his feet dangling in the pool in Uncle Auggie's backyard. Grace was beginning to wonder if he had ADD or some such other affliction, for all the distractions he seemed to find. "It must be cool, being so ahead on everything."

Grace shrugged. "It's actually kind of boring," she admitted, moving to sit beside him. She shucked off her sandals and plunged her feet in the water, sighing with pleasure as the cool water hit her skin. Indian summer had turned out to be standard for fall in L.A.: the weather so hot that week it made Grace long for the chilled mists back home. "I spend most of the time in class just waiting around."

"You don't know how lucky you are." Harry splashed happily, knee-length skater shorts red against the terra-cotta tiles. "I think it would be great, just kicking back, not stressing about everything."

"Sure, but it gets old." Grace sighed. "And the teachers really don't like having to give me extra work."

"Just be glad you have the time," Harry told her, splashing some more. "My parents are already bugging me about colleges. Yay Asian stereotypes!"

Grace laughed.

"It's not funny. They're making me join the baseball team, and do all kinds of extracurriculars. You should think about that too," he added. "Clubs and activities and stuff. I mean, it sucks, but they're kind of right."

"I guess." Grace was reluctant. "I'm not really a joiner."

"Tell that to the admissions people," Harry said darkly. "Yeah, sorry I only have a 4.0 GPA and no bull-shit student activities, I was actually studying, instead of pretending to be a well-rounded citizen."

Grace laughed again.

"No, I'm serious," Harry continued. "It's this big game that everyone keeps playing. You think anyone believes we're volunteering because we care, and not just for the credit?"

"But does that make a difference to the people you're helping?" Grace pointed out.

"A philosopher," Harry teased. "Great."

Theo was studying philosophy, Grace couldn't help but think. Studying it at Stanford, only six hours and six minutes away on the freeway—traffic depending. She'd checked.

"Listen," Harry said, his tone suddenly hesitant. "You, umm, want to get together later?"

"It's OK, we should have the chapters finished soon." Grace eased her feet out of the pool and went back to the table for her drink. She took a gulp, surveying the spread of textbooks and notes. "Don't worry, McLaren won't test us on the next section yet. We have tons of time."

"No." Harry coughed. "I meant, like, for a movie or something."

"Oh." Grace froze. She turned back to Harry, suddenly gripped with awkwardness. "I . . . I mean . . ."

"Or, we could just grab a coffee," Harry added quickly, looking about as agonized as Grace felt. "Or even go to this party Josh is having. His parents are out and he's having some people over to watch movies and hang out. . . . Whatever you want."

What she wanted. . . . Grace gulped. What she wanted was six hours away. "I don't think . . ." She trailed off. She'd never once been asked out by a boy before, not on an actual date, so how was she supposed to know how to turn him down? "I, umm . . ."

"Hey, guys."

Grace whirled around. Brandon was sauntering up

the path: casual in threadbare jeans and his usual two-day stubble, but to Grace, there could be no sweeter sight. Salvation!

"Brandon!" she exclaimed happily. Harry's face fell. "Hey! How are you? What's going on?"

"The usual." He stood by the pool, hands in his front pockets. "What's new with you?"

"Nothing!" Grace cried, quickly grabbing her notebook and chem file. "We were actually just finished here, right, Harry?"

He stared at her, clearly crestfallen. "Right. Yeah. OK."

"Great study session!" Grace could tell her voice was unnaturally high, but she couldn't help it. Those had been the most awkward thirty seconds in the history of the universe. "See you in school!"

Harry looked from her to Brandon, and packed up his things. "See you." He sighed, and loped off.

Grace collapsed in a chair with relief.

"Did I interrupt something?" Brandon asked, looking amused.

"Yes," Grace told him. "And for that, you have my undying gratitude."

Brandon laughed. "Aww, poor kid. Do you have any idea how terrifying it is to try to make a move on someone?"

"Do you have any idea how awkward it is to try and duck that move?" Grace countered. She exhaled. "Anyway, thanks. I owe you."

"No problem." Brandon looked around, the hope in his expression unmistakable. Grace felt a twist of pity.

"She's out," she told him gently.

"Oh." Brandon paused. "With him?"

"Yup." Grace finished packing up the study things. "She should be back later, if you want to come over then."

Brandon gave a shrug, as if he were trying to seem unconcerned. "No, it's cool. I'm helping clear out Miss Whitman's garage," he explained. "I thought Hallie might want to come see."

"Is she that old movie star, from all those fifties musicals?" Grace looked over in interest. The Whitman house was at the far end of the block: shadowed with elm trees, the front yard deep with weeds and flowers growing wild. "We drive past it all the time on the tour. One guy was totally obsessed, he took, like, a hundred photos of her mailbox and front gate."

Brandon nodded. "Yup. The house is like a museum. She has all these vintage clothes, and memorabilia from her movies. I figured, it was Hallie's kind of thing. . . ."

"It would be," Grace agreed. Brandon was looking about as downcast as Harry had, only moments before. She took pity on him. "Can I see it?"

"No, I mean, it's OK. You don't have to. . . ."

"I want to. It'll be fun to see inside."

Brandon finally smiled, and for a moment, his usually somber face was transformed into something youthful, even handsome. "OK," he agreed. "But I'm warning you, it's like hoarder heaven in there!"

Brandon wasn't exaggerating. Behind the overgrown, fairy-tale facade, the legendary Gray Whitman's mansion was knee-deep in old boxes, books, and mementos of her former life as an on-screen ingenue. The lady herself was taking a nap, Brandon said—apparently her code for a glass of sherry and the afternoon soap operas—so they started in the garage. He yanked up the door, flooding the space with light, Grace feared, it hadn't seen in years.

"These newspapers are from nineteen sixty-two!" Grace exclaimed, holding up a stack of crumbling yellowed pages. "Who keeps this kind of stuff?"

Brandon laughed. "The kind of person who also has every issue of *Variety* in their original wrappers." He hauled another box out of the way, sending up clouds of dust.

"How did you get roped into this?" Grace asked, filling the first of what she was sure would be many trash bags.

Brandon shrugged. "I volunteered to help. I don't have much else to do, and she's nice, really. Just kind of . . . prickly."

Grace raised an eyebrow. "Kind of? She set off the alarms over that tourist I was telling you about—chased him out with the sirens blaring."

"Can you blame her—people driving by every night?" Brandon argued. "She just wants to be left alone. I understand that."

Grace paused. She'd seen Brandon around all the time, but they'd never actually been alone together, to talk. "How are you doing?" she ventured, before wondering if that was too intrusive. "Amber said you were taking some classes," she added quickly. "Photography?"

Brandon nodded, slowly slicing his X-Acto knife down the side of another box. His shirtsleeve rode up, revealing the dark ink of a tattoo on the curve of his bicep. "My parents were on me to do . . . something," he explained. "Anything, really, to get me out the house."

"Do you like it?" Grace asked. "I tried it for an art elective once, it was pretty fun."

He thought for a moment. "I like the darkroom part: mixing the chemicals, and going through the different processes, but the actual taking pictures . . ." He gave her a rueful look. "This fancy psychologist they make me see suggested it. It's supposed to help me reengage with the world, pay attention to things. I just don't know what I'm supposed to be looking for."

"Maybe that's the point," Grace answered, after a moment. "Maybe it's enough that you're looking."

Brandon shrugged. "I guess." He methodically bagged another stack of old newspapers. "The thing is, they still believe everything's going to go back to normal. Like I'm going to wake up one day, and be the guy I used to be. All parties and beach volleyball, and trips down to Tijuana, like I used to. Before . . ." A shadow drifted across his face, and he turned away. "We need more trash bags," he said, voice changing. "You want anything from the house?"

"No, I'm good," Grace said quickly. "Thanks."

Brandon exited, and Grace unpacked in silence for a while. She could never imagine the horrors he'd experienced, but Grace felt a strange affinity with him all the same. Sometimes there was no going back to the life you'd once known. She could barely picture herself a couple of years ago: thinking that home would always be there; that her family was the constant in life, not a variable. It had been hard enough for Grace to try and rebuild some sense of normalcy after everything that had happened; she could see how Brandon would struggle to even pretend everything was OK now.

He came back in, bearing two bottles of fancy sparkling water, a package of Swiss chocolate cookies, and—to Grace's relief—no sign of that dark, shadowed look. "She insisted," he said, setting down the bounty on a dusty old dresser.

Grace laughed. "I guess one doesn't feed the help regular old Oreos." She grabbed a cookie and opened another box. "Ooh, costumes!" Grace lifted out a glittering bodice and a matching cape; holding them up to the light to examine the stiff seams and hand-stitched sequins. "You're right," she said, folding them carefully back into place and marking the box. "Hallie would love this stuff."

Brandon let out a wistful sigh that said just about everything on the topic of Hallie, and her nonpresence. He caught Grace looking at him, and changed the subject abruptly. "So what was wrong with your study buddy? He seemed nice enough. Why did you need rescuing?"

Grace cringed, reminded of the agonizing awkwardness she so narrowly escaped. "I don't know. I mean, he's a decent guy, and I guess we have fun. It's just . . ." Now it was her turn for the wistful sigh. "I don't feel it."

"It?" Brandon raised an eyebrow.

Grace blushed. "Like I want to do more than study with him."

Brandon laughed. "You sure made that clear, the way you kicked him out."

"Good!" Grace exclaimed. "I don't want to give the wrong idea. We're friends. End of sentence."

"Don't be too hard on the guy," Brandon said, his voice quiet. "It can be pretty tough, knowing someone you care about doesn't feel the same."

He didn't have to explain. It had been clear he had feelings for Hallie since the moment they'd met, but Grace knew that Hallie barely gave him a second thought—except to giggle about his scruffy wardrobe, or hark back to the day of the serial killer/knife breakdown. Maybe if they spent more time together, she would get to know him . . . but no; her sister was too wrapped up in Dakota to ever look Brandon's way, and Grace had to admit, she could understand why. The dashing musician, or the introverted army vet? It was no choice, and Grace suspected Brandon knew that all too well.

"Come on." Grace put down her water, and reached for the next box. "If we keep at it, we can get to at least nineteen sixty-four!"

It was past five by the time Brandon called time on the sorting. He insisted on walking Grace to her door, despite her protests. "You never know who's lurking around here," he warned her. "And my mom would kill me if I let you go home alone."

"Well, thanks," Grace told him, reaching for her keys. "I guess chivalry lives on."

She moved to open the door, but it swung open; Hallie breathless on the other side. "Finally!" she cried. "Where have you been?"

"Out—" Grace yelped as Hallie dragged her inside. "Bye, Brandon. . . ." The door slammed in his face. "Oww." Grace pulled away, rubbing her arm. "Did you have to be so rude? You didn't even say hi to him."

Hallie rolled her eyes. "Never mind Brandon!" She began pushing Grace through the entrance hall, back toward the kitchen. "You have to come see!"

"What?"

"Wait." Hallie stopped dead, not answering Grace. "Let me do something with your hair first." She fussed at Grace's braid. "Why couldn't you get it relaxed last week, when I did? And your outfit! Maybe you should go change . . . ? No, there's no time, you'll have to do."

"Do for what?" Grace exclaimed, equal parts frustrated and confused. She batted away Hallie's hands, now trying to smear lip gloss on her face. "Will you please tell me what's going on?"

Hallie beamed at her, and resumed the dragging until Grace stumbled out onto the back patio. Her mom, Amber, and Uncle Auggie were taking their seats at the dinner table, with . . .

Grace froze.

"Look who's come to visit!" Hallie cried, throwing out her arms like a game show hostess. "It's Theo!"

IV

"*Hey.*" Theo grinned at her. "Surprise."

Grace stared at him in shock. His hair was shorter, she noticed, and he had new glasses with black frames; wearing a crimson college sweatshirt and khaki pants. But for all the changes, he was still so unmistakably *Theo*—vivid and real in front of her for the first time in so long—that it made Grace's heart leap.

"Theo!" She flew toward him, arms outstretched, but Theo's answering hug was weak, and he stepped back almost right away. Grace stopped, confused, and dropped her hands to her sides. There was a pause.

"So what are you doing here?" she asked, recovering. "I thought you were slammed with classes all semester."

"Some of Theo's friends were driving down for the UCLA game," Hallie answered for him, "so he thought he'd drop by and say hi. Isn't that great?"

"You should have come down sooner," their mom added. "You're always welcome. After all, you're still part of the family!"

"Thanks, Mrs. W." Theo turned to Amber and Uncle Auggie. "And thank you both again for inviting me to dinner."

"Oh, look at you, so polite." Amber giggled. "Are you sure you don't want to stay the night? We have the room!"

"No thank you, I have to meet the guys after the game, and head back up to campus," Theo explained. "But I couldn't come to town and not see you . . . all. See you all." He caught Grace's eye for a second, then looked away, almost bashful.

Grace paused. Why was he acting like they'd barely even met, when just yesterday they'd spent a half hour arguing over word scores on an Internet Scrabble game? Was something the matter? Had she done something wrong? Grace grabbed a nearby seat, her happiness fading.

"No, silly, you go sit over there." Hallie shoved her around the table to a chair beside Theo. "I bet you've got tons of catching up to do!"

Grace dutifully slid into the chair. Theo reached for his water glass and began gulping steadily. "Easy there," she teased. "You know there's a global shortage, right?"

Theo put his glass down so abruptly it splashed.

"Well, isn't this great?" Amber cooed, beaming from the head of the table. "Theo here's been telling us all about Stanford, and your baby brother."

Theo nodded. "Dash is doing well," he told them. "He's getting really big now, you wouldn't believe. And Portia . . ."

Grace laughed. "We know Portia. What is it this week, baby Pilates classes? Early-years algebra?" She shot him a conspiratorial look, the kind they used to share all the time, but Theo just stared down, his gaze fixed firmly on the plate of lemon chicken Rosa had just deposited in front of him.

Grace felt her heart slip.

"Theo, Theo . . ." Uncle Auggie mused, furrowing his bushy eyebrows. "That's with a *T,* right?"

Grace froze.

"Uh, yes." Theo frowned.

"Yum, this chicken is great!" Grace said quickly, trying to derail the subject. "Do you know where Rosita got the recipe?"

They ignored her. "Theo with a *T,*" Auggie told Amber meaningfully. She looked blank for a moment, and then brightened.

"A *T*!" Amber looked from Theo to Grace and back again. "Of course! Welcome!"

Theo looked truly baffled. "Sure. Thanks for having me."

To Grace's relief, Amber's phone buzzed; she glanced down, distracted, and Grace leaped at the chance to redirect conversation away from the various consonants that made up Theo's name. "How's college?" she asked quickly. "Is that history professor giving you a break yet? Theo has this one guy who's a real dictator," Grace explained to the table. "He keeps springing tests on them with no warning."

Theo paused. "He's OK, but, my course load just doubled." He looked uncomfortable. "I decided to double major in business, as well. To keep them all happy back home."

"Oh, you never told me that." Grace frowned, but Uncle Auggie nodded.

"Smart move, keeping your options open. And in this economy—"

"No one cares about the stupid economy!" Hallie interrupted. "Theo wants to hear all the latest news. Like my acting career."

Finally, a smile tugged the edges of Theo's lips. "I'd love to hear about your acting," he told Hallie. "Tell me all about it."

Grace sat quietly through the rest of dinner, her first burst of joy long forgotten. This was all wrong: Theo had barely even looked in her direction all night. When it came to her mom, or Hallie, Theo laughed and joked like nothing had changed, but all of Grace's questions were met with awkward, half-hesitant replies until she gave up on trying to talk to him at all. What had happened?

Maybe she had screwed things up, back in San Francisco, Grace realized with a sudden horror. Maybe Theo had known exactly what she had been thinking about, well, the *kissing,* and now, in person, avoiding her unrequited feelings was just too awkward for him to deal with.

Hallie scraped back her chair. "I have to go meet Dakota."

The noise dragged Grace back to reality. She looked around. The light was fading now, nothing but empty plates and dinnertime debris on the table.

"Good to see you, Theo. Swing down anytime!" Hallie planted a kiss on his cheek, then left.

Amber and Auggie rose from the table too. "We'll make ourselves scarce," Amber said, winking at Grace. "Give you two some time to . . . catch up."

"It's fine!" Grace all but yelped. "You don't have to go anywhere."

But they disappeared into the house, her mother wafting after them, and suddenly, Grace and Theo were left alone.

"So . . ." Theo started, then stopped. He fidgeted with his napkin. "How have you been?"

"You mean, since yesterday?" Grace smiled, trying to keep the mood light, but Theo just looked even more awkward.

"Of course," he said. "Right."

"I'm good," Grace said quickly. "And I'm really glad you made it down. It's good to see you again. You know, for real."

The backyard suddenly lit up: dozens of tiny electric tea lights strung between the branches. Sultry jazz music began to play, low, through the outdoor speakers. Amber clearly thought she was doing them a favor: it was cozy, and romantic, and Theo looked as if he wanted to hurl himself straight into the pool to escape it all.

Grace leaped up. "Want a tour?" she said brightly.

"Yes!" Theo agreed immediately. "That would be great."

Grace led him inside, sending silent thanks that there were seven bedrooms, a gym suite, and a library to see. That, at least, would fill some time. "You need to see the viewing room," Grace babbled, heading up the sweeping staircase. "Uncle Auggie has a screen so big it takes up a whole wall, and the default screen saver shows pictures from Amber's modeling portfolio. And the guest bathrooms are done in hot pink and orange!"

Theo followed her up, looking around slowly at the sweep of marble and abundance of chandeliers. "You know, you've never really said if you're happy here."

"I guess so," Grace replied. "Amber's sweet, once you get to know her, and Uncle Auggie means well. He's so generous—he even tried to give me an allowance, but . . . I feel bad enough just taking over the guesthouse."

"That's not what I meant." Theo paused. "Does it feel like home?"

Grace stopped. "No," she said finally. "Not like before. Don't get me wrong: it's gorgeous," she added quickly, "and we're so lucky to be here. But, look around. It's like a different world. I don't know if I'll ever feel like . . . like I belong, the way I used to."

Grace opened the doors to Uncle Auggie's library: revealing a book-lined room of dark wood and hunter-green leather chairs. There were stuffed deer heads mounted above a huge flagstone fireplace, muted oil paintings on the wall, and a huge mahogany desk with ink pot and fountain pens at the ready. It looked like the quintessential gentleman's library. Uncle Auggie never stepped foot in it.

Theo blinked. "Wow." He drifted over to one of the bookcases, tracing the leather-bound volumes. "This is . . . kind of creepy, yet awesome."

"It's my favorite room in the house." Grace exhaled happily. "Nobody ever uses it, and, I mean, it's so wrong."

Theo stared up at the dearly departed livestock. "So wrong."

Grace collapsed into one of the wing chairs. "Check out the books. Take one."

Theo tried to pull one out of place. It didn't move. He frowned. "What . . . ?"

"They're not real." Grace grinned. Theo went to try another; this time, pulling out the whole row. "They're glued together," Grace explained. "Can you imagine? Amber said the designer bought them by the yard, just for the look. Some of them don't even have writing inside, it's all just for show."

Theo shook his head. "Sacrilege." He moved to join her, sitting in the matching wing chair across from the fireplace. "And this thing . . . ?" He looked at the heavy grate.

"Gas fire." Grace flipped a switch, and suddenly, the hearth glowed with the flicker of fake flames, projected on an LCD screen.

"Convenient." Theo grinned. "For when you want to warm yourself during those bitter Los Angeles winters."

"Right?" Grace laughed. "It got so hot over summer,

I could barely move. I just lay there for months, caressing the A/C dial."

Theo laughed, and Grace felt a rush of relief. There: a glimpse of normal.

"What about you?" she asked. "Tell me more about the Hamptons—you barely said a word about it all summer."

"It was fun." He shrugged vaguely. "Mainly family stuff, you know."

"Right." Grace didn't. "And now, college is . . . good?"

"Yup." Theo stared at the fake flames in the hearth. "What about you? Any new friends?"

"A few," Grace found herself saying. "You know about Palmer . . ."

"Right, with the hats."

"Uh-huh. And I'm hanging out more with Harry." Grace found herself adding, just to get some reaction. "And Brandon, of course. I was just with him, when you came over."

Theo blinked. "The guy from next door? But isn't he older?"

"Twenty-two." Grace shrugged, nonchalant. Sure, she hung out with twentysomething guys all the time.

"Isn't that kind of weird?" Theo looked thrown. "I mean, for him to be hanging around a junior?"

Grace stiffened. "Why? Because I'm such a kid?"

"I didn't mean—"

"We get along great, actually," she continued. "We have a lot in common." Grace folded her arms and gazed at Theo defiantly. Was that what he thought of her: too young to have older friends?

"That's great," he said unconvincingly. "That you're making friends."

"Yes, it is."

Silence.

Grace heard a car pull up outside; the familiar death rattle of Dakota's old engine. "That's weird," she said, glad to change the subject. "She only just went out."

She went to the window and looked out. Dakota's car came to a stop, slung at an abrupt angle across the driveway, and before he'd even shut off the engine, Hallie came tumbling out. She fled toward the house, slamming the front door behind her.

"Oh, boy . . ." Grace turned away from the window. She hadn't seen Hallie's face clearly, just a flash of distress, but that was enough. A sense of impending doom blossomed in her veins.

"What's wrong?" Theo leaped up at the sight of her face.

"I don't know. . . . Nothing good." Grace snapped back into action. "I should go, see if she's OK."

Theo's face fell. "Uh, sure. And I better be getting back, to meet the guys."

"Right."

Grace took him down to the front door. "Give my best to your mom, and Hallie," Theo said awkwardly. His shoulders were hunched, both hands in his pockets.

"You too. I mean, with Portia," Grace said.

There was a pause, then they both bobbed toward each other in what had to be the most awkward brief hug in the history of awkward brief hugs. Grace patted his back stiffly. "Have a safe trip back!"

"You too." Theo coughed. "I mean, stay safe."

"Uh-huh." Grace bit her lip. "Those mean streets of Beverly Hills!"

Grace closed the door behind him and rested her forehead against it for a moment, full of disappointment. What happened to "normal" and "nothing had changed?"; the casual emails and joking texts? Was this their friendship now: nothing but stilted conversation, and awkward hugs? She'd been waiting so long to see him again, but he'd been acting like they'd barely met—like all the afternoons they'd spent laughing together had never happened at all.

She headed for the guesthouse, trying to think of a reason, any reason at all why he would be so cold, but Grace could find only one explanation: that night up on the hill. She'd done this. She'd ruined everything!

The sound of Hallie shouting brought her back down to earth.

"I don't understand! Why don't you want me to come?"

"It's not that I don't want you to," Dakota's voice was pleading. "It's just, you can't, not right now."

Grace paused on the stairs. She felt awkward eavesdropping, like she was a kid again, hovering outside her sister's closed door, but she didn't step away.

"Why not?" Hallie cried, voice breaking. "Is it the band? Did they say something? I knew Reed never liked me!"

"Come on, Hallie, please. I'm going to be busy in the studio, I'd barely see you. And you can't leave your life here, I can't ask that."

"Why not? I'll do it. I'll do anything for us to be together!" Hallie cut off into loud sobs, and when Dakota spoke again, it was softer. Soothing.

"It's just for a couple of months," he said, voice faintly muffled. Grace could picture him holding Hallie close. "And then when things are more settled, you'll come visit, OK? Who knows, maybe they'll hate us, and put us on the next flight back."

"They won't." Hallie hiccupped. "They'll love you."

There was a long silence. Grace shifted uncomfortably, but just as she was about to turn and slip quietly back downstairs, Hallie's door flew open and Dakota emerged.

"Hey!" Grace exclaimed, flushing. "I didn't know you were here. I just came in!"

Dakota didn't seem to notice her embarrassment. He looked worn-out, the way Grace always felt after being caught in one of Hallie's maelstroms. "I have to go," he told her, then glanced back at Hallie's room. "Make sure she's OK?"

Grace nodded, but he was already gone: taking the stairs two at a time in a dull thud.

She ventured into Hallie's room. "What's going on?"

"The band got a deal." Hallie was sobbing, red eyed and wretched. "They're going to New York to record."

"But that's great!" Grace moved closer.

"No, it isn't!" Hallie cried. "He's leaving! Why does he have to go? Everyone I love always leaves me!" And she collapsed facedown on the bed and howled.

V

Dakota left for New York the very next week. Grace watched as Hallie spent every last minute trailing him from band practice to errands to bon voyage parties; clinging to his hand so tightly it was as if she could make him stay through sheer force of will. Too soon, the day of his departure came.

"You'll call?" Hallie clutched him, tears already flowing down her cheeks.

"Every day," Dakota promised, hugging her close.

Grace moved a polite distance away in the busy Departures concourse. Dakota was traveling with the rest of his band, but Hallie had never been one to overlook the drama of a passionate farewell scene: she insisted on waving him off at the airport, which meant that Grace, as the only Weston sister with a driver's license, was playing chauffeur.

She loitered by the newsstand while Dakota and Hallie murmured their good-byes.

"C'mon, D!" An impatient yell came from across the concourse. The rest of the band was waiting by the security line, toting guitar cases and duffel bags. Reed waved Dakota over. "We're boarding, get a move on!"

Dakota broke away from Hallie and gave her one last kiss, cradling her face in both hands. He whispered something—too soft for Grace to hear—and then hoisted his bag onto his shoulder and walked away.

"Ready to go?" Grace asked, but Hallie stayed glued to the spot, watching as he handed over his ticket and boarded the escalator. "Hallie . . ."

"Hold on." Hallie craned her neck to see, following the back of his head as he moved up toward the baggage-screening station; laughing and joking with the rest of the band. Grace watched too, waiting for Dakota to turn—to send Hallie one last smile, or wave—but he didn't look back. The line moved on, and he disappeared from sight.

Grace turned to Hallie. Her face had fallen, tears already starting again. "Let's go." Grace tucked her arm through Hallie's and steered her toward the exit. "We can stop by In-N-Out on our way back."

"I'm not hungry." Hallie's voice was listless, and Grace's heart fell as she remembered the black weeks after their father's death: the weeping, and the sleepless nights, and the way Hallie had barely touched her food.

"You will be." Grace kept her voice bright and upbeat. "The minute you smell those fries, you'll be stealing all of mine." She guided them across the street, Hallie still following obediently like a little child. "And I bet a hundred bucks, you'll hear from Dakota before they even land in New York. They have Wi-Fi on the flight, don't they?"

Hallie brightened, just a little. "I think so. . . ."

"See? With text, and e-mail, it'll be like he's not even gone," Grace insisted. "You can Skype on your phone, too. You'll see him every day!"

Hallie wiped her cheeks. "You're right. And anyway, I'm going to go visit in a couple of weeks. They'll be settled in then, and we can maybe look for a place together."

"Right," Grace agreed, too relieved that Hallie wasn't in total collapse to start asking about this new plan for her to go move across the country. "See? It's not the end of the world. He loves you, he's not going to just disappear."

But he did.

Not completely, and not all at once. No, it happened so gradually that Grace thought her sister was just exaggerating: playing up the wretched lover, abandoned by her soul mate. Dakota still called, and texted, and even sent mail during the first few weeks away: gift-wrapped care packages of N.Y.C. memorabilia; Polaroid pictures; scribbled lyrics. But the mail petered out, and his calls became farther and farther apart, until by the end of his first month away, Hallie was subsisting on occasional text messages that arrived at three a.m., and short fragments of phone calls that were always over too soon. Grace watched helplessly as Hallie sank into another dejected haze, watching TV all day—phone clutched by her side, just in case he called—and poring over every word and message like they held some kind of divine revelation.

"I don't understand!" she would say, blinking at Grace in confusion. "He said he'd call, but I haven't heard from him all week! Why is he doing this to me?"

Grace had no answers. She'd always thought Dakota was a good person. He'd cared about Hallie—about them all—so why would he fade Hallie out like this?

"Because he's an asshole." Palmer had no such qualms about Dakota's character. She slurped her iced coffee, sitting across from Grace at their usual café patio on South Beverly Drive. Their table was spread with homework, but studying was the last thing on Grace's mind.

"No, don't say that," Grace protested.

"Why not? He saw a chance for bigger, better things, so he cut loose and ran. Happens all the time in this town."

"But you saw them together," Grace argued. "He loves her."

"And?" Palmer shrugged. She propped her cowboy boots on their spare seat and sat back in the sun. "Trust me, love is the last thing these guys care about, not when their careers are on the line."

"But Dakota's not like that," Grace said weakly. "He doesn't care about being famous, he just wants to make his music."

Palmer hooted with laughter. "Please! It's not like we live in the Dark Ages, he could be talking to her all the time if he wanted. But he isn't. Which means he doesn't."

Grace slumped. "I can't believe it. He seemed like such a great guy!"

Palmer slurped some more. "They always do."

Grace stared out at the street forlornly. No matter what Palmer said, she couldn't accept it. He loved Hallie, he had to. Dakota wasn't just another ruthless, shallow wannabe: he'd driven Grace home from school, run out to fetch special oil paint glaze for their mom, and spent almost every night for four months with his arm draped around Hallie's shoulder, tenderly brushing hair away from her face. No, Grace was sure, this was all some terrible mistake. He was distracted by band stuff right now, but soon he'd call, or even fly back to make things right. Hallie would make him suffer and grovel awhile, and then everything would be calm again.

"Are you going to Harry's thing tonight?"

Grace blinked, turning back to Palmer. "What?"

"His 'gathering.'" Palmer made air quotes, the pink glitter on her nails flashing in the sun. "I heard some of the gloss posse talking about it, so I guess it's going to be a big deal."

"I don't know . . ." Grace tapped her pen restlessly. "That might not be a good idea."

"Why?" Palmer gave her a sly grin. "Because you might go crazy and hook up with him in a moment of wild abandon?"

Grace laughed. "That's never going to happen. You know I don't have feelings for him."

"So you're not in love?" Palmer rolled her eyes.

"We're sixteen, who is? He wants to date you, not get married. Go out, make out, have some fun."

"I couldn't." Grace blushed, glancing around in case anyone heard. "Not if I don't like him like that." She paused, studying Palmer. "Why, do you do it?"

"What, hook up?" Palmer gave her a look. "In case you haven't noticed, guys aren't exactly lining up to ask me out. Or in."

"But you're great," Grace said, confused.

"I like to think so." Palmer grinned. "But the male population of this town doesn't seem to agree. Apparently, I'm too intimidating."

"What?" Grace exclaimed. "How do you figure that?"

"Let me see." Palmer began to count off on her fingers. "There's my charm and beauty, obviously."

Grace laughed. "Obviously."

"Plus, my inability to tolerate bullshit; penchant for multisyllabic words; the fact I don't care what anyone thinks. According to the world, that all adds up to one angry feminist bitch."

"Then they're crazy," Grace told her. "And it's their loss."

"Sure, I know that." Palmer sighed, her sarcasm slipping for a moment. "But that doesn't stop me from sitting home alone, wondering if I'll ever get to go on an actual date."

"Then we'll stay home together," Grace said. "Because I'm not dating anytime soon either."

"Yes, but that's because you're all sensible and mature." Palmer tsked disapprovingly. "I want to have wild reckless adventures while I'm still too young to know better."

"Be careful what you wish for," Grace told her. "Hallie was wild and reckless, and now look at her: she hasn't changed her sweatpants in three days."

Hallie was still curled up in bed when Grace got back to the house, so she ventured to their mom's studio for advice.

"Just a second, sweetie," Valerie cried, not looking up from the huge canvas that covered half the wall. "I'm in my flow."

Grace idled in the doorway. The annex was a converted conservatory with a high glass roof and sharp light flooding through; unfinished paintings propped against the wall and dried paint palettes cracking on every surface. A corner was now devoted to Valerie's spiritual well-being: a yoga mat rolled up beside a small Buddha statue and bamboo plants, wind chimes tinkling from the window. It was easy for Grace to be dubious about the morning meditations, and the new love of Eastern philosophy, but the move had been good for her mother, Grace knew. She was still distracted and flighty, but it was an animated frenzy of activity, not the absent, glassy-eyed remoteness that had enfolded her after John's death. As Grace watched, her mom hurled great slashes of vivid purple paint at the abstract canvas that seemed almost alive with light and color.

"There." Valerie finally caught her breath. She lowered the brush and turned to Grace. "What do you think?"

"I like it." Grace didn't pretend to understand her mother's art. What had started with neat paintings of fruit in bowls and the bay at dusk had, over the years, spiraled into something wildly abstract, every canvas more obscure than the last. "The color's great," she offered.

Her mom smiled. "It's coming along. Now, what did you want to talk about?"

"Hallie." Grace sighed, still feeling like she was six years old, tattling on her sister for breaking the vase on the hall table. "You know, she hasn't gotten out of bed all week."

"She just needs time." Her mom began rinsing her brushes in the porcelain sink. "Her poor heart's been broken."

"But she did this before!" Grace protested. "For months, over Dad. It's not good for her."

"Grief is the air we breathe," her mom replied, a calm look on her face. "Our tears wash the past away."

"They're not washing anything away," Grace tried to argue. "She's drowning in them!"

Her mom moved closer, and pulled Grace into a hug. "You don't understand, this is natural. It's only when the well of sorrow has irrigated the plains of our heart that we can plant new crops."

Perfect.

"So you won't talk to her?" Grace asked, already defeated.

"She'll get up when she's ready." Valerie turned back to the canvas. "I can't rush her."

Their mom may not be in any rush, but Grace was.

She perched on the edge of the bed, watching her sister sniffle quietly. "Maybe a nice hot bath would make you feel better," she suggested hopefully. "You could use the one in the master suite, with the whirlpool jets, and all of Amber's aromatherapy candles."

Hallie shook her head listlessly. "What's the point? He's met someone else, I can feel it!"

"The point is, it's been days since you had a shower," Grace pointed out. "Do you want fungus to start growing in your toes?"

"That doesn't happen."

"You want to bet?" Grace looked at her, lying there helplessly as if someone had died all over again. But they hadn't. Was this really going to be Hallie's fate: to take to her bed indefinitely at every sign of heartache? Grace felt a flicker of impatience.

"Come on." She stood, and threw back the covers.

Hallie whimpered.

"You're getting up, and taking that bath," Grace informed her briskly. "And then we're going to do something about those sweatpants." She looked at the mangy gray fabric pooling around Hallie's legs. "Laundry is too good for them, I'm thinking we burn them."

"Leave me alone." Hallie rolled away, burying her head in the pillows.

"Nope!" Grace grabbed her arm and pulled her upright.

"A bath won't help." Hallie began to cry again. "Nothing will help. He's gone. He's not coming back!"

"But I'm here." Grace yanked her out of bed. "And I can't look at you like this another day. Or smell you like this. No offense," she added. "What if one of your friends comes over? Do you really want them to see you like this?"

Hallie paused, catching sight of herself in the mirror. "Well," she ventured in a small voice, "maybe that bath wouldn't be too bad. Can we light Amber's Diptyque candles?"

"Absolutely." Grace felt like cheering. Basic hygiene may not seem like much, but after seven solid days of moping, it counted as a major achievement for Hallie. "Go crazy with the candles. And use all the Crème de la Mer bath foam you can find!"

With Hallie soaking in five hundred dollars' worth of bath products, and those sweatpants safely dispatched to the garbage, Grace wandered into the kitchen, in search of snacks, and human interaction that didn't involve a pack of Kleenex.

"Grace, sweetie!" Amber was lounging at the table, drinking a glass of wine with one of her friends. Grace had tried to tell them apart, but it was hard: an identical sea of twentysomethings with the same blown-out hair, designer jeans, and oversize diamonds on their wedding finger. This one was dark haired and skinny in the way Grace had only ever seen in L.A. Professionally underfed, all sharp cheekbones and protruding clavicle. "You remember Missy, right?"

"Sure, hi." Grace smiled and went to the fridge.

"How is she doing?" Amber's forehead crinkled with concern. "Her poor sister," she explained to Missy, "just had her heart trampled by some scoundrel."

"Awww, poor thing. When I'm feeling the breakup blues, I always go straight to Fred Segal." Missy suggested, "There's nothing like a new purse to cheer you up. Except shoes!"

"Thanks," Grace said, trying not to smile. "I'll pass that on."

There was a noise behind her; Grace turned to find a girl about Hallie's age toting a toddler in her arms. She had auburn hair, and a smattering of freckles, with food stains trailing down her shirt. "She won't stay down," the girl said apologetically, her voice crisp with a British accent. "I'll just play with her here for a while, if that's OK?"

"Whatever!" Missy looked entirely unconcerned. "This is Lucy, my new gem of a nanny. She just moved out here, and doesn't know anyone. Maybe you girls could chat?"

"Sure." Grace smiled at Lucy, and joined her over by the range. "Welcome to L.A. I'm Grace," she added.

"Grace, of course." Lucy lit up. "So lovely to meet you! I'd shake your hand, but . . ." She held the baby up.

Grace grinned, holding up her plate of leftovers. "No need."

"Missy, babe, before you go, I need some advice." Amber looked deadly serious. "I have a benefit coming up, and I can't decide on the right shoes!"

Missy stood. "Black tie, white tie, cocktail, or casual?" she asked, with all the focus of a military sergeant, and followed Amber out of the room.

Grace waited until they were gone, then took their place at the table. "I didn't know there were so many variables when it came to shoes." She gave Lucy a friendly smile, remembering what it had been like to venture into rooms full of strangers when she first arrived in town.

"Obviously," Lucy replied. "That's not even starting on the open-toe dilemma!"

Grace laughed, assembling her leftovers into a makeshift sandwich. "So you're from England, huh? That's a long way from home."

"I'm on my gap year, before university," Lucy explained. "I always wanted to travel, and with nannying, I get to go all kinds of places."

"Sounds like fun."

Grace turned her attention to her midafternoon snack while Lucy stowed the child in the temporary playpen in the corner. When she looked up, Lucy was sitting across from her, fixing Grace with an unflinching stare.

"I have a confession."

Grace blinked. "Oh?"

Lucy smiled. "I actually asked Missy to bring me along today, so I could meet you."

Grace felt embarrassed. Reports of her social standing had clearly been exaggerated. "I'd be happy to show you around, and answer any questions, but I'm not really the social one out here—that's Hallie. Well." She paused. "It was."

"No. That's sweet of you, but it's not what I meant." Lucy smiled again, perky beneath the kind of ruffled bangs Grace could only dream of. "You see, we already have someone in common."

"We do?"

Lucy leaned closer, confidential. "Teddy Coates."

Grace stopped. "You know Theo?"

"Very well." Lucy nodded. "We met over the summer; I was nannying in the Hamptons with my last family."

"Oh. That's . . . nice." Grace swallowed. "I mean, Theo's a great guy."

"The best." Lucy sat back, and gave a little laugh. "This is such a relief! You have no idea what it's been like for me, having nobody to talk to about this."

"About what?"

"Teddy!" Lucy gave her a meaningful look. "You know what his family's like, of course, so we've had to keep everything hush-hush. But he always speaks so highly of you, I knew our secret would be safe with you!" She reached across the table and took Grace's hand, squeezing it. "You won't tell, will you?"

Grace's hand felt like deadweight in Lucy's bony grip. "Tell what?" she ventured, clutching at the faint hope that she was totally misunderstanding the British girl. Lost in translation, it had to be.

"About us, silly!" Lucy beamed at her. "Teddy and I are in love!"

VI

Grace stared at the strange girl in disbelief. Lucy was gazing at her serenely across the kitchen table, a tiny smile playing on the edge of her lips. Grace struggled to respond. "You . . . and Theo . . . You're . . . ?"

"Lovers," Lucy replied airily.

Grace choked on a slice of cold chicken. Even worse! "I . . . When . . . ?"

"We dated in secret all summer," Lucy told her, a romantic sheen to her gaze. "Walks on the beach, trips out on his boat. He swept me off my feet!"

"A summer romance?" Grace asked hopefully.

"At first," Lucy agreed, "but then we fell in love, and Teddy wouldn't hear about ending it. He even wanted to transfer to Columbia, to stay close to me, but I couldn't let him do that, so I found a job out here. It's still hard."

She sighed. "But we talk all the time, and visit. We'll make it work, until his family comes around."

"Right," Grace said faintly. She felt dizzy, like the earth was shifting beneath her. All this time, Theo had been with someone? In love! Why hadn't he told her?

"I can trust you, can't I?" Lucy suddenly looked at her, wide-eyed. "You can't tell anyone. If this got back to his family . . . I wasn't supposed to tell anyone but I've been dying to share it!"

"Uh-huh." Grace tried to recover. "I mean, of course. But, why the secrecy?" she asked. "Theo isn't the kind of guy to sneak around."

"I know," Lucy said, her tone sharper. She smiled quickly. "But his family wouldn't approve, with my being a nanny. You know his grandmother." She rolled her eyes.

"No," Grace admitted. "I never met her."

"That's right, you haven't." Lucy looked smug. "She's a sweet old lady, but she has all these outdated opinions, about class, and position. It's all rubbish, of course, but we have to be careful. We don't want her disinheriting him."

"She would do that, just for dating you?" Grace frowned.

Lucy laughed. "We're dating *now,*" she told Grace, with another smug look. "But this is only the beginning. One day, I'll be part of the family. See, he gave me this."

Lucy lifted a pendant over the neckline of her shirt. A simple silver chain, with . . . Grace gasped.

It was her necklace!

The periodic element pendant, the one she'd made for her craft project; the one Theo had helped her pack! He must have taken it instead of putting it in the storage box, and . . . given it to Lucy?

"It's the symbol for gold," Lucy explained, as Grace sat, reeling. Her blankness must have shown, because Lucy added, "You know, for commitment. Like a wedding ring."

Grace couldn't muster a response.

"You won't tell anyone, will you?" Lucy said again, still wide-eyed. "It has to be our little secret. Promise?"

Grace was still trying to understand how her necklace had wound up around another girl's neck as a symbol of undying love. "Sure," she managed.

"No, I need you to promise," Lucy insisted. "I'd be forever in your debt, and it's only the teensiest secret." She beamed at Grace across the table, so eager that Grace wilted in the face of her enthusiasm. What else could she say that wouldn't reveal her own pathetic—oh! so pathetic—hopes?

"OK." Grace nodded, the very word feeling like a betrayal. "I won't say a thing."

Amber and Missy soon bustled back in, and Lucy departed under a load of diaper bags, wafting promises to get together soon and "do lunch." "I'm so glad I met you!" She beamed at Grace on the doorstep. "I knew we'd be friends, just from the way Teddy talks about you. You know, you're like a sister to him!"

Grace managed a vague murmur of assent before shutting the door in her face.

"What a sweet girl," Amber cooed, moving to rearrange the vase of lilies cascading from the hall table. She plucked one from the heavy crystal vase, breathing in the scent. "I love that accent of hers, so classy. I bet she'll have the boys swooning over her in no time."

But Lucy already had. At least, the only boy who mattered. But why wouldn't Theo fall for her? Grace thought of the visitor morosely: her pretty auburn curls, and button nose, and light sprinkling of freckles. Yes, Lucy was cute, and sweet, and clearly more adventurous than Grace would ever be: venturing out half a world away from home.

Once she had the picture of them together, Grace couldn't stop the images from coming, just as Lucy had described to her: them walking hand in hand on the beach, taking romantic trips out on his boat, watching the sun go down, leaning in for a perfect kiss . . .

Grace turned abruptly to Amber. "I'm going out tonight, to a party," she said, before she could change her mind. "Do you think you could help me, with clothes, and my hair, and everything?"

Amber squealed. "Absolutely! I have this amazing black minidress, with diamanté spangles—!"

"I meant more, jeans and a shirt," Grace interrupted. "It's just a casual, hang-out thing."

Amber took a step back and assessed her with a well-practiced eye. "Shirt yes, jeans no. I have the cutest denim mini for you to borrow."

Grace must have blanched, because Amber laughed, scooping her into a hug. "Relax, girl. By the time I'm through with you, you'll have boys lining up to fill your dance card."

Worn out, Grace let Amber steer her upstairs, toward the great wonderland of her walk-in closet. She didn't have the heart to tell her that it didn't matter who was lining up—it didn't even matter what she wore. The boy Grace really wanted couldn't have been further out of reach.

Harry lived in a sprawling Spanish compound set in the hills above Bel Air. The moment Grace stepped through the doors, she realized what a mistake she'd made. Far from the small gathering Palmer had promised, the marble-floored house was thick with kids from school: juniors, seniors even, and a host of those designer-clad cliques. The air vibrated with a heavy bass, red plastic cups littering every surface. This was a full-on party, and Grace couldn't be further from the partying mood.

She paused in the marble-floored lobby. Every instinct said to turn back, but what was her alternative: pull on a pair of sweatpants, and join Hallie sitting shivah in the gloom of her bedroom, tormented by thoughts of Theo and Lucy together?

"You came!" Palmer ambushed her, a red cup in one hand; her trilby hat already askew, with one lone feather drooping over a kohl-rimmed eye. "What are you wearing?" She stood back to take it in.

Grace tugged the hem of her skirt. "Amber made me wear it," she said quickly. "It's dumb, I know."

"No!" Palmer grasped her hand and made Grace do a twirl. "It's hot! I just didn't know you had it in you." She giggled. "To paraphrase what a very inappropriate math teacher once said to me, 'Miss Weston, you've got *legs.*' "

Grace flushed. She tugged again, but the hemline on the denim cutoff skirt didn't budge: it remained six inches above her knees, which, in Grace's opinion, was a good four inches higher than necessary.

"Seriously, you look great." Palmer grinned, already dragging her into the crowd, pausing only to pluck a cup full of Lord knows what from the makeshift bar and thrust it into Grace's hand. "Look, there's Harry!"

Grace paused by the French doors at the back of the den. Outside, the backyard was lit bright with dozens of tiny lanterns, the brave exhibitionists already stripped down to their bikinis in the hot tub. She could see Harry hanging out with some of his skater friends, eating pizza from a stack of boxes by the pool.

"Ooh, and who's his friend? He's cute." Palmer's eyes widened as she noticed the boy beside him with dark curls and a punk-rock T-shirt. "Let's go say hi," she added, with a meaningful grin. "After all, he's our host. It's only polite."

"I don't know . . ." Grace hung back, reluctant.

Palmer rolled her eyes. "Don't give me that. You didn't come here, wearing *that,* if you didn't want to have some fun."

Grace's expression must have revealed something,

because Palmer lit up. "See, I know it. Deep down, your soul is crying out for some recreational flirting and light make-out action."

Grace couldn't help but laugh. "Recreational flirting? Who says that?"

"I do." Palmer beamed, pulling a lip balm from her pocket and swiftly smearing a fresh layer on her lips. "And I want some. So let's go!"

Grace saw the anticipation on Palmer's face and relented. "OK," she said. "But don't you dare leave me alone with Harry!"

"Why?" Palmer shot back. "Afraid you might succumb to your hidden passion and throw yourself into his arms?"

Grace laughed. "Sure, my heart beats for him alone!" She linked her arm through Palmer's and steered them outside. "Also, note for future reference? We have got to get you away from those romance novels!"

The dark-haired object of Palmer's desire was named Jesús, a senior from a public high school across town. "I feel a religious experience coming on," Palmer whispered to Grace as Harry pulled up a couple of lawn chairs for them and made room at the table.

Grace elbowed her. "Behave!"

Palmer stuck her tongue out in response and turned back to Jesús. "Those are cool pants." She smiled, edging her chair closer. "Do they have any secret pockets?"

Grace had to look away. Part of her was embarrassed by Palmer's outré flirtation, but part of her was just plain envious of her friend's confidence. Lines that would sound cheesy and desperate coming from Grace's lips took on a nonchalant power with one of Palmer's no-nonsense stares. If only Grace could be so bold.

"You want some pizza?" Harry asked, on her other side. "It's pepperoni," he added, "but there's veggie somewhere in the pile, if you want."

"No. I'm good." Grace caught her dismissive tone, and turned back. "Thanks, though," she added. "How's it going?"

"Pretty good." Harry nodded. "Everyone seems to be having a good time."

His words were punctuated by a group of jocks hurling themselves in the pool, whooping. Grace laughed. "Looks like it."

She paused, trying to look at Harry with fresh eyes. His hair flopped over his eyes appealingly, she could see, and the rumpled oxford shirt he wore with his baggy skater jeans was mismatched in a cute, scruffy way. Yes, Harry was more than eligible. He was sweet, and generally smart, and didn't have a secret girlfriend from the Hamptons, or think of Grace like a sister. He even liked her! So why shouldn't she like him back?

Grace noticed Harry's gaze drifting lower. She glanced down, and realized with horror that seated, the skirt was even shorter. She started to cross her legs, but realized that was even worse: the fabric riding up another perilous inch.

Grace downed the mystery punch in her cup and leaped up. "I'm, umm, going to get another drink."

"I'll show you!" Harry quickly got up too. Grace sent Palmer a desperate look, but she was leaning in close to Jesús, tracing the outline of the tattoo on his wrist with a dreamy expression. To drag her away would be cruel.

"Sure." Grace exhaled, turning back to Harry. "Thanks."

She followed him back into the house, and fought her way through the crowd. It was even louder now: punch splashing liberally onto cream carpets, and formerly spotless couch covers looking far more spotty. "Your parents don't mind?" she asked.

Harry frowned. "What?"

"The party!" Grace yelled. "Are they OK with it?"

Harry shrugged. "They're out of town. They said I could have a few people over to study." He guided her into the kitchen, quieter, but littered with empty cups, half-eaten dip, and a sink piled high with dirty dishes.

"How will you get everything cleaned up before they get back?" Grace asked, looking around. "This place is a mess!"

He grinned, rinsing her out a glass. "It's not a problem. I have a professional cleaning crew coming tomorrow. Nobody will ever know!"

"Oh. Right." Grace had forgotten for a moment: she was in Beverly Hills. Why race around trying to scrub vomit stains off hardwood floors when you could pay somebody else to do it?

Harry passed her the glass, giving her a shy smile. "I'm really glad you made it. I didn't think you were going to come."

Grace felt awkward under the hope in his gaze. "I needed to get out. Family stuff," she added, taking a tiny sip. Alcohol burned down the back of her throat, but she managed not to cough and splutter.

Harry nodded toward the living room: lights dimmed, seething with bodies. "You want to dance?" he asked. "Or, we could go back outside, where it's quieter. You know, talk."

Grace hesitated.

This was what she was supposed to do now, she knew: get drunk on mystery punch, dance wildly with inappropriate boys, and wind up making out with one of them in an upstairs bedroom somewhere, all in the name of "getting over Theo" and "moving on." It was expected; obligatory, even. She was supposed to cut loose, and go crazy, and all those other spring-break-worthy sentiments that people insisted on to bury their inner pain.

"I'm sorry," she said abruptly, putting her glass down. "I have to go."

Harry's face fell. "But—"

"Tell Palmer I'll call her, OK?" Grace was already backing away. "And I'll see you in school. Thanks for having me!"

She hurried toward the front door, pushing blindly through the crowd and not slowing until she was out of the house; sneakers crunching on the gravel driveway.

Grace gasped for breath, the night air cool in her lungs. What had she been thinking, coming here tonight? She didn't want Harry—she'd known that all along. She didn't want distraction, or drunken, crazy escapades, or whatever it was that the books and movies said she should be doing right now.

She wanted to go home.

To her surprise, Grace felt tears sting in her throat, and a hollow sadness well up from somewhere deep inside. She wanted to go home, to the house where her father still lived, and her mom still baked gingersnap cookies every fall, and her sister didn't weep for hours and threaten to throw herself off a tall building and mean it, even a little.

Grace wanted to be back there, up in the shaded tree house with her telescope, where everything had been so simple; before she'd even known what it was like to long for someone the way she longed for Theo.

Before she knew what it was like to have a broken heart.

But even as the sadness threatened to overwhelm her, Grace pulled back. She held tight. Crying wouldn't get her back there, she reminded herself firmly. It wouldn't change a thing. This was her world now: empty streets lined with palm trees, the quiet hum of money, a neat grid of city lights blanketing the valley below. This was her world, and she had to live in it. No father, no tree house, no weekend plays with Hallie, and no oven-warm gingersnap cookies.

No Theo.

Grace put her sadness away, pulled out her cell phone, and began to walk.

PART FOUR: *Winter*

I

It had been a month.

Only four weeks since Hallie's world was ripped apart; thirty days since her heart had shattered into a million anguished pieces. Lost in her sea of misery, she couldn't believe it. She felt as if she'd been broken forever, like years—decades, even; a lifetime!—had dragged past since the awful night Dakota had told her he was leaving.

"We're going to New York."

Hallie hadn't understood at first. She'd thought the "we" was them: her and Dakota, the way he'd always meant.

"Yes!" she'd gasped, already imagining the cool Brooklyn loft, and nights spent crawling dive bars on the Lower East Side. Bagels. Central Park. Ice-skating under holiday lights, her hands warm in mittens and Dakota's sure grasp. He would make his music, she'd find some off-off-off-Broadway play to launch her career. It would be perfect. Them against the world, the way they'd been planning.

"When do we go?" She slid around the diner table, so she was snuggled up against him in the red leather booth.

That's when his eyes drifted away from hers, face cloaked in a guarded look she'd never seen before. "No. I meant . . . the band." Dakota didn't meet her eyes, instead staring intently at the bottle of hot sauce on the table. "And I was thinking . . ." He paused, and Hallie felt a terrible shiver of dread. "Maybe this is a good thing for us, to take some time."

Hallie stared dumbly.

"You know . . . apart. Figure out . . . where this is going. I mean, we've been moving so fast . . ." Dakota trailed off, looking back at the hot sauce again. "It'll only be a few months."

Hallie couldn't speak a word the whole ride home. Dakota tried to fill the empty air between them, rambling about how busy he'd be in the studio, how he couldn't drag her across the country; her career, and his bandmates. "We just need to hit pause," he said, more than once, as if she were a movie screening in Uncle Auggie's den, and he needed to run out for pizza. "We'll make this work. When I get settled, we'll figure something out. It'll be OK."

But it wasn't.

Because despite all his reassurance and tender promises

to call her every day, Dakota drifted out of reach, disappearing into the new, exciting life he was leading in New York City. Without Hallie. Her phone calls started going to voice mail, her texts were left, unreplied. Even though Hallie filled his voice mail and in-box with plaintive messages until they were too full for more, Dakota barely answered, only checking in with messages that seemed more routine than heartfelt. And then there were the days that passed without a single word. Hallie found herself searching online for news of a tragic car accident, or random gang crime: anything to explain why he'd suddenly dropped out of contact. Maybe he was in a coma somewhere, unidentified; or stumbling around with amnesia, not even remembering his own name!

Except amnesiacs wouldn't pose for photos in their shiny new recording studio. Coma victims wouldn't be posting updates on the official band website about all their upcoming shows.

Hallie sank into a listless daze. To just leave, to ignore her pain like it meant nothing to him . . . ? This wasn't Dakota. It *couldn't* be. The boy who swore he couldn't sleep unless Hallie was nestled in the crook of his arms would never be so cruel and merciless. He at least would write back. Call. Check to make sure she hadn't drowned herself in Uncle Auggie's pool, the way she'd threatened in a moment of desperate rage.

But now it had been two weeks since she'd last heard from him, and Hallie couldn't dream up any more excuses. He was just gone.

"Hallie!" Grace burst into her bedroom, rudely interrupting Hallie's mental replay of the diner scene. "The dogs need walking. I can't keep taking them out."

"I'm napping." Hallie sank lower in her pillows; curtains still half-drawn to block out the hatefully cheerful sun.

"It's your job."

Hallie groaned. "So tell Amber to hire the old kid back."

"If you're going to quit, you need to do it yourself."

"Whatever." Hallie sighed, not caring. She was about to roll over, back to her mournful daydreams, when her phone buzzed, vibrating on the polished nightstand. Hallie bolted upright.

"Dakota!" She grabbed the phone to check the screen, heart racing. She knew it! He missed her, he was sorry for everything, he still loved her!

But it was only Ana Lucia.

Hallie let out a whimper. She hit DECLINE CALL and slumped back, pulling the covers over her head. Why was the cruel world taunting her with the promise of his call? Wasn't it enough that he was gone?

A moment later, the covers were yanked away. "Call her back." Grace grabbed her phone.

"No," Hallie replied, but before she could stop Grace, her sister hit REDIAL.

"Ana Lucia, hi. Hallie's right here, sorry about that." She thrust the phone at Hallie with a pointed glare and then stalked out.

Hallie lifted the phone to her ear reluctantly. "Hey." She exhaled, already exhausted.

"Hallie, where the hell have you been? I've been calling you for, like, years!" There was a steely note beneath Ana Lucia's syrupy concern. She clearly wasn't used to being ignored.

"Sorry, I've been . . . sick," Hallie managed. Heartsick.

"Aww, I bet you're missing Dakota," Ana Lucia cooed. "Long distance is the worst! I told the girls, you're probably calling each other twenty-four seven."

"Mmmm," Hallie murmured, the words like a dagger in her soul.

Ana Lucia chattered on, oblivious. "Want to grab brunch and tell us all about it? We're dying to hear how New York is working out."

"I don't know . . ."

"Come on," Ana Lucia insisted. "Girl time is exactly what you need. You'll feel tons better, I promise."

Hallie wavered. She hadn't left the house yet, and celebrity spotting at Urth Caffé never failed to lift her mood. . . .

"OK," she finally agreed. She had to reemerge from hiding sometime, and it may as well be with cheesecake. "Give me half an hour." Hallie paused. It had been a while since she'd picked up the loofah. "Better make that an hour."

The girls were clustered around a sidewalk table, already picking at their salads when Hallie arrived. "Sweetie!"

Ana Lucia leaped up, leaning to drop air-kisses on each cheek. "You poor thing, look at you, you look wrecked!"

Hallie's smile slipped. She'd done her best to polish up, but weeks moping around in abject misery had clearly taken their toll on her skin tone. "Don't worry, herbal tea is awesome for a detox," Ana Lucia added helpfully, gesturing to the staff to drag over another chair. "By the time the band is back in town, you'll look awesome again."

"Or are you going out to visit?" Brie looked up from her phone. Ana Lucia brightened.

"We could all go! Like a group vacation."

"No!" Hallie said quickly. "I mean, Dakota says they're really focused on the music," she explained, dismayed to find herself parroting the same weak excuses Dakota had given her. "Their manager doesn't want them to have any distractions," she added. "He wanted me to come out, but they laid down the law. No girlfriends. So . . ."

She trailed off, wondering if maybe there was some truth in her lie. Perhaps it was his bandmates urging Dakota to shun her; knowing his loyalties were split. Hallie frowned at the thought of it. She never had liked that AJ, with his Victorian gentleman hairstyle and suspenders—what grown man wore pomade?

"I'm sorry." Meredith squeezed her hand, giving Hallie a sympathetic smile. "That's the worst. You must miss him like crazy."

"I do." Hallie felt it, aching in every limb of her body. "I can't bear being away from him. It feels like part of me is missing."

The girls awwwed in unison. "So cute," Brie murmured.

"Has Reed said anything about me?" Ana Lucia interrupted. "I mean, to Dakota. We were going to get together before they left, but things were so busy. . . ."

"I don't think so," Hallie said carefully. Ana Lucia's lips tightened. "But, you know what Reed is like," she added quickly. "He doesn't really talk about his feelings."

"The strong, silent type," Meredith agreed. Ana Lucia relaxed again.

"You're right. He wouldn't talk about it, he's not that kind of guy—all sappy and emotional." She sipped her boba tea, confidence restored. "Anyway, it's not like we're dating or anything. You know I don't like to be tied down."

"That's not what I heard." Brie smirked.

Ana Lucia gave a tiny, satisfied shrug. "What can I say? He was older."

They all laughed, and for a moment at least, Hallie felt her ache ease. Maybe she should just come clean. They were her friends, right? Telling the truth could even help; let her wallow in sympathy and understanding, as warm as Amber's borrowed cashmere comforter.

Then Brie turned back to her with an expectant look. "So, tell us, how's recording? Are the guys writing any new songs?" And Hallie knew, she couldn't bring herself to tell the truth, and see that envy in their expressions turn to pity. Dakota was the one thing she had that these girls didn't. And, boy, did they have everything.

"Sure." She forced a smile—the nonchalant smile

of a girl whose boyfriend loved her, and couldn't bear to be apart—and began to tell them all about the amazing sessions the band had been recording, and how Dakota had written three new love songs, just for her. She was an actress through and through, she could play this part as long as it took, before Dakota came back to her, and the lies became real.

Because it could be true, Hallie told herself, after Ana Lucia dropped her back home. Just because he wasn't calling, didn't mean Dakota wasn't going through the same agony of separation, writing tormented love songs in her honor to soothe his broken heart. She slouched through the expanse of marble flooring and tasteless art, wondering if Dakota was really pining for her the same way she missed him, a thousand miles away. He had to be! Because otherwise . . . The idea left Hallie dizzy, too much for her to even contemplate. No, he still loved her. She knew it with every fiber of her being.

Hallie found Grace in the den, curled up in what had formerly been Hallie's own Chair of Misery, watching some boring Discovery Channel documentary about space. "Move." Hallie nudged her knee. "It's time for my soaps."

Grace didn't look away from the screen. "The TV's taken."

Hallie sighed tiredly. "Come on. You know I always watch now."

"Not today. They're running a Mysteries of the Cosmos marathon, and then five episodes of *Firefly.* And sit on the couch if you want," Grace added, lips set in a determined pout. "I was here first."

Hallie felt a burn of irritation. She'd spent the afternoon telling one painful lie after another, now all she wanted was to collapse in peace. "Why are you being like this?" she demanded. "You know I'm depressed here!"

Grace shrugged, staring back at the screen. "So? Maybe I'm depressed too."

Hallie snorted. "Over what? Your stupid crush on Theo? Oh, no, he's so far away in *Northern California*," she mimicked. "In case you forgot, Dakota is on the other side of the country!"

"That's how you win?" Grace was clearly unmoved. "Geographical distance. Big deal."

Hallie gasped. So unfeeling! "What is wrong with you?" she cried. "I've got a broken heart. I've been separated from the man I love!"

Grace's expression changed. "So you have to fall apart and mope like you always do." She got up from the chair, jabbing a cruel finger at Hallie. "He left! So what? Get over it!"

Hallie reeled back in shock. "How can you say that? And what gives you any right to talk about love?" Hallie felt her temper rise, sharp in her chest. "I bet you've never even kissed a boy!"

"You don't know anything about my life," Grace said quietly. Her voice had a tremor to it, but Hallie was too furious to stop.

"I know that you're a coward!" she shot back. "You sit quietly in the corner, watching life just pass you by.

And then you have the nerve to judge the rest of us for actually *doing* something about it."

"Oh, yeah? And what have you done?" Grace folded her arms. "Built your whole life around some guy, so you fall apart the minute he leaves? Thanks, but I'll pass!"

Hallie felt sobs come, hot and stinging. This wasn't fair!

"You're just jealous." She hurled the words at her sister. "You're a coward, and you're jealous because I have a real relationship."

"Don't you mean, *had*?" Grace's face was sharp with spite.

"You never liked him." Hallie's voice rose, hoarse through the tears. "You hate seeing me happy, because you're too scared to ever make something happen with Theo." She shook with anger, furious Grace could be so cruel. Furious that Dakota was gone, and she was in agony, and nobody seemed to understand.

"You don't know how lucky you are!" she wailed. "You like him, he likes you; you could be with him anytime you want! There's nothing keeping you apart—except *you,* and the fact that you're too scared to ever go after what you want!"

"Stop it!" Grace protested, like she didn't realize she had everything Hallie could only dream about. She was blessed!

"I'm right, aren't I?" Hallie pushed. "There's nothing standing in your way. You're just too pathetic and immature to make it happen."

"You don't know anything!" Grace yelled fiercely.

"So give me one good reason why you can't be together!" Hallie waited, tapping her foot in an exaggerated gesture. "Well?"

Grace was silent.

"See! You don't have any!" Hallie was overwhelmed with the injustice of the world. She'd had her true love ripped away from her, and there Grace was, moping around like her little crush was the worst thing to ever happen to her—and all along, she could have her guy!

"Fine, take the stupid remote!" Grace suddenly hurled it at her. It flew wide, bouncing off the coffee table with a clatter. "Because everything's always about you. *You're* hurting, *you're* in pain, and nobody else in the history of the world knows what that's like!"

She stormed out, leaving Hallie alone with the low drone of the documentary narrator. How could Grace be so *cruel*? She'd been sarcastic, but to Hallie, it was true: the longing that ached with every breath she took, it was *hers*. How could anyone understand how it felt, let alone make it better? Only Dakota knew her pain, and he was gone.

Gone.

Hallie sank into the chair and began to sob.

II

Without school or a real job to force her out into the world, Hallie retreated into a dull haze—days slipping past in a lethargic blur as mornings in bed faded into afternoon naps that led to early nights snuggled beneath the blankets. Her bed became a sanctuary: a warm, cotton-scented retreat where she could safely spend hours daydreaming about happier days; replaying scenes of her time with Dakota over and over, as if she could conjure them back to reality by sheer force of will.

Her grand plans for Hollywood success faded; auditions passed unnoticed on her calendar. Sure, she left the house occasionally—when Amber insisted on dragging her to the salon, or Ana Lucia and Co. invited her out for lunch or to shop at glossy stores far beyond her budget—but those trips were less indulgences than trials to be endured. Hallie made conversation, and kept up the pretense that she and Dakota were still together, but in her heart, she was only waiting until she could return to the comforting folds of her duvet, and dream of the day when Dakota would come back to her, and make everything OK again.

And then Thanksgiving came.

"I have a surprise for you!" Amber beamed at Hallie, her perky smile barely visible over the feast of food spread over the table. She and Auggie had gone all out for the occasion, with streamers and lights and Pilgrim-themed decorations; tiny silver placeholders in the shape of turkeys at each setting.

"Uh-huh?" Hallie prodded her potatoes, barely mustering enthusiasm. Her mom had surfaced long enough to order Hallie dressed and out of bed for dinner, and it was all she could do to sit quietly, passing the yams, while the bustle of holiday cheer whirled on around her. Holidays should be illegal, she thought morosely; cruel and unusual punishment for those suffering from a broken heart.

"Well, for both of you girls," Auggie added. He and Amber were resplendent in matching knit holiday sweaters adorned with tiny turkeys. "Guess!"

There was silence. Grace stayed slumped, mirroring Hallie's pose. Since their fight, she'd barely spoken to Hallie, and although it was a welcome break from her usual orders to snap out of it and get up, Hallie still felt it was all wrong. What did Grace have to be upset about? Hallie was the one suffering here!

"Well?" Their mom prompted them, a knowing look on her face. "What do you think it is?"

"I don't know." Hallie shrugged. "Amber's pregnant?"

There was a pause. Auggie and Amber looked at each other, then exploded in a chorus of laughter. "Ha!" Uncle Auggie hooted. "Are you kidding? You don't know my girl!"

"A baby?" Amber shook with laughter. "Hollering and bawling all hours of the day? And my figure . . . ! Oh, honey, no! Marilyn and Monroe are my babies. Aren't you, girls? Yes you are!" She scooped one off the floor and nuzzled it happily.

"Okaay." Hallie rolled her eyes. "So what's the big announcement?"

Amber looked up again. "Do you want to tell them?"

Uncle Auggie shook his head. "No, you do it, it was your idea."

"But you're the one who organized everything. . . ."

Hallie sank lower in her seat as they bickered. Who cared who said what? Who cared about the surprise at all? Unless they were going to announce that Dakota was out waiting in the kitchen with the five kinds of pumpkin pie Amber had ordered, she wasn't interested. What could possibly matter more than the fifty-plus e-mails, thirty-two voice mails, and forty texts she'd sent Dakota since he'd left; all of them unanswered?

". . . to New York."

Hallie's head jerked up at the words. "What?"

Uncle Auggie laughed. "See, I knew that would get her attention."

Hallie looked around the table. Amber was beaming

proudly, and even Grace looked perkier. "What about New York?" she asked, breathless.

"Amber's taking you girls for a trip," their mom explained, smiling.

"A little preholiday getaway!" Amber clapped excitedly. "We can go shopping, and to a show, and see the lights—"

Hallie leaped up and flew around the table. "Thank you, thank you, thank you!" she squealed, smothering Amber with a hug. "Oh, my God, this is perfect! I'll be able to see Dakota!"

Amber laughed. "There, that smile's what we wanted."

"You've been moping around too long," Uncle Auggie agreed. "It's not healthy."

Hallie bounced in the air, unable to contain her joy. New York! Dakota! They would be reunited, and the past silent, lonely weeks would be forgotten. Everything would be all right again!

"Eeee!" She let out a delighted shriek. The universe had aligned again; fate was on her side once more. "When do we leave?" she demanded, ready to go race to the airport that very second. "How long are we staying? What do I need to pack?"

They didn't leave for another two weeks, but for Hallie, the days passed in an excited blur. Time may have dragged by unbearably slowly since Dakota left, but with the prospect of seeing him bright on the horizon, Hallie rushed breathlessly through her preparation and packing. There was so much to do! Salon visits, and shopping, and picking out the perfect outfits that would make him fall right back at her feet where he belonged. She barely paused to think of the alternative — there was none, surely! — fervent with excitement until the moment they arrived in the bitter cold of New York; whisked away from the airport in a plush limo and delivered to the Waldorf-Astoria for the week.

"You're in the Empire Suite." The concierge passed over their room keys at check-in.

Amber giggled, bundled in a huge white ski jacket with fake-fur trim around the hood. "You hear that, girls?" She nudged Hallie gleefully. "The Empire Suite. And would you look at that tree?"

Hallie couldn't care less about the holiday decorations. "Are there any messages?" she demanded. The concierge glanced at his screen.

"Nothing, Miss Weston."

"Are you sure?" she checked. "No flowers? Or chocolates? Six-foot stuffed teddy bears?" Dakota had always been more subtle with his gifts, but you never knew.

"I'm sorry." He gave her a vague smile. "We'll call up to your room the moment anything arrives."

"Fine." Hallie exhaled, looking carefully around the gleaming lobby, in case Dakota was lurking behind the twenty-foot tree, waiting to serenade her in person. Now, that would be an apology! But there was nothing except a ten-part all-boys choir, fa-la-la-ing in front of the blazing log fire.

"I should call him again," Hallie decided as they

headed for the elevators, two bellhops trailing them with Amber's full collection of designer luggage. "I sent him all my flight details, but he'll want to know we landed safely."

The doors closed behind them. Grace studied her with an unreadable gaze. "So he called you back?"

Hallie paused. Trust Grace to start speaking to her long enough to drag down Hallie's good mood. "Well, no," she admitted, "but I'm here now. He'll be in touch to see me, for sure."

Amber patted her arm. "Of course he will. And until he does, we've got plenty to do!" A dog yapped in agreement, poking its head out from the flaps of a monogrammed leather carry case. Amber couldn't bear to be parted from them, even for a week, so Marilyn and Monroe had flown with them, tucked in their own seat in the first-class cabin. "I love the city in winter." Amber sighed happily. "It's just like my favorite movie."

"*Manhattan*?" Grace suggested.

"*Legally Blonde*?" Hallie couldn't help but offer.

"No, silly." Amber beamed. "*Serendipity*!"

Their suite was vast and luxurious: a master suite for Amber, huge queen beds in Grace and Hallie's shared room, with a view of Central Park, and a whirlpool tub big enough to fit a small army. Not that it mattered to Hallie: she left the others to tour, gasping, and made straight for the gift basket waiting on the polished walnut table, full of chocolates and expensive spa products.

Hallie snatched up the card. Of course he hadn't let

her arrive without some small—or not so small—token of his affection! "'Enjoy the break. My girls deserve their fun . . .'" She trailed off. "It's from Uncle Auggie," she said, disappointed.

"Awww," Amber cooed. "How sweet. And he sent Godiva, my favorite!" She popped a chocolate truffle into her mouth. "That man is a gem."

Gem was the right word. Namely, diamonds. Somehow Hallie didn't think Amber would be cooing if they were checked into the Holiday Inn, eating vending machine Cheetos.

Hallie left them to the candies and went to check her e-mail. Girls like Amber made their choices, but some things were more important than money and status—like true love. She and Dakota had talked about it all the time: about how they wouldn't sell out like everyone else. It didn't matter if they were starving off in a garret somewhere, they would stay true to their art. And each other.

No new messages.

"Ready?" Amber appeared in the doorway, changed from her in-flight Uggs to three-inch-heeled snow boots. "We've got time to hit Bloomingdale's, and then some dinner before the show!"

"You go ahead," Hallie decided. "I've got a headache coming on, so think I'm just going to relax here today. Recover from the flight."

Amber gave her a look. "You're not waiting for him to call, are you? Because that's never the way to get a guy, just sitting around. You've got to be out there, making him jealous!"

"No!" Hallie forced a laugh. "I'll take a bath, order room service. I'll be fine! Really," she insisted.

"Well . . . OK, then." Amber blew her a kiss. "Order the lobster. Whenever I go anyplace fancy, I always order the lobster."

They headed out, leaving Hallie alone in the quiet of the empty suite. She sank into one of the lounge chairs, taking in the silence.

He would call. She knew it.

But he didn't. Hallie idled in their room all afternoon—restlessly playing with the TV, unpacking her entire wardrobe, even taking a long bubble bath—until darkness fell outside, and New York was spread in a grid of glorious lights outside the hotel. Hallie curled in a window seat, gazing out at the winter wonderland. It was beautiful, but all she could think of was those nights she spent up on Mulholland Drive with Dakota, watching L.A. crawl by in the distance as they planned their grand adventures; the hope and dreams they were going to make real.

And now he was somewhere out there in the city, having his grand adventure. Alone.

The headache she'd faked to Amber became real: blossoming behind her eyeballs in a hot rush of pain as Hallie traced her fingertips over the glass, trying to imagine it. But she couldn't. Everything they'd said, all the plans they'd made, they had all been about the two of them—together. He'd promised her!

Hallie found herself dialing, the number she knew by heart. "Hey, it's me. Hallie. I, umm, just wanted to let you know, we're here. In New York. You can reach me at the Waldorf-Astoria, or on my cell, like usual. . . ."

As she rattled off the details, Hallie tried not to think of how many messages had gone unanswered; how many calls he'd just ignored. Dakota must have a good reason for being so busy these last weeks. Maybe he'd lost his phone, months ago, and had no idea she was in town. Maybe he was on some no-technology detox and hadn't checked his e-mail. Maybe . . .

Before she knew it, it was nine p.m., and Amber and Grace bustled in, toting armfuls of crisp paper shopping bags and the dogs in their carry case.

"Sweetie, how are you feeling?" Amber asked, dropping her bags in a heap. She collapsed onto the couch, unzipped her boots, and gave an ecstatic sigh. "Lord, that's better." She looked over at Hallie. "You missed a hell of a show. And dinner . . . The maître d' looked just like an elf. A little, snooty, French elf!"

"She's right." Grace joined her in the lounge area, setting a takeout container down. "He kept looking down his nose at us, so Amber ordered the most expensive bottle of wine on the menu. And then she only drank half a glass!"

"Carbs." Amber nodded. "Alcohol calories are empty calories!"

Hallie didn't respond. Grace's expression changed. "No word from Dakota?"

Hallie paused, reluctant, then slowly shook her head.

There was silence for a moment. "Well, we can't just

sit around!" Amber declared brightly, getting to her feet. "Go get changed, we're going to hit the town."

"It's OK." Hallie sighed. More pity was the last thing she needed, but Amber was not to be dissuaded.

"No way." Amber crossed to the window and tugged Hallie to her feet. "There's a whole city just waiting for us. Drinks and dessert, and then some dancing!"

Grace coughed. "Umm, we're underage."

"Oh." Amber paused. "Well, how about just the dessert?"

Hallie considered. If she kept her cell phone on, with the ringer set to loud . . .

"OK," she agreed, sending Amber skipping with delight. "But only to the hotel restaurant, so they can come get me, if anyone calls." Hallie caught Grace's look, and bridled. "He will call," she said, for what seemed like the hundredth time. "I know he will."

III

It didn't take Hallie long to realize: if Dakota couldn't come to her, she would just have to go to Dakota.

"This is a bad idea." Grace trudged along the Brooklyn sidewalk beside her, bundled in a coat and earmuffs and a scarf wound so tightly that it took a moment for Hallie to decipher what she was saying. "Please, Hallie, let's just go back to Manhattan and meet Amber. She wants to go ice-skating, and to that Serendipity café they used in the movie."

"No!" Hallie strode on, trying to ignore the bitter winds numbing her legs. She was determined that the first time Dakota saw her again, she would look fabulous: no thermal underwear or ugly parkas, no, she was wearing the dress he'd always said made her look like a 1940s movie star, and the borrowed leather jacket she hadn't had the heart to send back to him.

Perfect. If her limbs didn't drop off from hypothermia before she reached him.

"But Hallie—"

Hallie cut her off. "You didn't have to come! I didn't ask you to, so stop complaining." She checked the cross street. The band had updated their blog with news about the recording studios, so it had been easy for Hallie to track the address down. "Ooh, we're here!"

She looked up at the ugly industrial building and tried to quell her nerves. It would be OK. Whatever his reasons for not calling her back, they were nothing compared to love. One look in her eyes and he'd realize what he might have lost. He'd never risk that again.

"I wasn't complaining," Grace said quietly. "I just don't want to see you get any more hurt."

Hallie ignored her and hit the studio buzzer. A moment later, the door clicked open. She turned back to Grace. "Are you going to keep whining, or are you going to come inside?"

Grace rolled her eyes, but followed her in out of the cold, and up to the second floor, where a bored-looking boy with a blue Mohawk was chewing gum behind a vast desk; exposed brick walls covered with mounted CDs.

"Hey." Hallie breezed up to the reception desk. "I'm here with Take Fountain. Which studio are they in . . . ?"

He raised one pierced eyebrow. "You're *with* them?"

"Yup!" Hallie's smile didn't slip. "Just got in from L.A. They're through here, right?" She gestured down the nearest hallway.

"They were." Mohawk guy spun idly on his chair. "They wrapped recording last week."

Hallie's heart sank, but she tried to seem unaffected. "Oh, shoot. I have a bunch of papers from their manager. Can I get a forwarding address . . . ?" She trailed off hopefully.

Mohawk guy just shrugged. "Sorry. They come, they go."

"But you must have something." Hallie clenched her fists with frustration. "The place they're staying? A number, to check-in?"

Another shrug.

There was a sudden burst of noise. One of the far doors opened, and a group of guys emerged from a studio: low-slung jeans and backward caps, their necks heavy with bling.

"Hallie . . ." Grace tugged her sleeve. Hallie ignored her, focusing all her attention on the desk guy, who was, for some unfathomable reason, standing between her and a reunion with Dakota.

"You don't understand, I need to see them!" Her voice rose. "It's important!" The guy's expression changed—disdain skittering across his face. "They're my friends," she insisted quickly. "Dakota is expecting to see me!"

"So call him." Mohawk guy snapped his gum and smirked. "If he's such a good friend."

"But it's a surprise!" Hallie's lip began to quiver, and tears rose, hot behind her eyes. Why was he being like this? "You don't understand," she yelled. "We came all the way from L.A. I *have* to see him!"

There was laughter behind her. "Someone better call the cops," one of the rappers cracked. "Superfan's gone crazy!"

"What?" Hallie demanded, glaring at them. "You think this is funny? Do you?"

Grace tugged on her arm again. "Please," she whispered. "Hallie—"

Hallie shook her off, whirling back to Mohawk guy. "All I want is an address! One tiny, stupid, little address, and you're acting like I'm a crazy person. Well, I'm not!" she screamed, banging the desk. "Do you hear me? *I'm not crazy!*"

Silence.

Hallie looked around. Even the rapper guys blinked at her, wide-eyed. She exhaled, all her anger suddenly draining away.

"Come on." Grace nudged her gently toward the elevator. "Let's go."

"OK," she agreed tiredly, following Grace back to the exit as her sister murmured apologies to everyone. She didn't care. This was it: her last route to Dakota, and it had turned out to be nothing but a dead end.

"Maybe this is for the best," Grace said softly as they headed back down to street level. "I mean, what could he say, to make it better?"

Hallie stared at her in disbelief. "Everything! That he still loves me, that all this was a mistake, that he wants to be with me again!"

"But wouldn't he be with you already, if he wanted to?"

Hallie's body felt like ice. "It's not that simple," she snapped, striding out of the elevator. "You're too young. You don't understand. Love is . . . Love is complicated sometimes, OK?"

She was almost at the door when she noticed the flyers, pasted haphazardly on the bare brick wall. Guitar lessons, amps for sale, session singers wanted . . . and live shows. Take Fountain—their name leaping out from the mess as if it were printed in three-foot-tall lettering.

Hallie gasped, tearing the blue xeroxed page down. "Look!" She waved it at Grace excitedly. "They're playing a showcase, at a club in the city next week. Monday!"

Grace said nothing.

"We can go, meet Dakota there!" Hallie clasped it to her chest. Of course! This was the reunion they were meant to have: a single spotlight on the stage, Dakota's eyes meeting hers, in the middle of the darkened crowd . . . "I told you." She linked her arm through Grace's and strode happily back out into the cold. "Everything's going to work out. It's a sign!"

Their date with destiny set, Hallie was finally able to relax and enjoy New York, swept up in Amber's giddy whirl for the rest of the weekend as they reenacted all her favorite on-screen holiday moments: ice-skating in Rockefeller Center; hot cocoa and cake in the Serendipity 3 café; taking photos up in the Empire State Building in what Amber swore was the exact same spot where Meg Ryan and Tom Hanks had rendezvoused in *Sleepless in Seattle*—Hallie smiled serenely through it all. Even when Amber met up with one of her bobble-headed L.A. friends, Missy, and spent three hours camped out in the lingerie section at Bergdorf's, her good mood didn't slip. Dakota was safely scheduled for Monday night, and nothing in the world was going to stand between them this time around.

"Oh, this is darling, don't you think?"

Hallie looked up to find Missy's nanny, Lucy, stroking a silk negligee, five inches from Hallie's head. She ducked out of the way. "I guess."

"What do you think, Grace?" Lucy turned, holding it up. "Men love blue. At least, *some* guys do. . . ."

Grace gave a sharp shrug and sat on another of the lounge chairs with Missy's gurgling baby.

"Or maybe I'll get something in black." Lucy wandered over to another rack, wispy bra and panties hung like tree decorations on thin silver wire. "It's sexier. And it's always better to be sexy. Especially since we won't have seen each other in a while."

Lucy was talking so meaningfully, it was clear she wanted someone to ask more. "Do you have a boyfriend?" Hallie asked obligingly. The girl seemed sweet enough—upbeat even though she worked for a woman who dressed her baby in head-to-toe leopard print.

"Yes!" Lucy beamed. "It's soooo romantic. We're dating in secret, because his family wouldn't approve."

"Scandalous," Hallie teased.

"He's in town, too, visiting his family for the holidays. I couldn't bear to be away from him, so I suggested Missy come hit the shops." Lucy winked.

"Smart," Hallie agreed.

"Isn't it? Now we can slip away and get together for some *alone time.*" Lucy waggled the negligee suggestively. "What do you think, Grace?" she asked again. "Should I get the blue or the black?"

"Whatever you want." Grace suddenly leaped up, grabbing her coat. "I'm going back to the hotel. I want to take a nap before dinner."

"Me too." Hallie yawned. "I didn't think it was possible to do too much shopping, but this is it. Just let me pay for this stuff." She turned to Lucy. "Good luck with your secret meeting," she said, pulling on her jacket. "And I say go with the black. It's a classic."

Lucy looked between them. "We'll come too!" she quickly declared. "It's time for Angelina's nap, and the apartment is in your direction. We can split a cab."

"OK," Hallie agreed. "Grace?"

"Sure." She sighed, impatient. "I'll see you guys out front." Grace hurried ahead, leaving Hallie to find a register and pay for her motley assortment of gifts. It had been hard to find anything on her budget—let alone in Amber's kind of store, where even a pair of gloves seemed to cost three figures—but Hallie had prevailed. So what if Uncle Auggie might not want another pair of golfing socks: it was the thought that counted!

"So what's the story with your sister?" Lucy asked, waiting alongside her in line for a register. There was only one salesclerk on the floor, and he was busy flirting with the Ivy League guy in front of them: studying engraved business-card cases like they were the Holy Grail.

Lucy bounced baby Angelina in her arms and fixed

Hallie with an eager gaze. "Is she, you know, seeing anyone?"

"You think she tells me anything?" Hallie snorted.

"Come on, there must be someone. A crush, someone from back in San Francisco, maybe?" Lucy's expression was sharp for a moment, then it smoothed into a sunny smile again. "I was just thinking, you know, maybe I could fix her up!"

Hallie laughed. "Don't bother. She's got our neighbor Brandon over all the time, and this guy from school, Harry, and then there's—" She stopped, suddenly glimpsing a tangle of dark curls on the other side of the menswear section. Her heart leaped. Could it be . . . ?

"Who?" Lucy asked. "You were about to say something."

"Huh?" Hallie squinted eagerly across the room. The guy was too far away to see clearly, half hidden by a display of tuxedo jackets.

"You said there's another guy," Lucy asked, "for Grace?"

Hallie didn't take her eyes from the stranger. She'd thought she'd seen Dakota everywhere in L.A. too, but this was different—it really could be him! But as Hallie watched, a blond girl approached: shaking her head at his selection, and passing a new jacket for him to try. He did so obediently, stepping out of sight behind the rail of clothing.

Hallie sighed. Of course it wasn't him—why would Dakota be browsing tuxedo jackets in Bergdorf's? He was a strictly vintage guy, at home in threadbare band shirts and worn jeans. She turned back to the line as the Ivy League guy finally tucked his platinum credit card—and the salesman's phone number—away.

"Hallie?" Lucy prompted again.

"Oh, yeah, it doesn't matter." Hallie strode up to the register and dumped her gifts on the counter. "So, where in England are you from?" she asked Lucy, changing the subject. "I've always wanted to go to London!"

Lucy filled the cab ride back with chatter about life in England, and then insisted on stopping off at the hotel with them to take a look at the lobby. "It's so Christmassy," she trilled happily, gazing around at the baubles and tree.

"Miss Weston?" The concierge called over from the front desk. "You had a visitor. A young man . . ."

Hallie gasped. "When? Where? Did he leave a note?"

"No message," the concierge said, "but I saw him head into the lounge. He might still be there. . . ."

Hallie was already hurrying across the lobby, heart pounding. He'd come! Her boots skittered on the marble floors as she ducked past tourists, sliding to a stop as she reached the lounge area. She scanned the couches, desperate for a glimpse of Dakota. Not him, not them, no . . .

"Oh."

Her heart sank as she spied the boy sitting in front of the fire. Messy brown hair instead of Dakota's dark curls; a preppy parka and khakis where skinny jeans and leather should be.

"It's you," she said, disappointment in every syllable.

Theo turned at the sound of her voice. "Hallie, hey!" He got up to greet her, then paused, noticing her expression. "What's wrong?"

"Nothing." Hallie sighed. "I just thought you were someone else."

"Sorry." Theo gave her an awkward hug.

"What are you even doing out here?" Hallie asked. She could hear the petulant note in her tone, but she didn't care. Everyone was showing up except the one person she wanted more than anything!

"We're spending the holidays with my grandma here in the city," Theo explained. "There's a holiday party, tomorrow night. I thought maybe you'd want to come. Both of you," he added, looking around hopefully.

"I'm going to Dakota's show," Hallie told him. "But I guess Grace could come. Why don't you ask her?" she added as Grace reached them, Lucy following behind. "Look who came to visit," Hallie told Grace meaningfully. "Isn't that great?"

Grace didn't speak. Instead, it was Lucy who lit up. "Teddy!" she cried. "Oh, my God. I didn't think you were coming until next week!"

Hallie looked back and forth between them. "Wait, how do you two know each other?"

Theo flushed. "I . . . um . . . we . . ."

"They met over the summer," Grace said, her voice dull. "In the Hamptons."

"Huh. Small world." Hallie shrugged. Theo was still

frozen, turning redder by the second. “Anyway, his folks are throwing some party tomorrow, he came to see if you’d come.”

“I’d love to!” Lucy piped up. Hallie was about to point out that he hadn’t actually meant her, when Grace backed away, knocking into an antique side table.

“I need to go,” Grace said, looking strained. “Headache. I have to lie down.”

“But Theo came to see you.” Hallie stared at her, confused. Was Grace completely oblivious? This was her one true love in front of her, with that puppy-dog look and everything! “You should have a coffee. Catch up!”

“I can’t. But, thanks.” Grace gave Theo a weak smile and then took off across the lobby, almost at a run. Hallie watched her go, frowning. That had been downright impolite, and her sister, no matter what, was *never* rude. Even when creepy homeless guys accosted her on the subway, Grace would always smile and tell them she was sorry, but she didn’t have any change.

“I better go too,” Hallie told them. “Make sure she’s OK.”

“Right,” Theo said, looking downcast.

“That’s OK!” Lucy trilled happily. “I’ll keep him company.”

Hallie caught up with Grace by the elevators. “Are you crazy?” she asked. “Why did you blow him off? He came to see you, anyone could tell.”

Grace just shook her head, but when the doors closed

behind them, Hallie heard a muffled sob. She looked over. Grace was crying.

Crying!

Hallie gasped. "What's wrong?" She couldn't remember Grace crying since . . . since never. Not even at their father's funeral!

"He's with Lucy," Grace told her, lips trembling. "They hooked up over the summer. She's been visiting him at college. They're in love." Her voice twisted on the last word.

"No . . ." Hallie breathed, remembering Lucy's smug comments about lingerie and secret rendezvous. "That bitch!"

"It's not her fault." Grace sniffed, clearly miserable. "It's mine, for ever even thinking . . ." The elevator doors opened. Grace slumped miserably down the hall to their suite; swiping uselessly with her key card until Hallie took it from her and let them in.

"Look at me," Grace sniffled. "I can't even open a door."

Hallie shook her head. Doors weren't the problem here, no, their problem was five six, with freckles and a snooty British accent. She knew there was something off about the girl. Nobody was that nice to small children without hiding some dark, twisted heart.

"How do you know all this?" Hallie demanded. "Wait, did she tell you?"

Grace threw herself on the couch. "Why wouldn't she? She thinks I'm her friend. She doesn't know . . ."

Hallie wasn't so sure.

"And Theo?" she asked. "What does he say?"

"He didn't." Grace sat up, eyes puffy. "He didn't say a thing. Not that he'd met someone, or that they were still together. It's probably the real reason he was he in L.A., that time he came to visit. He came to see her."

She gave Hallie a dejected look, so defeated that it took Hallie's breath away. She sank on the couch beside Grace, guilt suddenly blossoming in her chest. All this time, she'd figured Grace's feelings were a childish crush; something to tease her about. But this wasn't the end of something light and silly, this was real heartbreak on her sister's face.

"How long have you known?" she asked gently.

"Since October." Her sister curled up. "It was this big secret, she swore I couldn't tell."

"So all this time . . . ?" Hallie remembered their fight—how she'd accused Grace of being a coward, when, really, she'd been suffering just the same as Hallie: pining for a boy who was out of reach. "Oh, Grace . . ." She reached out and stroked her sister's hair.

"It's my own fault." Grace sighed. "I shouldn't have thought we could . . . That he felt . . ."

"But he did. He does!" Hallie insisted. "Everyone can see."

Grace shook her head. "No, he's just a friend. He was being nice to me, that's all, after Dad died. I was the one who wanted it to be something more."

Hallie tried to smile. "At least you finally admit it." Grace stared back blankly. "Your feelings," Hallie explained. "That's the first time you've ever come out and said you like him."

Grace laughed, hollow. "Right. Because that helps me now."

They sat in silence for a moment. "Sorry," Hallie offered at last. "For being so, you know . . ."

"Oblivious and self-involved?" Grace suggested, but there was a ghost of a smile on her lips all the same.

Hallie grinned, relieved. "I was going more for single-minded, but sure."

"It wouldn't have made a difference"—Grace sighed—"even if you had known."

"But we could have been in it together: losing them."

Grace looked at her, plaintive. Resigned. "No. You were right. He was never even mine to lose. You at least had Dakota."

"Have," Hallie corrected quickly. "Or, at least I will, come Monday."

Grace rested her head against Hallie's shoulder, snuggling closer, the way they used to do as kids, bundled up in the den watching Disney movies. "I hope so," she said. "I really do. Because nobody should have to feel like this. Not even you."

"Thanks!"

"You know what I mean."

IV

Hallie wanted to skip the Coates Family's Christmas Nightmare altogether, but Grace insisted they at least drop by. "Theo will know something's wrong, otherwise," she said forlornly.

"So?" Hallie blotted her lipstick, already breathless with excitement for Dakota's show. "It is!"

"But I can't have him know that. Please, Hallie," Grace added, "I mean it. The one thing that would make all of this worse is if he knows I'm upset about Lucy. It would ruin everything!"

To Hallie, it seemed like Theo had done all the ruining himself, but Grace was insistent, and so early Monday evening found the sisters outside the penthouse of a snooty doorman building on the Upper East Side. "Another penthouse." Grace sighed, stamping her feet on the rug.

"It's because they like looking down on people," Hallie replied, before the door swung open.

"Girls!" Portia cried, blinking at them. She was wearing a severe white dress with diamonds twinkling at her throat—not so much the merry widow, Hallie noted, as the positively glowing one. "What are you . . . ? I mean, welcome!"

Hallie smirked. Ruffling Portia's precious feathers? That was worth coming for all on its own.

Grace exhaled. "Didn't Theo say he invited us?"

"No, no, it must have slipped his mind." Portia gave them a smile that didn't reach her eyes. "Anyway, come on in. The more the merrier!" She waved them inside.

The girls followed her in. It was one of those echoing, old-style apartments: tall windows and bare floorboards, cluttered with antique furniture and tight little groups of stiff-backed guests in cocktail outfits sipping wine. Only the tree in the corner, and the faint sound of carols on the stereo, gave any hint that it was a holiday party. "Help yourself to a drink." Portia waved at the circulating waiters. "Juice, of course. Dash is in the playroom, but I'm sure he'd love to see you."

"Thanks." Grace smiled politely. There was a pause.

"Well, then . . ." Portia blinked. "Lovely to see you. We'll catch up!" She turned on her perilously high heels and quickly disappeared into the crowd.

"These people sure could use some Christmas spirit," Hallie murmured, looking around. "They look more like Scrooges in here."

"Shh," Grace hissed. "They're family."

Hallie rolled her eyes. As far as she was concerned, family was something you chose, not got lumbered with because of your father's brief lapse in sanity. These people may be tied to her by marriage and law, but they were clearly no relation. Just look at all this tweed!

"We only stay an hour, max," Hallie reminded her. "I don't want to be late for the show."

"We're not even going in," Grace argued. "It's sold out. And I'm not going to freeze on the sidewalk for hours when—"

They were interrupted by a burst of laughter. Lucy was in the corner, wearing a demure pale-pink dress and chatting happily with a trio of white-haired old ladies in pearls. Hallie felt Grace tense beside her. "Pink?" Hallie snorted quietly. "With her hair? Please."

Grace gave a weak smile, then took a deep breath, as if bracing herself. "We better circulate. Go say hi to everyone."

"Make it loud," Hallie added. "So the old folks can all hear."

After explaining for the fifth time that, yes, they really *were* related to little Dash—and wasn't that just amazing?—Hallie was ready to bail.

"I'll pay you a hundred bucks to leave right now," she offered, gulping the grape juice that all the children had been relegated to. Hallie supposed she should just be happy they hadn't offered it in a sippy cup.

"You don't have a hundred bucks," Grace pointed

out. "I bet you don't even have ten after buying that dress."

Hallie grinned, giving a little twirl. "Worth it, though, right? Anyway, I'll owe you."

Grace shook her head.

"Pretty please?" Hallie begged. "Seriously, one of those old men just asked where I went on vacation to get so tan."

Grace sighed. "We can't go yet, it would be rude."

"And he wasn't?"

"Grace!" Lucy's breathless cry made them turn; the British girl descended, lavishing air-kisses on both of their cheeks in turn. "Isn't this party the best? I chatted with Theo's grandmother for half an hour. I don't know what he was so worried about, the woman's a doll!"

Grace's smile was thin. "That's great."

"Isn't it?" Lucy's eyes were wide, but now that she knew what to look for, Hallie could see the steel behind them. "Now that I'm getting to know them all, there's no reason for us to keep our relationship a secret anymore. Theo will be so relieved."

"Will he?" Hallie asked. Lucy blinked at her.

"Of course. It's been so hard on him, not being able to tell anyone."

"Right." Hallie kept a smile fixed on her face. "Except usually, if a guy really likes you, he wants to tell the whole world. Unless, it's like some dirty little secret." Grace's elbow dug into her side, but Hallie couldn't resist finishing. "You know, a mistake, that he's ashamed about."

Lucy's smile dissolved so fast it could have set a record. "Theo and me are in love," she said, practically hissing.

There! Hallie knew that whole Mary Poppins routine was an act!

"I," she corrected, not able to resist a tiny dig. Lucy frowned. "It's *Theo and I,*" Hallie explained, smirking. "I thought you Brits were sticklers for grammar."

Grace coughed. "Ooh, look, cookies!" She tried to drag Hallie away. Hallie stood fast.

"If you're so in love, why aren't you over there with him now?" She fluttered a wave across the room at Theo. He saw them all, froze, and then promptly turned and headed in the other direction.

Sure, like that was a boy in the grips of a secret wild passion.

"Whoops," Hallie said, sarcastic. "He must not have seen you."

"He saw me." Lucy pulled herself up to her full height, giving Hallie a smug look. "We just agreed not to go public tonight. Agreed it last night. Which we spent together. At his place."

Hallie heard Grace's pained intake of breath and snapped. She lurched forward, spilling red grape juice all down the front of Lucy's dress.

"Oh, no!" Hallie cried. "I'm so clumsy. You better go wash that out before it stains!"

Lucy glared at her, openmouthed, but no sound came out. Finally, she spun on her heel and fled toward the bathroom.

"Hallie!" Grace dragged her into the empty kitchen, countertops full of hors d'oeuvre platters and empty wine glasses. Grace shut the door behind them and turned on Hallie. "I can't believe you did that!"

"It was for you!" Hallie protested. "I was helping!"

"I don't want your help," Grace told her. "It was mean, and immature, and . . . and . . ." A tiny smile bubbled to her lips. "Did you see her face?"

Hallie grinned. "Priceless. Now, the stain should keep her busy for a while, so you go get back out there with Theo and fight."

"But I don't want to." Grace sagged against the kitchen cabinets. "I don't want to fight. It shouldn't be a competition. Either he likes me or he doesn't, and, well . . . clearly he doesn't."

"There's no clearly about it," Hallie insisted. "Did you hear her story? Something's not right. I bet you she's lied about everything."

"But why?" Grace countered. "Why go through all the trouble pretending, when we could easily find out just by asking Theo?"

"So why don't you?" Hallie asked.

Grace looked away.

There was a noise in the doorway. "Hey, you two, champagne's running thin."

They both turned. It was the Ivy League guy from Bergdorf's, Hallie realized: floppy blond hair and an expensive watch. He looked at them impatiently. "The trays. We need fresh bottles out there."

Hallie blinked, confused, but Grace snorted under

her breath. "He thinks we're the help," she explained to Hallie, voice brittle. "I can't imagine why."

They exchanged a look.

"Who are you exactly?" Hallie asked him.

Ivy League looked thrown. "Rex Coates. This is my family's party."

"And we're part of the family." Hallie gave him a deadly smile. "Your step-sisters."

There was a beat, but Rex didn't even have the decency to apologize. He frowned again, processing the information, then shrugged. "If you do see the real staff, tell them about the champagne, OK?" He turned to go. "Oh, and happy holidays."

The kitchen door closed behind him. Hallie shook her head in disbelief. "This family! They are all freaking insane," she declared.

"Except Theo," Grace said quietly.

"Keep telling yourself that." Hallie wasn't so sure. "You still care if these people think you're polite or not?"

Grace wavered, then shook her head. Finally! Some sense. Hallie linked her arm through Grace's. "Then let's get the hell out of here."

Hallie didn't have tickets for the sold-out show—or the money to spend two hundred bucks on scalped passes from the seedy guys lurking around outside the club—so she figured the backstage entrance was her best bet. Simply wait by the stage door once the show was over, intercept Dakota on his way out, and voilà! The reunion she'd been dreaming about. Sure, the back alley was strewn with garbage instead of rose petals, but the setting didn't matter; once she and Dakota were together again, they could retire back to the Waldorf-Astoria to catch up; the important part was that she was finally—finally!—going to see him again.

"You're sure it's not too late to talk you out of this?" Grace asked, following Hallie around to the back of the club. There were two dozen fans waiting there already, and the line out front of the show had stretched around the block, easily their biggest audience to date. Hallie couldn't help feeling a glow of pride on Dakota's behalf. They were doing it: the band was really breaking out!

"We could go back to the hotel and splurge on room service," Grace continued, bundled up and blowing on her hands like she was deep in Arctic Russia. "The warm, toasty hotel. With heated towels and an adjustable thermostat."

"Don't be such a baby," Hallie told her. She was shaking too, but her tremors were from pure nervous excitement. "A little cold never hurt anyone!"

"Except for all those people who die from hypothermia!"

Hallie ignored her protests, cutting ruthlessly right to the front of the crowd. She quickly scoped out her competition for the band's attention. Underage fangirls, she decided: clutching posters for the band to sign, their cameras at the ready. Dakota wouldn't give them a second glance.

Grace ducked in behind her, apologizing as she went. "What are you going to do if this doesn't work out?"

"It will!"

"No," Grace said, "I mean it." She put her hands on Hallie's shoulders, forcing her to look into her eyes. "What will you do?"

Hallie blinked. For a moment, something inside her slipped—icy cold and fearful—but then a sudden excited cry went up, and the crowd pressed forward. They were coming out! Hallie broke away from Grace, breathlessly straining for the first glimpse of him.

And there he was.

Dakota came sauntering out behind AJ and Reed; hair damp with sweat, that Sex Pistols shirt Hallie picked out peeking from under a jacket, and looking every bit as beautiful as Hallie remembered him. She felt her body wilt with pure relief. He was there, right in front of her! Everything was going to be OK!

"Dakota!" she called, but her voice was lost in the din. The crowd swelled, filling the small space in the alley, and the band was quickly surrounded.

"Whoa!" The guys laughed, clearly reveling in their moment of glory. "Back up!" A couple of club bouncers hurried out, trying to fend off the adoring masses.

Hallie struggled against the surge. "Dakota!" she yelled, louder. "Over here!"

He didn't hear her, busy scribbling autographs on T-shirts, tickets, even random limbs girls thrust his way. He looked completely happy, Hallie realized, not even fazed by the crush of people screaming out for his attention. This was what he wanted, after all: to be seen, recognized.

A black limo arrived, driving slowly through the alley. The crowd began to scatter, happily clutching their autographs and camera phones. "Wait up," Dakota called ahead, over the noise of the crowd. "We can't go without her."

Hallie brightened. He'd seen her. He'd—

The stage door opened again, and security ushered a girl out. Face obscured by huge sunglasses, she was dressed in tight black jeans and leather boots, long blond hair spilling in a glossy wave over a silky shirt.

Hallie blinked in recognition at the same time as an audible gasp went up from the crowd.

"Is that . . . omigod! Talia!"

Talia Talbot: Hollywood starlet, tabloid staple. And . . . the girl Hallie had seen in Bergdorf's the other day, she suddenly realized.

The tide of people pressed Hallie forward again as they grabbed for the star. Dakota reached Talia first: throwing one protective arm around her shoulder and blocking their faces from the dizzying flash of cameras. Talia sank against him, resting her head against his chest as if she hadn't been stalked by the paparazzi since the day she'd "accidentally" torn her dress and flashed the entire Emmy Awards her perfect derriere.

Hallie froze, staring at the pair in bewilderment. They were just ten feet away from her: Dakota's arm around Talia's slim body; her hand clutching at his jacket. His brand-new, designer tuxedo jacket.

And then, as if Hallie were trapped in some cruel nightmare, Dakota leaned down and kissed Talia. A long, slow kiss that left the crowd screaming, and turned Hallie's body to ice.

How was this possible?

The couple broke apart, smiling. Talia climbed into the limo, but Dakota turned back to give the crowd one last wave. That's when he saw her.

Their eyes locked. His smile slipped.

Hallie finally unfroze. She ducked under the arm of one of the security guys and closed the distance between them, unsteady on her heels. "Dakota?"

"H-Hallie?" Dakota stuttered, glancing anxiously toward the car. "What are you doing here?"

"I came to see you." Hallie stared back at him. Everything she'd imagined telling him was gone from her mind: wiped blank by the sight of his lips on someone else's. "I don't understand," she managed, ignoring the sound of the overexcited crowd. "Why won't you talk to me? I've been calling you for weeks!"

"I, um, I got a new phone."

Hallie gasped. All this time, he hadn't even *listened* to her pain? "But you still know my number. Why didn't you call?" she demanded. "You just disappeared. I didn't know what to think!"

Dakota shifted, not meeting her eyes. "I told you, things got crazy. I needed some time."

"For what?" Hallie cried. "*Her?*"

He stiffened, and pulled her to the side. The bouncers closed around them, forming a solid wall of muscle between them and the crowd. "Look, it's not like that," Dakota hissed. "The label, they've sunk a ton of money into us, but without publicity . . ." He jammed his hands in his jacket pockets—the jacket she'd seen some other girl pick out, just the day before—and looked at her plaintively. "Please, try to understand!"

But she did understand. That was the problem. For the first time in months, Hallie understood perfectly, and the truth was so simple, it took her breath away. The reason he'd stopped calling? The reason he hadn't invited her out, or visited, or done anything to assuage the terrible misery and heartache she'd been going through?

He didn't want to.

Not enough to do something about it, anyway. Not enough to send her even a simple note explaining that he couldn't see her anymore—give her some kind of closure, or power to put him behind her for good. Hallie had spent the last weeks making so many excuses to herself for the way he was acting, but finally standing there in front of him, she realized: there was none.

It was over, she saw that now, but worse than that, it had *always* been over. Dakota had just been too much of a coward to ever say it to her face.

"Hey, D, get in the damn car!" Reed's yell came from through the tinted window, and the limo began inching its way slowly back toward the street. Dakota looked between them, torn.

"Hallie . . ." he began, those blue eyes pooled with regret.

Hallie cut him off. "Go," she spat, something new forming: a sharp blade in her chest that cut through the melancholy haze that had shrouded her ever since he left.

"Go to your precious after-party, with all your fancy new friends. It's what you wanted, isn't it? To be seen. To *matter.*"

She was shaking—not with grief, or any of the pitiful emotions she'd been weighed under for so long. No, this was rage, chasing the icy numbness away with a furious power. Hallie peeled his leather jacket off and thrust it at him. "*Go!*"

"Please, you don't understand. . . . It's not just about me. I have the band to think about. . . ." Dakota looked to the car, then back at her. He seemed suspended there a moment: caught between them, unmoving, with an unreadable expression in his eyes.

"Dakota, sweetie." A honeyed voice emerged from the limo. "They're holding our table!"

Dakota seemed to sag. He took one final look at Hallie, took the jacket, and slid into the limo. The door slammed shut, the tinted window slid up, and slowly, it rolled away—leaving Hallie there in the dark alley with nothing but her thin vintage dress and a bitter rage so thick she could taste it.

"Hallie?" Grace approached her, wide-eyed. "What happened? Are you OK?"

Hallie spun around, turning her back on the club, and the crowd, and her terrible humiliation. "It's over," she told Grace bluntly. "It couldn't be more over. Let's go home."

V

He changed his mind.

That was the thought Hallie wrestled with the entire trip back home, fighting to keep her blazing new anger contained through airport security lines and the bright, cheerful sound of holiday carols at every turn. *He'd changed his mind.*

She sat, fuming in the dim silence of the first-class cabin. All around her, people were dozing, or staring glassy-eyed at their seat-back screens, but Hallie felt like yelling at the top of her lungs. How *could* he? She didn't think it was possible; it shouldn't be allowed! To make promises one day, then turn around and be with someone else . . . ? Of all the reasons Hallie had imagined to explain Dakota's silence, this had never even figured. And why would it? She had meant it, every time she said she loved him. She had believed with all her heart and soul that they were made for each other, that the future they planned would actually come to be.

And he'd believed it too! Even in her fury, Hallie couldn't bring herself to think he'd lied; that the words murmured softly to her late in the night were all false. An act. No, Dakota had loved her, which made it even worse. Because if mankind was really so fickle—acting as if love could be stumbled out of, as easily as fallen into—then her whole philosophy on life was a joke. Dakota hadn't just broken her heart, he'd shaken Hallie's very faith in love itself!

By the time they touched down at LAX, her rage had hardened into an almost Zen-like calm. If it was Zen to craft a voodoo doll of your ex-boyfriend out of plastic straws and a cashmere sleep mask, that is. Hallie was happily twisting its malformed limbs by the baggage carousel when her cell rang.

"Is it true?" Ana Lucia demanded. "We all said it couldn't be, but my stylist swore his cousin did makeup for her at the premiere and they were, like, all over each other!" There was a hushed whisper in the background.

"I'm talking to her," Ana Lucia said, voice muffled. "Shut up! So?" Her voice got louder. "What the hell is going on?"

Hallie took a few steps away from Amber and Grace, hoisting Amber's parade of excess baggage onto the carts. "It's true," she admitted quietly, the words burning her from the inside out. "I found them together, in New York."

Ana Lucia gasped. "She walked in on them!" she told her audience. "Totally caught in the act!"

"No, not like that," Hallie hurried to explain, before the story was all over Hollywood. "Ana Lucia? Hello?"

Another rustle, and then Ana Lucia was back on the line. "So, I don't get it. Was he cheating, or did you break up?"

"It's . . . complicated," Hallie answered slowly. There was a call from across the concourse: Grace waved her over to where they were waiting with a driver. "Listen, I have to go, but I really need to get out. What are you guys doing tonight?"

"We were heading to Soho House," Ana Lucia replied. "But, are you sure you're up to it? Maybe you should just chill. You know, alone time."

"I'm fine," Hallie insisted. "Really. See you guys there."

Hallie hung up, determined. That was it: she needed to go out, and have a fabulous time, like nothing was wrong. Show Dakota and all her friends that she couldn't care less about him and his tabloid bimbo. She was fine—better!—without him.

Hallie hurried out front of the terminal and bundled into the waiting car. "Hey, Amber, you remember you offered to loan me that dress one time. The black one with the—"

"—asymmetrical neckline and amazing diamanté

shoes?" Amber finished. "Why? Are you hitting the town?"

Hallie nodded. "Just hanging out with some friends, but I want to look . . . spectacular."

Amber winked. "Say no more. I'll get my stylist over ASAP, and we'll have you looking like a supermodel in no time." She pulled out her cell phone. "Philippe, sweetie, I need you!"

Hallie felt a strange wave of affection. Amber may act like Miss Gold Digger nineteen fifty-two sometimes, but at least she cared.

Unlike some people.

The brief pause for goodwill passed; Hallie's anger returned with a vengeance. She would show him. She would show them all. Hallie Weston didn't mope around, heartbroken—at least, not this time. She would rise, triumphant. She would win this goddamn breakup, and she would do it all in four-inch designer heels!

But it turned out not to be so simple. From the moment Hallie stepped out of her cab that night, resplendent in Amber's borrowed outfit, the only thing anyone wanted to talk about was . . . Dakota. New friends from Ana Lucia's clique; random acquaintances she'd met at a Take Fountain show three months ago—it felt like everyone Hallie had ever met in Hollywood was lining up to demand the inside scoop on the breakup, and give her that knowing little smile, like they didn't believe for a second she was really so happy to be rid of him.

"You guys were so perfect together!" a random blond girl Hallie didn't even recognize cooed to her in the elevators.

"And to find out like that!" A cluster of tight-shirted men rolled their eyes knowingly by the bar. "Drinks on us, sweetie."

"You need it," another guy added, in that faux-sympathetic tone she'd come to know so well. "You poor, poor thing!"

"No, I'm fine!" Hallie's cheeks already ached from forcing her 'I'm so much better off without him' smile. She winked at them. "But if you insist, make mine a margarita!"

At least that was a perk of being the latest object of Hollywood gossip: free drinks. By the time midnight rolled around, Hallie was on her third cocktail of the night, but even the hazy glow of alcohol couldn't soothe the furious burn of righteous indignation in her chest, or shake the image of him emerging from the stage door, and how goddamn *happy* he looked, strutting around for all those cameras.

"He never wanted to be famous!" Hallie cried, collapsed on a crushed-velvet couch beside Meredith. She gestured wildly, almost spilling their latest round of sympathy margaritas. "He agreed with me, so many times. Celebrity is meaningless, his music is what matters!"

Meredith made a supportive noise, dabbing at the skirt of her lacy maxi dress.

"All that talk about artistic integrity, and now he's nothing but a big freaking sellout." Hallie laughed bitterly.

"I mean, how desperate: faking a relationship with Talia just for the sake of some tabloid headlines. *Talia!*" she said again, voice scornful. "That girl couldn't play a serious role to save her life. She's showed her tits in, like, three different movies!"

"Shh!" Meredith hissed, looking over her shoulder. "You want to get us kicked out? That's her best friend over there!"

Hallie shrugged, pulling herself to her feet. She wobbled a moment, unsteady in those borrowed heels. "I could take her. Bet she hasn't eaten all week!"

Meredith checked the other girl again. "Just, try not to start any catfights on your way to the bathroom, OK?"

Hallie threw her arms out. "Anyone wants trouble, they can just try!"

She tottered across the lounge floor, glad to see heads turn her way. The girls' favorite hangout wasn't a lounge, or regular bar, but a private members' club, set on the top two floors of a swanky building on Sunset Boulevard. You had to be signed in to even step foot in the elevator, and once upstairs, there was a luxurious spread of lounge rooms, restaurant, even a 24-hour gym—not that the girls had ever used it. They were too busy staking out prime couches in the lounge area to watch the various celebrity makeups and breakups that took place away from the prying eyes of the paparazzi.

Hallie slipped into the bathroom and found Ana Lucia and Brie propped up by the sink. "There you are!" Hallie cried happily. "You disappeared, forever ago. Where have you been?"

"Around." Ana Lucia wiped her nose. "How are you holding up?"

"Fabulous," Hallie declared. "But I swear, if another bobblehead blonde asks me how I'm doing, I'm going to snap her oversize head right off her tiny body." She laughed loudly. "You guys excluded, of course."

"Uh-huh."

Hallie fumbled with her clutch to find her lipstick. "I'm serious, Dakota can go screw himself. Or that bitch. I don't care!" She caught Ana Lucia exchanging a look with Brie. "I don't!" Hallie insisted. "It's so over. I mean, I deserve a guy who's not going to sell me out for the sake of some stupid magazine covers."

"Right," Ana Lucia murmured. "You already said that. Like, five times."

"Well, it's true!" Hallie focused on reapplying her lipstick. "So, what do you think: you want to hang here some more? Or come back to my place? Ooh, slumber party!"

Ana Lucia shrugged vaguely. "I think we're going to bail soon. Keisha is having some people over."

"Who's that?" Hallie frowned, trying to remember a face from the blur of new introductions.

"Just a friend of mine."

Brie piped up. "She's the girl from that new sitcom, you know, with the three party girls in the city who inherit the baby twins?"

Hallie lit up. "But that's perfect! I need to get my head back in the acting game, now that I don't have any distractions. Where does she live—up in the hills?"

There was a pause.

"It's more of a private party," Ana Lucia replied at last. "And you should probably be heading home. But take care of yourself, OK, doll?"

They were out the door of the bathroom before Hallie could even process the brush-off. She stopped, gloss wand halfway to her lips, as Ana Lucia's dismissive tone sank in.

Wait, what *was* that?

Hallie hurried out of the bathroom after the girls. "Ana Lucia? Hey, hold up!" she called, catching up to them in the middle of the main lounge area. "What's going on?"

Ana Lucia and Brie exchanged another look. "Like I said, it's a private party," Ana Lucia said with a shrug. "No offense."

Meredith arrived with an armful of their jackets. "Ready to roll?" she asked Hallie, oblivious. Brie jabbed her in the ribs. Meredith looked around. "Huh? What did I miss?"

"I wish I knew." Even through the margarita haze, Hallie was getting a very bad feeling—one that only got worse when Ana Lucia took a step closer, and gave Hallie a faux-awkward look, all rueful and apologetic.

"I didn't want to say anything, but, well, the thing is, it's getting kind of uncomfortable." Ana Lucia blinked at her, the very model of regret. "You know," she added, with another tiny grimace, "the way you act around my famous friends."

Hallie gaped. "What? I don't understand. How do

I act?" She turned to the other girls for support, but Meredith just stood looking uncomfortable, while Brie tapped away delightedly at her cell phone.

"The way you bug them about their agents, and auditions," Ana Lucia explained, with a smug smile. "It's just, tacky. Especially when we're all just hanging out."

Hallie stared back, horrified. The way Ana Lucia was looking at her . . . she knew it way too well: it was the look Ana Lucia gave to wannabes, and hangers-on, and those poor souls with the misfortune of wearing last year's wet-look leather leggings.

And now, for the first time, Hallie.

"But, you're the one who introduced me to everyone!" Hallie protested. "You told me to talk to Rachel about audition reels, remember?" Hallie insisted. "And when we met Zoe, at that party over the summer, you're the one who said I was trying to break in. They were happy to talk to me!"

"Well, sure, because they didn't want to be rude." Ana Lucia's smile became more frozen—barely a smile at all. "I'm just saying, it's been uncomfortable. For all of us. I know you're an outsider, but, this isn't how we do it here." She shrugged, and turned on her heel to leave—as if Hallie were nothing more than an embarrassing inconvenience now, and not the girl who had been right beside her at every brunch and shopping trip for months; supplying them with backstage passes, and invites to all of Take Fountain's private after-show parties.

Suddenly, Hallie's anger bubbled up again.

"This is about Dakota, isn't it?" she demanded furiously. "All along, you've been using me to get near Reed. But now that we've broken up, you're done with me!"

Ana Lucia hardened. "Me? Using you?" She snorted. "Please. What do you have that I could possibly want?" She took a step closer to Hallie and glared, all pretense of friendship gone. "We let you tag along for long enough, but just because you lucked out in the right zip code, and have some rich relative taking pity on you, it doesn't make you one of us!"

Brie finally looked up from her cell phone. "Your uncle isn't even in features," she added, like it was the ultimate put-down. "He does *TV.*"

She and Ana Lucia whirled on their spiked heels and stalked away. Meredith paused a moment, and gave Hallie a regretful look. "Sorry. She's just . . ." Meredith sighed. "You know Reed slept with her, right before they all went to New York? And now he's not returning her calls."

"So she *was* just using me." Hallie's anger returned, only this time, she didn't know whether to be mad at Ana Lucia, or herself—for not seeing the blatant exchange that had been holding up their entire friendship. She looked at Meredith, arms folded. "What about you? Are you done too?"

Meredith glanced over to the elevators, where Ana Lucia and Brie were waiting. Ana Lucia glared at them impatiently. "We go way back," Meredith offered, the feeble note in her voice telling Hallie everything she needed to know. "They're my best friends out here. They know everyone."

And there it was again. Who you knew—or didn't know—made all the difference in this town.

"You'll miss your ride," Hallie told her harshly, turning away. She didn't wait to watch Meredith leave with the others; for once, Hallie needed to be the one to walk away first.

VI

Hallie made straight for the bar, blood still singing from her showdown with Ana Lucia and Co. She waved for the bartender's attention, keeping one eye on the far doors. For all she knew, Ana Lucia would send security up to bounce her out, now that she was there without a precious member's permission. Hallie may be drunk, but she was nowhere near drunk enough for that. "Another margarita, please."

He didn't ask for ID. They never did here, just mixed the drinks and waited for their tips. Hallie scrabbled in her bag for the money.

"I've got this." A voice came from her left-hand side: a tanned, blond guy in his twenties wearing designer denim and an ultra-white smile. Hallie hesitated. Getting hit on was the last thing she wanted, but as if he could read her thoughts, the guy took a step back, glanced at her shoes, and gasped. "Are those Prada? Oh, sweetheart, you look *fierce*!"

Hallie relaxed. "Thanks!" she replied. "And for the drink too. I'm Hallie, by the way."

"Roger," he replied, pronouncing it like a European: Ro-ZHAIR. "And I know. I saw your scene over by the elevators with that skinny girl," he explained, rolling his eyes. "What a be-yatch!"

"Isn't she?" Hallie cried. "She calls me the user, when all along, she only wants access to Take Fountain, and a guy who couldn't care less about her!"

Roger tutted sympathetically. "People in this town are the worst," he agreed, laying a fifty down on the bar for their drinks. "They only use you to get what they want, and then, *BAM*, they're done with you. You can't let them get to you, they'll get what they deserve in the end."

"Yes! You're right." Hallie nodded at her kindred spirit. "You're so right."

"Why don't you come sit?" Roger nodded toward a free couch in the corner. "And tell Uncle Roger all about it."

Roger turned out to be the perfect audience to Hallie's woe: attentive, sympathetic, and full of disdain at the cruel and thoughtless way Dakota had treated her.

". . . and then he got in the car!" she finished, stifling a yawn. It was three a.m. and the lounge was emptying out now, but she was still ensconced in the corner with her new BFF and *his* BFF, a bleached blonde in her twenties with a raspy Brooklyn accent.

"Bastard!" Roger declared. "I can see it now: you standing proudly like Vivien Leigh in *Gone with the Wind.*"

Hallie nodded tiredly. Yes! Scarlett O'Hara. That was her all the way: dignified to the end.

"So Talia was right there?" the girl—Kay, Hallie thought she was called—asked, wide-eyed with interest. "Did she say anything?"

"Not to me." Hallie scowled. "She just ordered him to get in the car, like I wasn't even there. But I could tell, she knew exactly what was going on. You could see it in her eyes, she loved watching me suffer."

Kay and Roger shook their heads in dismayed unison.

"You know, you should get your side of the story out there," Roger suggested, resting one arm on the back of the couch behind Hallie.

"He's right." Kay leaned in from her other side. "No one even knows what you went through."

"To the world, you're just some crazy fan who made a scene outside his show."

"And he's the charming rock star who swept Talia off her feet," Kay finished, nodding. "People deserve to know the truth."

Hallie looked back and forth between them, the rapid motion making her dizzy. She reached for her drink, gulping down the weak dregs of melted ice. She frowned at the empty glass. "I think I should get going. . . ."

Roger squeezed her shoulder. "No way, the night is

still young! Another round!" He gestured to one of the roving waitresses before turning back. "So, what do you think?"

"About what?" Hallie tried to focus.

"Telling your story," Roger prompted.

Hallie was still blank. "I don't understand. Tell my story to who?"

There was a pause. Roger and Kay exchanged a look. "That's the great thing. See, I actually know some editors. . . ." Kay pulled a business card from her leopard-print purse. Hallie took it, squinting at the blurry print.

"You're a . . . journalist?" She froze.

"Writer," Kay corrected quickly. "Celebrity biographies, mainly, but I do some freelance work. It would be totally tasteful," she reassured Hallie. "Your story, some photos—"

"Professional hair and makeup, naturally," Roger interrupted.

"They'd make you look fabulous. Not that it's hard—look at you!" They laughed again, a high-pitched chorus, but this time, their voices sounded weird to Hallie: discordant.

Yup, definitely time to go.

Hallie tried to hand the card back. "No, thanks." She managed a smile. "It's not my thing."

"But we'd pay." Kay leaned in so close Hallie could see the places her lipstick had faded, leaving only the harsh red line around the edge of her mouth. "It could be a lot, depending on what you can give us."

"Give you . . . ?" Hallie echoed, penned in. Already,

she wished she'd left back when Ana Lucia had; that she'd never even come out tonight at all. How much had she been drinking? She wondered through a haze. And why was Kay looking at her with a hungry edge to her smile: all teeth, like she was about to take a bite out of her?

"Details. About Dakota," Kay pressed. "What kind of stuff is he into? Did you ever see him take drugs? Do you think he'd offer Talia drugs?"

"No, no, he's not like that." Hallie shook her head. Mistake. The room began to spin gently.

"Are you sure?" Roger asked.

"She's only just out of rehab," Kay added. "Did she look high when you saw her? Maybe with some white powder . . . ?" She wiped her nose meaningfully. "That's the kind of detail that would really raise your price."

Her price? The harsh word finally cut through Hallie's fog. That's what this was about? They thought she was as bad as Dakota: willing to sell out their relationship for the sake of some publicity, and an easy paycheck!

"If not drugs, then maybe sex?" Kay was still pressing, hand on Hallie's arm. "Did he like anything . . . different? Kinky. Threesomes—"

"Stop!" Hallie leaped up. The world lurched alarmingly, and she had to grab on to a nearby chair for support. "I don't care how much you're paying. I'm not doing any story!" She paused. That wasn't right. "It's not a story," she corrected, glaring at them. "It's my life!"

Hallie hurried away—or rather, stumbled. What kind of people were they: exploiting her pain for profit, preying on her in her moment of weakness? But she hadn't even reached the elevators before Kay and Roger caught up with her, pulling Hallie into a dim hallway away from the main floor.

"I don't think you understand." Their smiles had dropped: now Kay narrowed her eyes, calculating. "It's too late to walk away now."

"What do you mean?" Hallie backed up, but found herself against a damask-covered wall.

"You already told us everything. We don't need your permission, we can run with what we've got." Kay held up her cell phone—the same phone that had been sitting innocuously on the table all evening. She pressed a couple of buttons, and Hallie heard her own voice play back.

"You could see it in her eyes, she loved watching me suffer."

Hallie gasped. "I didn't . . . But . . . You set me up!" she cried.

"How?" Kay smirked. "You were the one pouring your heart out."

"But . . . you . . ." Hallie was lost for words. A moment ago, they'd been dripping honey, so sweet and supportive, but now she could practically see the dollar signs glowing in their eyes.

"It'll be OK," Roger reassured her. "Just do the interview, on the record, like a good girl. Otherwise . . ." He paused. "Well, maybe the story will turn out to be about them, and how they're being stalked by Dakota's psycho ex-girlfriend."

Hallie felt tears well up. "You wouldn't!"

"Stalkers sell copies." Kay shrugged. "Maybe we'd even put them on the cover. America loves a victim."

Hallie looked back and forth between them, her heart sinking. She was trapped, and it was her own stupid fault. Why had she trusted them? All the margaritas in the world couldn't excuse this mess. And what had she told them? Hallie couldn't even remember what she'd said ten minutes ago, let alone before that last round of shots. . . .

"It's up to you." Kay shrugged. "Cooperate, or see what it feels like to be the biggest joke in town. Your choice."

But it wasn't her choice, it never was! This whole year had been one long list of everyone else making important decisions, while she was left desperately trying to handle the fallout. Dakota chose to leave, her mom chose to move them to L.A., her father chose to drop dead on her . . . Hallie didn't get a say in any of it!

Well, no more!

Hallie drew herself up to her full height—four-inch heels and all—and stared down her nose at Kay. All her bitterness, and loneliness, and anger over the past year channeled into a beam of pure fury shot straight at them.

"No."

"Fine, then." Kay shrugged. "Psycho stalker it is."

Hallie looked around for her out, gaze landing on a table of empty glasses. There. "Was that a threat?" she asked, her voice like ice. "Because you've already been feeding me drinks all night—delinquency of a minor, isn't it? Coercion, maybe. And now blackmail? My uncle's lawyers will have fun with that one."

Kay and Roger didn't look so confident anymore.

"We still have your story." Kay brandished the phone. "You can't get out of that one."

"You think?" With one swift movement, Hallie snatched Kay's phone from her grip and dropped it on the floor; slamming her fabulous heel into the screen and grinding down until the whole gadget shattered. "Whoops!"

Kay gasped. "You didn't!"

"I did." Hallie glared at them. "And if anything I said to you ever comes up in print, my family will sue you so fast, you . . . you . . ." She tried to think of something suitably threatening, but her mind was still fuzzy. "You'll be sorry, that's all I can say."

She pushed past, and this time, they didn't follow. Hallie could hear them arguing furiously as she waited for the elevator.

"How could you let her take the recording?"

"What about you? You said she was drunk. Easy money, you said!"

Hallie grinned as the doors closed behind her. There! She wasn't just waiting around anymore, while other people made the big decisions. She was back in control, she was independent, she was—

Broke.

Hallie rifled through her purse as she stepped out into the lobby, but all she had was three dollars and a fetching shade of lip gloss. She groaned. It was way too late to call Grace, and she'd told Amber and her mom that she was sleeping over at Ana Lucia's. Even if she got a cab to take her back, would she even be able to dig up the cash once she got home?

Hallie pulled out her cell phone, and dialed.

VII

Brandon arrived in a half hour, his Jeep looking out of place in the line of Porsches and BMWs that slowly rolled through the valet stand. Hallie hopped up in the passenger side. "Thank you, thank you, thank you," she told him fervently. "I'm sorry, but I didn't know who else to call."

Brandon shrugged. He looked like he'd just rolled out of bed: gray sweatpants, and a dark zip-up hoodie open over a Disney T. "It's OK, I couldn't sleep."

He passed her a bottle of water, then popped the cap on a pack of Advil, handing Hallie two pills. "It's better to take them now, before the hangover kicks in tomorrow," he advised with a wry smile, shifting the car back into drive and easing out of the exit.

"How could you tell?" Hallie gulped them back. The wooziness had worn off waiting for him to come, now she just felt empty; a metallic edge to her nerves.

"Four in the morning, scraping you off the floor at some club?" Brandon looked amused. "Sure, you've been hanging out drinking hot cocoa and knitting."

Hallie managed a smile. She curled up in the seat and took a long breath as they turned back onto Sunset Boulevard, bright with billboards and headlights. It felt like she'd been in that club for a lifetime, bouncing between insincere smiles and vicious bitchy showdowns, and now, now, her head was finally clear. She rested her cheek against the cool glass, watching the city slip by.

"I didn't say welcome back." Brandon glanced over as they paused at a red light. "Did you have a good time in New York?"

"Not at all." Hallie sighed. "Dakota . . ." She paused, embarrassed. "We kind of—"

"It's OK." Brandon cut her off. "Amber came over to gossip with my mom. I kind of overheard. . . ."

"Oh." Hallie flushed. "Yeah, it didn't really go the way I planned."

"Sorry," Brandon offered, with another awkward smile. "I know you wanted to make it work."

"Understatement," Hallie agreed. "But, maybe it was for the best, to have it thrown in my face like that. I mean, at least I know it's over now. For real, this time." She gazed out of the window—they were heading down into Beverly Hills now, but Hallie felt something pull her in the other direction, back up into the hills.

"Would you mind if we made a detour?" she asked suddenly. "I know it's late—"

"You mean, early."

"Sorry," Hallie said again. She knew she should just head home, and not test Brandon's chivalry any further, but there was a restlessness still in her veins; a sharp itch she needed to set to rest. "It won't take long, I promise. It's just, that way." She pointed behind them.

Brandon looked at her for a moment, then sighed. "You're lucky I'm an insomniac," he told her, pulling a U-turn in the middle of the street.

They parked off the side of the road, up on Mulholland where Dakota had taken Hallie that first night, a lifetime ago. She left Brandon by the car and made her way out to the edge of the cliff, shucking off her shoes so she was barefoot on the gravel and rocks.

Hallie gazed down at the snaking lights of the freeway and felt an unexpected calm. It was all still here. The sprawling, glittering grid; the dark horizon. Dakota may be gone, but all of this—the world—was still right there like it had always been.

Just because she'd built all her dreams with him beside her, it didn't mean she couldn't go on and make them come true on her own.

"Hey." Brandon's hand was tight on her arm. "Watch the edge."

"Why?" Hallie laughed. "You think I'm going to throw myself off or something?"

There was a pause.

"I don't know," Brandon replied, his expression even. "Would you?"

"No!" Hallie spluttered. "I would never . . ." Her protest died as she took in the calm set of his face. "I wouldn't!" She tried again to reassure him. "Really!"

Brandon nodded slowly, but the grip on her arm didn't loosen until Hallie drew back from the cliff edge.

She stood there, shaken, suddenly remembering every time she'd claimed she'd die without Dakota; every desperate sob that life wasn't worth living without him. Hallie was horrified. When had she become the girl who talked like that?

And, worse still, when had she become a girl who would even *consider* it?

"It's late," Brandon told her. He slipped off his hoodie and draped it over her shoulders. "We should get back."

Brandon headed for the Jeep, but Hallie lingered a moment, thinking back over the last months of listless wallowing with fresh shame. All the time that had slipped past; all the agony Hallie had clung to—holding on for dear life, as if her misery were somehow noble. As if weeping for hours in a dark room were the only way to make her wretched love mean anything at all.

She hadn't been the brave heroine, in the play of her life. She'd been the fool.

Hallie finally joined Brandon back in the car. "I need you to know, I wouldn't do anything like that," she told him. "I know I said some stuff . . . but I was just being dramatic. I didn't mean it. I promise."

He nodded, but didn't start the engine; instead, he sat in silence, staring straight out into the valley. She could tell he wanted to say something, so Hallie waited, seconds ticking past before he finally cleared his throat.

"I thought about it," he said in a low voice, still not looking at her. "When I first got back. When I was out, surfing sometimes." Brandon paused. "A wave would break over me," he told her, "and I'd think about not swimming. Just, going under."

Hallie caught her breath. His tone was so matter-of-fact, but that was Brandon all over: he didn't exaggerate, or make a scene, even when his words were the most dramatic thing she could imagine. Hallie instinctively reached to cover his hand with hers. "What stopped you?" she asked quietly.

Brandon shrugged. "A bunch of stuff. My family, the guys we lost out there. They would have kicked my ass for even thinking about it." He gave her a wry smile. "In the end, I guess it was just . . . hope. That I wouldn't always feel that way. That the world would start making sense again."

Hallie nodded slowly. "And does it?"

Brandon glanced down at their hands, then back to her. "Sometimes."

Hallie looked at him, really looked: the square of his jaw beneath the five-day stubble, the harsh red line of his scar. For the first time, she recognized his quiet self-possession: not creepy, or unnerving, but something stronger. A hard-won calm after the storm.

"Good," she said, giving his hand a brief squeeze before releasing it. "I mean, who else would come get me from my . . . knitting parties?"

Brandon laughed. "Sure. Priorities."

"Exactly." Hallie smiled, just to cover her shame. Priorities. She hadn't had any; she'd been so deep in self-pity, she hadn't seen anything at all. She changed the subject quickly. "And don't forget Amber's big plans for the holidays. She's talking about some Hanukkah-slash-Kwanzaa party, with a ten-piece carol choir and a hog roast stuffed inside an ox. You want to be around for that."

"It's the simple things, that make life worth living," Brandon quipped back. Hallie gave him a look to let him know she didn't mean all this joking; that she understood the weight of what he shared. Brandon nodded slightly, then started the ignition. "You won't say anything, will you, about—?"

"No!" Hallie exclaimed. "I promise, that's just between us. And if you ever need to talk," she added, "I'm here. Anytime."

"Right next door." Brandon smiled slightly.

"Exactly," Hallie agreed, surprised to find that thought reassuring. "Right next door."

VIII

After all the drama of New York and her return to L.A., Hallie was relieved to find Christmas and New Year's pass uneventfully—save, of course, for Amber and Auggie's blowout holiday party. Two hundred of their closest friends crammed the house and backyard, partying until dawn under the vast swathes of Christmas lights and inflatable reindeer perched on every square foot of roof.

Hallie didn't mind. It was good to be surrounded by noise and laughter—rather than stuck alone wondering what exclusive party Ana Lucia hadn't invited her to. Besides, half those friends of Auggie's turned out to be producers and casting agents, who offered Hallie their cards the minute Amber started gushing about what a talent she was, and about how she had *just this very minute* decided to try her hand at acting.

"You don't have to say that." Hallie pulled Amber aside, embarrassed. Ana Lucia's comments were still burned in her memory; the last thing she wanted was to make a nuisance of herself. "Please, let's not even talk about me acting at all. These are your friends."

"Exactly!" Amber cried, flushed and tipsy as the party whirled on around them. She wore a silver-sequined minidress, reflecting the holiday lights like a walking mirror ball. "And I bet every one of them got where they are today because someone helped them starting out."

Hallie wavered. "Are you sure? I don't want to make things weird, or uncomfortable—"

"Honey, no!" Amber cried. "You're doing *them* the favor. They're all looking to find the next big thing. Trust me!"

So Hallie let Amber sweep her off on another round of the party, throwing her in the path of every available agent and manager she could find, until Hallie was weighed down with a confetti of business cards.

It felt good, Hallie realized, to have some purpose again, and as the weeks passed, and she chased down her new leads—turning e-mails into meetings, into afternoons spent waiting in the bland back hallways of every audition in town—she was reminded again just how much she had let fade away in the face of her grief over Dakota.

What had she been *doing*?

It had been her mistake too, she could see that now: not the end, but everything that came after. The further Hallie got from it, the clearer it became, like those paintings that are just a blur up close but take on new shape and meaning from across the room. Sure, it still hurt; she still missed him, but when his absence hit her at night with a hollow ache in her chest, Hallie climbed on out of bed and went to watch TV with Brandon, or pulled out her latest audition script to memorize. She didn't sit around, thinking about the time they spent together, anymore. No, the key was not to think of him at all.

"How'd it go?" Grace met her at the door after Hallie's latest audition.

"Good!" Hallie dumped her bag and kicked off the heels Amber had insisted she wear. "Socialites-slash-cat-burglars don't wear sneakers!" she'd cried, and she'd been right: the waiting room had been filled with girls in their best stilettos. Hallie massaged her poor arches. "Actually, I think I nailed it, but you never know."

"This was for that cable crime show, right? Dead Sorority Girl Number Three?" Grace followed Hallie into the kitchen, where she made straight for the fridge full of—yes!—cold pot roast and Rosa's famous cheesecake.

"No, that was this morning," Hallie replied, her mouth already full. "This was the big one, it's one of the main parts on a new heist show. I wasn't even supposed to be there, but Amber does her strip-hop dance class with one of the executives' wives and managed to get me in for a first read." She collapsed at the table and began to eat, straight from the Tupperware containers. God, that was good! The months she'd spent limply wasting away, barely eating a thing, were a distant dream. If there was one thing she could say for sure about mental health, it made her *hungry.*

"And a first read . . . ?" Grace joined Hallie at the table, pushing aside the stack of Amber's magazines. Hallie forgot, her sister didn't read the trades like she did.

"Is like the very first stage," Hallie explained. "Then you get callbacks, until you make the short list, then cast reads—where they have you try out with the other people they've already hired—and then you get test shoots, in front of the camera. And then, if you're still in the game, you read for the producers and network heads."

"Wow." Grace blinked. "That's . . . a long process."

"Yup." Hallie scooped up a spoonful of creamy topping. "But I made it to the third round of callbacks on the last thing I went out for, remember that cough syrup ad?"

"The taste to chase your tickles away," Grace quoted. "You were saying nothing else for two days straight. Believe me, it's burned into my brain,"

Hallie laughed. Sure, these weren't the Oscar-worthy roles of her dreams she was trying out for, but everyone had to start somewhere. These were the bit parts that would get her an agent, which would get her speaking roles with more than five seconds of screen time. Who knew? By the end of the year, she might even have more than ten lines of dialogue in a major network show!

Grace glanced absently at the pile of magazines, then froze.

"What?" Hallie asked.

"Nothing!" Grace yelped, flipping the magazine over.

Hallie sighed. "It's OK. I know they went to that

premiere of hers together. The photos are all over the Internet."

Grace looked at her cautiously. "You can talk about it, if you want. You haven't really said anything for a while about . . . him."

Hallie rolled her eyes. "You can say his name. Or just call him the Heartless Sellout with No Soul. Either way, talking won't help. Double-double-chocolate cheesecake, on the other hand . . ." She took another mouthful. "What about you? Have you heard from Theo since New York?"

There was a pause. Grace took a spoon, carved out a chunk of dessert, and then shook her head, mouth full. "Lucy's e-mailed a bunch of times, though," she said, swallowing. "You know she quit to go work for Portia? Portia looooves her theories on organic early-childhood education. They're practically new BFFs."

"Bitch."

Grace didn't disagree.

"So what now?" Hallie asked.

Grace shrugged. "I don't know. Back to normal, I guess. School. Work. Friends. The usual." She glanced at her phone. "I should go meet Palmer. We're going to go see a movie at the Grove, maybe get some food." She paused, looking at Hallie again. "You can come, if you want?"

Hallie waved her off. "I'm fine. Go, have fun."

Alone, she turned her attention back to the pressing issue in front of her: cheesecake. But the lure of those magazines was too much, and despite her every instinct, Hallie found herself reaching for them. Dakota's face stared back at her from the glossy cover of the latest *Us Weekly.* TALIA'S NEW LOVE HEATS UP! the headline screamed, above a photo of them together on the red carpet. Dakota looked dashing and hot, and Talia was gazing up at him with such a giddy expression of bliss that Hallie had to hurl it through the open French doors into the backyard so she didn't have to look at them another moment longer.

There was a muffled yelp, and then a crash.

"Hello?" Hallie went outside to investigate, and found Brandon collecting a box of small canisters, now scattered over the lawn. "Oh, sorry. I didn't know you were out here."

Brandon laughed. "You sure it's not just payback for making you watch *Hellfire 3*?"

"There was no plot!" Hallie cried, for what felt like the fifth time since going to the movies with him. "It was just two hours of stuff blowing up!"

"Yeah, well, what did you want us to see, that French thing?" Brandon curled his lip. "I don't do subtitles."

"Philistine," Hallie declared, helping him pick up the canisters.

"Snob," he teased back. She shook her head in despair.

"One of these days, you're going to raise your cultural awareness higher than robots and zombies." Hallie straightened up, handing him the final roll. "What are you doing with all this . . . ?"

"Film," Brandon finished. He showed her the box,

full of canisters like the ones Hallie remembered from when she was a kid, and cameras came with film and negatives and trips to the drugstore, instead of digital memory cards and USB cables. "I've been taking a bunch of new shots," he explained. "Now I get to spend the week in the darkroom, getting high off chemical mixes." There was a pause. "That was a joke."

"Duh." Hallie weighed a roll in her palm, amused. They'd been hanging out more, but Brandon was still awkward sometimes, fumbling his words or jolting if she brushed against him. She guessed he wasn't used to people these days, period: Amber said that when he came back from Iraq, he barely left the house for months. "Can I come see your stuff?" Hallie asked hopefully. "It's OK if you don't want to," she added quickly. Brandon hadn't offered to show her yet, and she knew some of it might be personal. "But, you did always say you'd help me with my headshots. . . ."

To her relief, Brandon didn't seem reluctant. "Admit it," he teased. "You want to see if I'm up to the job."

"Well, sure." Hallie smiled back. "I need to have complete creative synchronicity with my artist."

"I don't even know what that means." Brandon laughed. "But sure, step into my office. . . ."

He led her across to the far side of Amber and Auggie's house, and a small side door that led into a windowless passage. Hallie looked around at the unfamiliar walls. "What is this place? I can't believe I've never been out here."

"Servants' quarters, storage, I don't know." Brandon

opened another door into a small, dark room. He flipped on a lone lightbulb, revealing trays laid out on a bench, and walls lined with shelves of chemicals and paper. Photographs hung across the room, pegged to a laundry line. "Auggie had it light-proofed a few years back, but no one ever used it, so he said I was welcome."

Hallie reached up to look at the photos, drying on the line. The line nearest to her was a series from the beach. Surfers preparing for the waves: pulling on wet suits, waxing down their boards. Brandon had captured their focus, a calm concentration painted in black and white against the far gray sky. "These are good!" she exclaimed.

Brandon gave her a twisted smile. "Don't sound so surprised."

"I'm not! I mean"—Hallie caught herself—"OK, I am. But come on: everyone calls themselves a photographer these days. They just point and snap, and post everything online."

"But there's so much more to it than that. Here." Brandon set down his box and pulled out an old-school camera with all kinds of knobs and settings. He passed it to her, almost reverently. "See, this is a Pentax, from the eighties."

Hallie held it up to look through the viewfinder at him. For a moment she was caught, looking into his eyes. They were a dark shade of blue Hallie had never noticed before, almost gray. . . .

She lowered the camera quickly. "It still works?"

"Sure. These things last forever, if you take care

of them. The hard part is finding the film," Brandon explained. He took the camera back, and showed her how to twist the lens to focus. "I get it off auction sites online, and at estate sales around town. Last month, I found a whole lot of untouched film: sealed, no damp, nothing."

He snapped the cover shut, and handed it back to Hallie. "Go on, take something."

"Now?" Hallie paused, the camera an unfamiliar weight in her hand. "OK . . ." She held it up quickly and snapped a shot of Brandon before he had a chance to cover his face.

"Not me!"

"Why not?" Hallie kept clicking. She had to wind the film between shots, and only got in a couple more before he took the camera back.

"I'm not that kind of guy," he said, and under the harsh light, Hallie could swear he was blushing. "I don't like being the center of things. I'm more a behind-the-scenes kind of guy."

"I think that's a good thing," Hallie decided, hopping up on one of the counters. He started shooting her, and she struck a pose, blowing kisses until the film ran out. "I mean, people who want to be in the spotlight, they have this hunger, you know? Like they'll do anything to make it, even if it means crossing the line."

"Oh, yeah?" Brandon raised an eyebrow.

"Not me!" Hallie protested. "But, you know, people."

"I know." Brandon looked at her carefully, so carefully that Hallie shifted, uncomfortable.

"What?"

"Nothing." He turned back to the camera. "Just, you seem different now."

"Different bad or different good?"

Brandon smiled. "We'll see. Now, turn off the light, we have to do this next part in pitch-black, so we don't wreck the film."

Hallie stayed in the darkroom for the rest of the day, watching as thin spools of negatives were transformed into actual prints under Brandon's careful hands. "We made them, from scratch!" she exclaimed, delighted, looking at the final print of her photos of Brandon.

He groaned, trying to snatch them away. "You can't keep those! The exposure's all wrong, and the focus is smudged—"

Hallie held them close to her chest, out of reach. "But they're mine!" She paused, looking around the tiny room, pictures dangling at every turn. "It's pretty cool, what you do here: taking moments and making them last."

Brandon looked bashful. "My therapist says it's supposed to remind me how everything is fleeting, but that doesn't mean it isn't real, in the moment, you know?"

"I know." Boy, did she know.

Hallie followed him out onto the back lawn. It was dark now, she was surprised to see, the house silent in the glow of the security lights. "I guess nobody's home. Amber said something about a charity thing. . . ."

"Want to come over?" Brandon suggested. "We could get pizza and watch something."

"You mean, *Hellfire 4*?" Hallie grinned.

He laughed. "Nope. That doesn't come out until next year. You can pick."

"Ooh." Hallie clapped, heading around to the front of the house. "There's that new Russian movie . . . or did you see *The Artist*? It's a French movie—"

"No subtitles!"

"There aren't any, silly," she reassured him, with an evil grin. "It's a black-and-white silent movie!"

Brandon stopped dead.

"It's good, I promise," Hallie told him. "It won a bunch of Oscars, and . . ."

The words died on her lips. Standing in the driveway, with his hands in the pockets of his leather jacket, was the one face she'd never expected to see.

Dakota.

"Hey," he said, with that familiar smile. "Brandon." Dakota gave him the guy nod. "How's it going, man?"

Brandon didn't respond. He was frozen next to Hallie, tension radiating from his body as he glared at Dakota. Dakota stared back, his expression changing as he looked from Brandon to Hallie and back again.

Hallie nudged Brandon, breaking the face-off. "You go ahead," she told him. "I'll be over in a minute."

He gave her a searching look. "You sure?"

Hallie nodded. "Order extra-crispy," she said, amazed to find her voice emerge steady and sure. "But no—"

"Anchovies," Brandon finished, finally relaxing. "Got it." He glared one last time at Dakota and then sauntered past.

Dakota cleared his throat. "So . . ." he started, moving closer. "Hey."

Hallie stared back evenly. "Hey." She expected a rush of feeling—anger, longing, regret, *something*—but instead, she felt nothing. Nothing! As if the months of pained longing and fervent sobs had burned all her emotion away.

"You guys look pretty friendly." Dakota tried a teasing smile. "Is there something going on I should know about?"

"I don't think so," Hallie said coolly. "I don't think you have the right to know anything about my life anymore."

Dakota's smile dropped. "I guess I deserve that," he said quietly.

Hallie sighed. "What are you doing here?"

"We're back in L.A. now," Dakota explained, "doing final mixes and promo for the album."

"And going to movie premieres."

He looked away. "Yeah. I'm, sorry about that. I wanted to warn you, about the photos, and events, but—"

"It's fine." Hallie bit out the words. "It's nothing to do with me anymore."

Dakota looked back at her, eyes full of something she could swear was regret. "I never meant . . ." He trailed off. "What I mean is . . . I'm sorry, about the way everything went down. I should never have treated you like that, or even ended it at all."

Hallie was still trying to process those last words, when Dakota stepped forward. "You have to know," he said, pleading, "it wasn't because I stopped loving you. Hallie . . ." He clutched her hand. "Things just got so confusing, and then the label, and Talia . . ." He held on, as if for dear life. "Please, I loved you. I still do."

Hallie stood there, still numb. His words seemed to drift somewhere, just out of reach—not connecting, not making her feel anything at all. But that made sense, she realized, looking at that face that had consumed her every thought since the night she first laid eyes on it—nothing so desperate as the way she'd felt about him could ever last for long. She'd exhausted every last ounce of love for this boy, blazing through it like a wildfire, and now Hallie was left with nothing more than a small, empty place in her heart where he used to be.

It was over.

Hallie sighed, feeling the last breath of devotion leave her body. "I hope it's worth it," she said quietly. "I hope you picked right."

Dakota's face seemed to slip for a moment. His eyes were pained, and as his hand held on tight to hers, the touch took Hallie back: to those nights driving around downtown, her fingers laced between his.

Nothing else in the world had mattered. She'd belonged to him, completely.

That was the problem.

"Good-bye."

Hallie kissed him gently on the cheek, and walked away.

PART FIVE: *Spring*

I

It was March; the tree-lined streets of Beverly Hills were bright with blossoms, and Grace was turning seventeen.

"Are you sure you don't want a party?" Amber asked hopefully as they sat over coffee in the sun-drenched kitchen. "Just something small. A hundred people, top DJs, a cake in the shape of the periodic table . . . You know, intimate!"

Grace shook her head vigorously. After the dramas of the past year, she would have happily chosen a quiet evening in with a book, but Amber, she suspected, would keel over at that suggestion. "I want to keep it simple," Grace said instead. "Just family, and maybe Palmer."

"And Brandon too," Amber added, with a meaningful grin.

Grace turned, following her gaze out to the back lawn, where their neighbor sat running lines with Hallie. It looked like a death scene, but every time Hallie fell to the grass in her final writhings, Brandon would say something, or poke her with his toe, and Hallie would fall about in hysterics.

"She looks happy," Grace said, the knot of worry she kept for her sister loosening another notch. Since the day Dakota had come by, they hadn't heard another word about him. Now Hallie was taking acting classes, and booking jobs, and making plans to move out; passing newsstands plastered with updates of his love affair without a second glance.

"She sure is." Amber turned back. "But what about you? Are you sure you don't want a big blowout? We could book out a restaurant, and get a band you like to come play—"

"No!" Grace cried again. "Small. Simple. A family dinner, or a beach picnic. Promise?"

Amber sighed, pouting.

"I mean it," Grace warned her. "I hate surprises. The last thing I want is to walk in and find half my class at school pretending like they're my best friends. I'll turn around and walk right out."

"Fine," Amber agreed reluctantly. "I promise. But I'm taking you for a girl's day out, pampering at the salon, and there's nothing you can do to stop me!"

Grace's birthday dawned warm and sunny, and—after Grace spent five solid hours being pummeled, smeared, straightened, and polished by Amber's team of quasi-sadistic spa experts—a caravan of cars wound their way out to the Malibu shore.

"This is your idea of simple?" Grace laughed, as Auggie and Brandon struggled to unload a trunk full of gourmet foods, complete with wicker picnic baskets and matching designer blankets.

"But it is!" Amber protested, wide-eyed. She had a silk scarf wrapped over her hair, and a bright-pink bikini under her sheer white cover-up. "I only had them pack three different freshly squeezed juices, and two flavors of cake!"

"Don't listen to her," Hallie interrupted, passing their mom a stack of pillows. "This is fabulous!"

"That's because you're not carrying it all." Brandon staggered past them toward the beach path. Hallie let out a noise of protest.

"These blankets are pure wool cashmere. They're *heavy*!" she cried, following him.

"It is OK, isn't it?" Amber looked distressed, surveying the bags of bone china and silverware. "I know I got a little carried away with the decor, but I wanted it to be special—"

"I'm just teasing," Grace reassured her, with a hug. "It's perfect. Thank you!"

Grace fell back with Palmer as their motley crew headed through the lagoons to the beach. "It's so nice out here, with the hills, and the ocean . . ." She took a deep breath. "How did you find it?"

"Jesús showed it to me last year." Palmer grinned. "There are tons of private places to stop and—"

"Eww, enough!" Grace quickly cut her off.

Palmer gave her a withering stare. "I was going to say, share a chaste kiss."

"Sure you were." Grace laughed. Palmer and Jesús hooked up for a while after Harry's party, until Palmer decided that even a casual, no-strings kind of dating was too much of a demand on her time. The star tours were still going strong, and she'd been talking about adding a handbag line to her portfolio—apparently there being piles of Italian leather goods waiting to be imported, and sold to the fashion-hungry girls of L.A. at ridiculous markups.

"So . . ." Palmer began meaningfully, when Amber and Valerie disappeared around the next bend. "Any word?"

"Nope." Grace hugged her box of glasses to her chest and kept walking.

"Aww, I'm sorry."

Grace shrugged. "He hasn't contacted me since before Christmas, why should he start now?"

"Because it's your birthday." Palmer gave her a sympathetic look. "And if he doesn't call, then he's a stupid selfish asswipe who deserves that stuck-up British bitch."

Grace cracked a smile. "You never even met Lucy."

"And that matters?" Palmer paused to kick off her flip-flops as they rounded the last corner and emerged onto the fine golden sand of the secluded beach. "She hurt you, and you're my friend, thus by the laws of polite society, I get to call her a bitch. But, I am sorry. It's his loss."

Grace shrugged. "There was never anything to lose," she said, not able to hide the wistful note in her voice. She shook her head quickly; this wasn't the day for pining, not with two flavors of cake and a vast array of fresh-squeezed juices to enjoy. "Come on, I need to set this box down before something breaks!"

They basked for hours in the afternoon sun: making toasts, and tossing Frisbees, and eating more cake than Grace thought possible. Her mom wandered off with her paint set to capture the "magnificence of nature, unkempt"; Amber slathered on her sunscreen; and Auggie slept blissfully under the shade of his half-read book.

Grace relaxed, her eyes closed and toes buried in the sun-warmed sand. She could hear the steady roll of the ocean, and Hallie's cries of protest as she lost her game of boccie to Brandon; Auggie's intermittent snores on her other side. A wash of contentment slipped over her; an even, steady calm.

This was it, she realized. Home. Her family. The world that had splintered into so many new directions had reformed into something bright and enduring. Her year of pained, fearful change was done.

She didn't have to worry anymore.

"Grace!" A boccie ball thudded against her foot, and Grace sat up to find Hallie waving to her from the water's edge. "Come, swim!"

"No, thanks!" Grace called back. Palmer and Brandon were already splashing in the shallows, their laughter carrying on the breeze. "You guys go ahead!"

But Hallie didn't. Instead, she jogged over and pulled Grace to her feet. "Come on!"

"But it's cold!" Grace protested. "And your hair—"

"You've got to stop this watching from the sidelines," Hallie told her. "It's your birthday! You've got to *do* something!"

Grace hesitated. But Hallie was right. In one swift move, Grace stripped off the sundress covering her bikini and raced toward the water, shrieking as the cold waves broke around her legs. But it was too late to back out; Grace plunged on, until her whole body was submerged.

"See!" Hallie laughed, treading water beside her in the shallows. "Isn't it *gorgeous*?"

Grace grinned. It was. Behind them, the lagoons nestled beneath the hills; the whole coastline stretching in a haze of golden sand and blue, blue water. She swam lazily, flipping onto her back as Hallie let out a contented sigh.

"Every time I'm out here, I feel like . . . I don't know, like there's something bigger." Hallie looked over at Grace, her expression thoughtful. "Maybe we could come out again next month. For Dad."

"Sure. I mean, if you want. I didn't think you'd want to do anything." It would be the anniversary of their father's death—a day Grace wished she didn't have to mark, but knew she must, all the same.

"Sarabeth says I need rituals, to help the grieving process," Hallie explained.

Sarabeth was Hallie's new therapist. Grace still couldn't believe her sister was going to therapy at all, let alone talking about their father, but it seemed to be helping. Her tantrums and crying jags had dwindled, and now, Grace could even have a reasoned argument over who got control of the remote without Hallie storming off and slamming doors.

"You don't have to come," Hallie said quickly. "I mean, if you want time to remember him alone."

"No." Grace gave her a small smile. "That sounds nice. We'll do it together."

They drifted there awhile longer, until their fingertips puckered and the cold was finally too much. Palmer met them on the shore with a hopeful look. "Want to go get gelato?"

Grace groaned. "Are you crazy? I can barely even float, I ate so much."

Hallie brightened. "Wait, is this the place across the street?" Palmer nodded. "Oh, we have to go. This place is, like, the *best* in the whole world!"

"So . . . full . . ." Grace murmured.

"It melts into liquid," Palmer protested as they arrived back at their camp. "It's like having a drink of water."

"See?" Hallie agreed. "Science!"

"Oh, my God!"

They all looked up at Amber's cry. She was clutching her cell phone, eyes wide with shock. "I don't believe it! Oh, Grace!"

"What's happened?" Grace asked. "Is everything OK?"

"No!" Amber cried. "Missy just texted. That Lucy girl, her old nanny, she's run off to Vegas. Eloped! With Theo!"

They all gasped.

Grace felt faint. Her legs seemed to fold under of their own accord, depositing her onto the blanket with a thump.

"That's crazy, she must have it wrong." Palmer quickly sat next to her, voice full of scorn. Hallie agreed, squeezing Grace's shoulder.

Grace gulped. "She said they were in love," she offered, feeling a terrible ache. Of course Theo hadn't called—not when he was off getting married. Married! At nineteen! He must really be in love with her.

"Uh-huh." Hallie pulled out her cell phone and began typing. "I don't believe it. Even Theo isn't stupid enough to do something like that."

"Check his profile," Palmer suggested.

"Already there." Hallie clicked onscreen. "Ha! See? Status: single." She held it up as evidence.

But Grace wasn't going to cling to false hope. "He wouldn't have time to change it," she said, miserable. In an instant, all her happiness and contentment had been ripped away, and by what? Confirmation of something she'd known for months already. It was foolish. "He's probably been too busy dealing with wedding stuff, and the honeymoon . . ."

Oh, God. Grace wasn't even going to go there.

Hallie kept clicking. "No, don't give me that face. You don't get to cry until there's absolute proof that—" She stopped, and let out a cackle of laughter. "There!" Hallie shoved her cell phone in Grace's face. "Told you!"

Grace blinked at the screen. It was Hallie's newsfeed,

full of updates from her friends and family. "What? I don't see it."

"Lucy's photostream from Vegas. She didn't marry Theo," Hallie declared, gleeful. "She married Rex!"

"Theo's brother?" Palmer asked. "But I thought you said he was . . ."

"Gay! I know!" Hallie pulled Grace into a hug. "See? It's OK! Whatever's going on here, it has nothing to do with Theo. He's not married, and he's definitely not with Lucy anymore! He's free!"

Grace caught her breath, reeling. In barely three minutes, she'd plunged from joy, to misery, and back again, and now the relief was almost too much to take—a sharp thunder of adrenaline in her veins. She clambered to her feet, unsteady.

"I have to go." Grace took another breath, lightheaded, and then said it louder. "I have to go. Now. To Stanford. Where are the keys?"

Hallie shrieked in delight. "Yes! Oh, my God, road trip!"

"I'm in!" Palmer exclaimed.

"No." Grace scrambled for her bag, pulling her dress back on. "I have to do this on my own, I—"

"Will chicken out the minute you get past Santa Barbara," Hallie interrupted. "Are you kidding? Of course I'm going to come. Brandon!" she yelled. "Brandon!"

"I'm right here." He was behind them.

"Oh, OK. Get your stuff," Hallie ordered. "We're taking Grace to Theo."

Brandon raised an eyebrow.

"Please!" Hallie wheedled. "It's true love! You can't stand in the way!"

"It's six hours on the freeway."

"And you drive so *masterfully.*" Hallie beamed.

He sighed good-naturedly. "One of these days, I'm going to have to teach you how to drive."

"Stop!" Grace yelled, interrupting them all. They turned. "You've got it wrong," she insisted. "I just need to talk to him, that's all. Alone."

There was a beat.

"We can get the gelato before we go, it's right by the gas station." Palmer hoisted her purse.

"Great idea," Hallie cried. "Road snacks!"

"You girls take my credit card," Amber added, digging in her wallet. "You'll need someplace to stay, and I'm not having you at one of those roach-motel places."

"And no backseat driving," Brandon warned. "My wheels, my rules."

Hallie giggled. "Isn't he so cute when he gets all dour and manly?"

"Come on!" Palmer called, already ahead by the path. "It's a long way to Stanford!"

Grace sighed. She wasn't sure whether to scream, or hug them for being such good friends. She suspected hugging would be easier.

"Fine!" Grace told them, as if she'd ever really had a choice. "But I call shotgun!"

II

Hallie turned out to be right. By the time they cleared Malibu city limits, Grace was already having second thoughts; as they cruised past San Luis Obispo, she was begging them to turn back; and by the time they headed up past San Jose and turned into the campus itself, Grace knew without a doubt that this was the most foolish, reckless, doomed-to-humiliation thing she'd ever done.

"Well, quite possibly, yes," Palmer told her, in what Grace supposed was a comforting voice. "But we're here now! Remember why you decided to come at all."

"A brief mental break?" Grace replied, looking around at the sprawl of Spanish-style buildings, their red-tile roofs lit up under streetlights and spotlights. It was almost midnight, but the campus was still lively—students heading out to parties, or returning to their dorms. Grace swallowed. Her elation at discovering that Theo was not, in fact, joined in holy matrimony had faded a while back. About a hundred miles ago. "Guys, this is a really bad idea. . . ."

"Exactly." Hallie reached forward from the backseat and gave Grace's shoulder a squeeze. "But when was the last time you went running off on some random quest, or cared enough to risk everything? Never! This bad idea could be the best idea you ever had."

Grace didn't quite follow her logic, but it was too late: Brandon was pulling up outside an ivy-covered residence hall. "Roble Hall . . . that's him, right?"

Grace didn't move. "What am I supposed to do, just march in there and tell him how I feel?"

"Pretty much." They all nodded.

"Brandon, you're the sane one." She turned to him, pleading. "Tell them this is crazy."

"Hey, I'm just the driver!" He softened, looking at her clearly panicked face. "Do it like a Band-Aid: just rip it off, fast. Then, at least, it'll be done."

Fast. Painful. That sounded about right.

"But what will he say?"

Brandon gave her a rueful look. "Does it matter?"

Grace stared. Did it matter? She was about to go pledge her affection for a guy who hadn't even bothered to e-mail in months, who might turn around and run—or, worse still, laugh in her face! Of course it mattered!

And yet . . .

No. It didn't. Grace realized with a shock that the reason she'd come all this way, the reason she'd even wanted to in the first place, didn't have anything to do with what happened after she told Theo how she felt. The only thing that mattered was that she tell him. Finally.

Grace took a breath and reached for the door handle. "I'm going in."

"She's going in!" Palmer cheered.

"I saw a café-slash-juice-bar-type-place just back around the corner," Hallie told her. "Come meet us there after. Or, you know, bring Theo along." She winked.

"Uh-huh." Grace stumbled down from the car and paused a moment, looking up at the building. This must be how pro athletes felt, trying to psych themselves up for the big game. Or those men who ran with the bulls in Spain: embarking on a reckless mission that may well end in bloody, painful death.

"You can do it!" Palmer called.

She could. Do this.

Oh, God.

Grace hurried up the steps, slipping into the building behind a group of girls in matching team sweatshirts. She waited for the elevators with them, her skin prickling; never so glad that nobody could see the hot flush that was spread across her face. Theo lived on the third floor, and too soon, Grace was standing outside his room.

She raised her hand to knock, then lowered it. He might not even be in. He could be in the library, studying, or out with friends, or even some other girl—

Grace knocked. There was a pause, and then the door swung open.

"Grace?" Theo gaped at her.

Grace felt a pang. He looked exactly how she'd been remembering him: glasses, a college sweatshirt, and striped pajama bottoms; chestnut hair sticking up in unruly tufts.

"What . . . ? How . . . ? I mean, hi." He finally recovered, standing back from the door. "Sorry, come in. I'm just . . . surprised to see you."

"Me too." Grace followed him into the small single room, her heart racing. It was earnestly neat: no posters or clutter, just a stacked bookcase, some ficus, and a framed Rothko print. Theo swiftly kicked some laundry under the bed and straightened his duvet.

"So, hey," he said again, loitering awkwardly in the middle of the room. "How are you? Is everything OK?" His eyes widened with sudden concern.

"Yes!" Grace said quickly. "Everyone's fine. No emergency, I promise."

"Oh." He exhaled. "Good."

There was silence.

This was it, Grace told herself. Time to rip the Band-Aid. Just a few short words, and she'd be done. Hell, she could even turn and run right after if she wanted.

"I, umm, heard about Rex," she said instead, drifting closer to the desk. "And Lucy."

"You did?" Theo seemed to brighten, or maybe that was just Grace's imagination. "It was all pretty sudden.

I've been on the phone all day with everyone. Portia's in meltdown."

"What happened?" Grace perched on the desk chair, swiveling back and forth. "I mean, really."

Theo sank onto the edge of the bed. "Honestly, I don't even know half of it yet. Portia fired Lucy a couple of days ago, and I guess her visa was running out. She needed a way to stay, and Rex was up there visiting Portia . . ." He trailed off.

"That part, I don't get." Grace paused. "I mean, isn't he . . . ?"

"Gay? Yup." Theo looked about as baffled as she felt. "But he's run through all his money; our parents cut him off. The only way we can get our trust funds early is if we're married. So, the next thing anyone knows, they're in Vegas."

"I'm sorry," Grace murmured. "You must feel awful."

"Why?" Theo stared.

"Because of Lucy, leaving you like that."

Theo looked shocked, but Grace added quickly, "It's OK, she told me everything, about you guys falling in love, and keeping it secret, and—"

"Love?" Theo interrupted. "No, wait, you've got it all wrong."

Grace stopped. "I have?" She couldn't help the hopeful note that crept into her voice. "You mean . . . you weren't seeing her?"

Theo flushed. "I . . . well, yes. But not like that," he added quickly. "We were never serious."

"Oh." Grace didn't know if that was worse; that Theo had just been hooking up with Lucy, and it didn't mean anything to him. Her feelings must have shown, because he sighed, frustrated.

"I'm not explaining this right." Theo took a breath. "The truth is, I met Lucy in the Hamptons over summer, and we, well, we dated." He looked away at that last part. "It got too serious, way too fast," Theo continued, "and I realized that we weren't right for each other, but by then . . ." Theo's voice was heavy with regret. "I didn't want to be one of those guys that just cuts and runs, you know?"

Grace nodded. Of course he didn't; Theo couldn't have been further from the type.

"So I tried to let her down gently," he continued, "but she wouldn't take the hint. When summer ended, I figured, that was it. She kept calling and e-mailing, and I kept blowing her off, but I didn't even know she was talking to you until we all met in New York." Theo looked at her earnestly. "I'm sorry. I know what you must have thought of me."

"Why?" Grace said simply. "You didn't owe me anything."

It was true, he didn't. Grace could have so easily hooked up with Harry that night at the party, or started dating someone else herself. As much as it had pained Grace to think of him with Lucy, Theo didn't belong to her—they'd said nothing at all.

"And then, your necklace . . ." Theo continued,

awkward. "I thought I'd just misplaced it, but then I saw her wearing it at Christmas, and I realized . . . I didn't give it to her," he swore. "I would never do that. I only kept it because . . ."

He stopped.

Because what? But before Grace could find the words to ask, Theo leaped up.

"I got you something," he said, crossing to the desk. Grace stepped back, out of his way, as he opened a drawer and pulled out a gift box. "For your birthday." He gave her a rueful smile. "I can't believe I didn't even say anything yet. It should have been the first thing."

Theo held it out, awkward.

"Thank you," Grace said, slowly taking it.

"I know it's not wrapped, or anything. I was going to drive down, to visit, and give it to you in person." Theo bit his lip. "But then, Lucy and Rex happened, and everyone needed to talk, and—"

"I get it." Grace laughed. "I mean, it's a good thing you didn't. Otherwise, I'd be here, and you'd be there, and . . . well. You know."

She opened the lid. "Theo!" Grace looked up at him in delight. "Where did you even get this?"

He looked bashful all over again. "I had it made. Is that OK? I know it was your idea, but I just thought . . ."

"Are you kidding?" Grace lifted out the necklace, the gold pendant dangling. A central atom, and then electrons circling it like the rings on a planet: the chemical equation for silver. "I can't believe you did this for me!" She reached to fasten it around her neck, lifting her hair aside.

"Here." Theo took it and fastened the clasp, his fingers brushing against her skin.

Grace turned back around, and found Theo looking at her.

"It looks great on you," he said quietly.

"Thanks." Grace toyed with the pendant, suddenly self-conscious. "It's perfect."

"Good."

Grace fell silent. Theo was close now, standing just inches away. Neither of them moved. She caught her breath. This was it, this had to be it. She couldn't wait anymore, she couldn't keep hiding, not when the only thing she had left to lose was the possibility of this becoming real. But it wouldn't, not until she found the courage to say what she'd been feeling all this time. To own her emotions, whatever they were.

"I . . . like you."

Theo's head jerked around, and Grace felt a rush of pure panic. Oh, God, what had she done? It sounded so stupid out loud like that, but there was no stopping now, it was there, hanging in the space between them, she had no choice but to stumble on; cheeks burning.

"Not like a friend, or family—God, not at all like family!" Grace forgot how to breathe. "I *like you* like you, I mean. And it's OK if you don't feel the same," she babbled, "or even want to be friends, I just had to tell you because I've been carrying this around forever and I can't keep it in anymore—"

She stopped, she had to. Theo was kissing her.

Oh.

His lips were warm, soft against hers, almost featherlight, until Grace leaned in, instinctively. The kiss deepened. His hand went to her cheek, the other light on her waist as Grace tasted him: toothpaste and cola and *Theo.*

She surfaced for air, giddy. They blinked at each other.

"I—" Theo began, and this time, it was Grace who silenced him.

Postscript

Hallie's impassioned death throes on the hit teen supernatural drama *Vampire Kisses* so impressed the producers that they resurrected her the next season to star as the newest beautiful (yet tormented) bloodsucker in the mysterious town of Darkness Falls. She soon had her pick of agents, and landed her very first film role in an indie comedy. The part was for a reckless, self-centered drama queen. It would, Hallie said at the time, be a real stretch, but she would dig deep and do the part justice.

Despite receiving regular invitations to club openings, premieres, and celebrity parties, Hallie prefers to lead a quieter life out of the glare of the spotlight. When she does walk the red carpet, she's usually accompanied by her sister, or boyfriend, Brandon—a critically acclaimed photographer whose series on returning war veterans recently won a National Press Photographers Association prize, and remains on exhibition at the Whitney Museum in New York. They live together in Venice Beach, with a view of the ocean. He's still trying to teach her how to drive.

Lucy and Rex were married for thirty-two days, until his grandmother—via Portia's urging—threatened to disinherit him. Since Rex could not acknowledge that he hadn't consummated the relationship with his new wife, a divorce was the only option. Joint-property laws in Nevada being what they are, Lucy reached a very comfortable settlement. She is currently vacationing in Paris, while Rex prepares his dissertation: *The Reign of the Phallus: Sexual Politics in Ancient Greece.*

Dakota's band, Take Fountain, had the most illegally downloaded album of the year with their debut record, *Lights of Mulholland*. Paid sales, however, disappointed, and after a lackluster sophomore effort (which *Rolling Stone* called "a shadow of their former selves"), they were quietly dropped by their label. Dakota continued to date his way through Hollywood's C-list starlets, in pursuit of column inches and a solo deal, to no avail. He is currently living in London, writing songs for British-reality-contest-winners Nu-Edge, who have gone on the record about wanting a "fresh rock sound" and "like, authentic emotionality" in their music. He watches *Vampire Kisses* every week, and tries drunk-dialing Hallie when his regret gets too much to take. She changed her number.

Auggie Jennings continues to produce, receiving wide commercial (if not critical) acclaim for *Please, Daddy, No: The Jody Leigh Simmons Story,* now Lifetime's highest-rated true-crime movie of all-time. Amber—retired since twenty-two—is still active in the charity, shopping, and strip-hop-exercise-class communities of Beverly Hills. They recently welcomed a new addition to the family: Elizabeth Taylor, a purebred snicker-poodle.

Valerie rose to prominence with her moving, provocative series in oils entitled *The White Witch Cometh.* The *New York Times* called it a "bold, almost violent expose of humanity's selfish urges," while the *New Yorker* heralded her as "one of our undiscovered African-American talents." All speculation that the unnamed, dark-haired figure in the paintings was inspired by Portia has been, of course, denied.

Palmer's foray into the leather-goods market took an unexpected turn when Kyra Lane (star of the hit reality show *Spa Wars*) used her trademark leopard-print tote bag to assault her cheating rapper boyfriend outside the launch party for his latest album. The resulting paparazzi photos led to a 1,000 percent surge in demand; Palmer incorporated before her eighteenth birthday, and is now well on her way to that first million. Her latest venture is a line of jewelry based on periodic table elements. Grace is chief designer and equity partner, but has forbidden the use of the symbols for silver and gold. Palmer is attempting to change her mind.

Portia moved to Connecticut with Dash and married a third-generation investment banker who played golf with her father, went yachting with her brother, and could trace his family's lineage back to the *Mayflower.* After six months, she discovered him in bed with the latest of her nannies, a plump Irish girl named Bridget. Worse still, he declared that they were in love. He divorced Portia, married the nanny, and is now happily raising alpacas in New England—and wearing his shoes indoors. Portia is now considering an *Eat, Pray, Love*–style journey of self-discovery—only without the pesky praying, of course. Or the eating.

Grace dated Theo all through high school, to his family's enduring disappointment. They took turns visiting every other week, and found that six hours on the freeway wasn't very much at all when it came to love. Theo dropped his business major after one disastrous semester, and is happily pursuing his utterly useless degree in philosophy, while Grace recently graduated valedictorian. They are currently backpacking together through Europe, before Grace starts school at MIT. She's convinced herself another few years of extra-long-distance will be fine, but Theo isn't so sure: he's already looking at transfer applications to East Coast schools. Preferably within walking distance.

Grace still kisses him at every opportunity, just because she can.

Acknowledgments

A huge thanks to Rosemary Stimola, Rebecca Friedman; Kaylan Adair, and the rest of the team at Candlewick for all their hard work. Thanks to my wonderful friends for their support and enthusiasm: Elisabeth Donnelly, Stu Sherman, Leigh Bardugo, Gretchen McNeil, Jessica Morgan, Julia Collard, John Cei Douglas, Jennifer Bosworth, Laurie Farrugia, Amy Stern, and Robin Benway. And thanks to my mother, Ann, as always—for everything.